Crown Publishers
New York

For Christopher

Copyright © 2001 by Megan McCafferty

All rights reserved. No part of this book may be reproduced or transmitted in any form or by any means, electronic or mechanical, including photocopying, recording, or by any information storage and retrieval system, without permission in writing from the publisher.

Published by Crown Publishers, New York, New York.
Member of the Crown Publishing Group.

Random House, Inc. New York, Toronto, London, Sydney, Auckland
www.randomhouse.com

CROWN is a trademark and the Crown colophon is a registered trademark of Random House, Inc.

Printed in the United States of America

Design by Elina D. Nudelman

Library of Congress Cataloging-in-Publication Data
McCafferty, Megan.
  Sloppy firsts : a novel / Megan McCafferty.
    p. cm.
  1. High school students—Fiction.   2. Teenage girls—Fiction.
  3. New Jersey—Fiction.   I. Title.

PS3613.C34 S58 2001
813'.6—dc21   2001028143

ISBN 0-609-80790-0

10 9 8 7 6 5

First Edition

sloppy firsts

January 1st

Hope,

I guess your move wasn't a sign of the Y2K teen angst apocalypse after all. I'm still here. You're still there. Fortunately, I've been way too busy basking in the golden glow of adolescent adulation to be the least bit depressed about your departure. . . .

I'm kidding. Sort of.

The pathetic truth is this: I have become somewhat of a Pineville High celebrity in the eighteen hours since our good-bye. Everyone is paying more attention to me. Of course, I still lack the Oscar-caliber star power that would win me instant acceptance into the Upper Crust or make Paul Parlipiano worship and adore me. No, mine is a Z-level celebrity, comparable to an actress who makes her mark in Lifetime made-for-TV movies with titles like *Daddy, May I Dance with Danger?*

The real reason I'm writing this letter is because I want it to get to your new zip code before you do. I figure you'd want something other than your grandmother's Shalimar-soaked hug to greet you upon your arrival at your new Home Sweet Home. Plus, there's no better way to ring in this oh-so-Happy New Year than by exercising my right to make good on the first of our **Totally Guilt-Free Guidelines for Keeping in Touch:**

1. Snail-mail once a month.
2. Call once a week.
3. E-mail/IM once a day.

Remember: ONLY IF YOU WANT TO. The minute our correspondence becomes obligatory, there's no point in keeping touch at all. I miss you. Already.

Quasi-famously yours, J.

january

the second

Tonight I've been thinking about the mosaic Hope gave me the night she U-hauled ass out of Pineville. I wasn't supposed to open it until my birthday, but I couldn't wait. I tore off the wrapping paper and finally had an explanation for the mysterious slivers of shredded magazine pages all over her carpet. For months, Hope had been tearing out pictures of school buses and pumpkins to capture the color of her curls. Hershey bars and beer bottles for my bob.

I hung it on the wall next to my bed. I've been staring at it, trying to figure out how she glued all those tiny pieces of paper so they would come together to re-create my favorite photo: Hope and me at four A.M.—wide awake and laughing, waiting to sneak out to watch the sunrise.

I remember that summer sleepover at Hope's house two and a half years ago more vividly than anything I did today.

We watched the video of her Little Miss Superstar dance recital. She was the most coordinated of the dozen or so yellow-bikini-clad four-year-olds shuffle-ball-changing to a Beach Boys medley. (Hope's review: *Hello, JonBenét Ramsey!*)

We tried to outdo each other in round after round of "Would You Rather" *Eat nothing but fish sticks OR wear head-to-toe *NSYNC paraphernalia for the rest of your life? French kiss your dog, Dalí, OR have sex with the Chaka, the Special Ed. King? Be zit free forever OR fill a D-cup bra?*

We flipped through our eighth-grade yearbook and decided that being voted Class Brainiac (me) and Class Artist (her) just about guaranteed geekdom in high school. We thought that Brainiac Who Will Actually Make Something of Her Life and Not End Up Managing a 7-Eleven and Artist Who Will Contribute More to This World Than Misspelled Graffiti sounded so much better. Then we literally rolled on the rug laughing as we stripped other Class Characters of their titles and gave them what they really deserved . . .

Scotty Glazer: *from Most Athletic to Most Middle-Aged Yet Totally Immature*
Bridget Milhokovich: *from Best Looking to Best Bet She'll Peak Too Soon*
Manda Powers: *from Biggest Flirt to Most Likely to End Up on Jerry Springer*
Sara D'Abruzzi: *from Class Motormouth to Future Double Agent Who Would Betray Her Country for Liposuction.*

Mrs. Weaver made German pancakes with lemon juice and confectioners' sugar for breakfast. Hope's then-sixteen-year-old brother, Heath, snorted the powdery sugar up his nose and imitated some crazy seventies comedian all hopped up on coke. This made me laugh so hard I thought my stomach was going to come out my ears. I felt bad when Hope later explained to me why she and her mom weren't so amused by his antics. And when Heath died of a heroin overdose six months ago, I felt even worse.

My brother would've been in the same grade as Heath. Hope and I always thought that was a really freaky coincidence. I never knew him, though. Matthew Michael Darling died when he was only two weeks old. Sudden Infant Death Syndrome. No one in my family talks about him. Ever.

Mr. and Mrs. Weaver made countless excuses for the sudden move back to their tiny hometown (Wellgoode, Tennessee: Population 6,345, uh, make that 6,348). They *had* to get Hope down there in time to start the third marking period. They *had* to move in with Hope's grandmother so they could afford to pay for college. But Hope and I saw through the lies. We knew the truth—even if we never said it out loud. The Weavers wanted to get Hope out of Pineville, New Jersey (pop. 32,000, give or take three people), so she wouldn't end up like her brother. Dead at eighteen.

Now I—I mean, *we*, Hope and me—have to pay for *his* mistakes. It's not fair. I know this may sound a little selfish, but couldn't they have waited another seventeen days? Couldn't they have waited until *after* my birthday?

I told my parents not to even dare throwing me a Sweet Six-teen party. The very thought of ice-cream cake and pink crepe paper makes me want to hurl. Not to mention the fact that I can't even imagine who would be on the guest list since I hate all my other friends. I know my parents think I'm being ridiculous. But if the one person I want to be there can't be there, I'd rather just stay home. And mope. Or sleep.

Besides, I have never been sweet. Maybe not *never*, but defi-nitely not after the age of three. That's when my baby blond hair suddenly darkened—and my attitude went with it. (Which is why my dad's nickname for me is "Notso," as in Jessica Not-So-Darling.) Whenever anyone tried to talk to me I'd yell BOR-ING and run away. I probably picked it up from my sister, Bethany, who was fourteen at the time and spent hours in front of the mirror rolling her eyes and practicing pissy looks to advertise her so-called angst. Of course, the difference between Bethany and me is that I've never had to practice.

the fifth

When I was a kid, I loved playing with the *Charlie's Angels* dolls I inherited from Bethany. I'm talking the old-school Angels: Sabrina, Kelly, Jill—even Kris. (They never made dolls for Tanya Roberts or Shelley Hack.) They all wore a navy blue scarf and matching go-go boots but their polyester jumpsuits came in differ-ent colors: Sabrina's in red, Kelly's in yellow, Jill's in white, and Kris's in green. I thought they were so cool, even though everyone else I knew played with Barbie and the Rockers.

This was back when I wanted to be my pretty, popular older

sister more than anything, back when I was young and impression-able and stupid. I loved everything she loved. Anything she thought was cool, I thought was cool. Though my Bethany-worship was short-lived—thank God—her pop cultural impact lives on. She is directly responsible for my freakish lack of interest in nearly all forms of entertainment targeted at my own generation (Gen Y? Gen i? Gen What-*ever*?) in favor of all things anachronistic.

The irony does not escape me.

One day when I was brushing the Angels' hair, getting them ready for their next bad-guy-whupping adventure, I noticed that Sabrina didn't have eyelashes. All the Angels had painted-on eye-lashes but Sabrina. First I thought it was a mistake—like I'd gotten a messed-up doll. But then I asked Bethany if her friends' Sabrinas had eyelashes and she said she didn't think so. I tried to figure out what it was about Sabrina that would make her undeserving of eye-lashes. I never did.

Until last night. I caught a rerun on TV Land in which Kelly and Jill went undercover as hot-pants-wearing hookers while Sabrina—in a turtleneck, no less—gathered case-cracking clues with Bosley. Suddenly, her eyelashlessness made sense. Sabrina was the *brainy* Angel. Yet another example of how every girl had to be one or the other: Pretty or smart. Guess which one I got. You'll see where it's gotten me.

By the way, this is the type of thing that Hope and I talk about. But I won't rehash our convos here. I'll show and tell on a need-to-know basis. The rest is off-limits. Private.

I know it's bizarre that I don't gush on and on about someone who means so much to me. But that's exactly why I won't. When you say too much about anything important, it always ends up sounding more trivial than it is. Words trash it. Plus, my conversa-tions with Hope are like Farsi or some other foreign language. It sounds like *blah-diddy-blah-blah* to everyone *except* those who speak it. If you read a word-for-word transcript of our last conversation, you'd come to the conclusion that Hope and I were total morons.

I wanted to talk about *Charlie's Angels* with Hope in person today, which I obviously couldn't do. Even though my dad used his network administrator clout to hook Hope and me up with the most state-of-the-art Web cams, it doesn't help much when Hope's computer isn't as jacked-to-the-max as mine. We spend the artificial face time griping about how we can't see or hear each other. I might as well use an abacus.

Truth be told, this is fine by me. My dad would love it if I were a computer wonk—it would give us something to talk about besides running—but I'm not. Firewalls be damned. I just don't trust technology, especially since a PHS hacker E-mailed the contents of a freshman's E-journal to every student in school. (He transferred out, so harsh was his humiliation.) Hope has no problem spilling her guts all over the information superhighway, but she's a far less suspicious person than I am. The point is, if I can't talk to her or see her, I prefer handwriting a letter instead of venting over E-mail, or scribbling in this journal instead of cyberchatting with total strangers with screen names like 2kewlchick or buffyrulz04. I'm all too aware of the fact that *I'm* not Y2K compliant. It's nothing short of a miracle that my brain didn't blow up on January first.

In lieu of Hope, I settled for asking Bridget if she remembered playing with the *Charlie's Angels* dolls when we were kids. Bridget is my age and lives across the street. For the first twelve years of my life, these qualifications were all I needed in a best friend. But that was before Bridget's braces came off and her boyfriend, Burke, got on, before Hope and I met in our seventh-grade honors classes.

"Hey. Do you remember when we used to play with the *Charlie's Angels* dolls?"

Bridget shook her golden ponytail and stared like I'd just grown horns out of my forehead.

Bridget is pretty. Very. Actually, she's beautiful. She's usually compared to Grace Kelly or Gwyneth—depending on the age of the eye of the beholder.

Her looks are directly responsible for the demise of our friendship.

One afternoon in August, before we entered seventh grade, Bridget and I went shopping for back-to-school clothes with my mom and my sister. More than one salesperson commented on the trio's classically beautiful, high-quality genes. They all had straight, flaxen hair. (Me, a frizzy brunette.) Their eyes were as large and blue as swimming pools. (Mine were as small and brown as mud puddles.) Their skin, lightly tanned and unblemished. (Mine, sunburnt and zitty.) They were petite, yet curvy in all the right places. (I was long-limbed and skinny with orangutan arms.) Who wouldn't have assumed that *I* was the neighbor's daughter? They thought it was hilarious. I laughed along, hiding my humiliation.

Our friendship was never quite the same after that. But it was okay. A month later, I met Hope and Bridget met Burke Roy (an *eighth*-grader, no less) and we didn't need each other anymore anyway. My mom still clings to the idea that Bridget is my bestest bud, an assumption based on the fact that I've known Bridget since the crib, versus the paltry three and a half years I've known Hope. This is one reason why my mother can't comprehend why one weekly sixty-minute long-distance phone call to Hope is not enough. Another one of those reasons is that my mom knows nothing about me.

Seconds after Bridget's *Angels* dis, Manda and Sara joined us at the table. "Honors" is a relative term in our school district, so I met them in my seventh-grade classes, too, through Hope. Or Hope through them. See, Hope, Manda, and Sara had been quite the clique in their own elementary school. This is as unfathomable as me being friends with Bridget back in the day. Once Hope and I discovered that we were of like minds, we christened Bridget, Manda, and Sara the Clueless Crew. Now they're still here and Hope is gone. My luck sucks.

Once all three members of the Clueless Crew were assembled, they commenced their daily ritual of not eating and alternately trashing/worshipping the models and actresses in a teen mag.

"How could they have put her on the cover? Her ass is like, totally huge," cried Bridget.

Bridget is always zeroing in on the hugeness of models' asses.

That's because Bridget herself is an aspiring model who is convinced she has a huge ass. This is the burden of being beautiful, apparently. In Psych class I learned that the hotter you are, the more paranoid you are about the way you look. That's because born beauties get so much pretty-girl praise that their appearance becomes crucial to their oh-so-delicate self-worth.

Boo-freaking-hoo.

Anyway, Bridget has been modeling for about a year but has yet to make it in the pages of any of the major teen publications. She's one of those anonymous, magalog models. But that's goddamn glamorous for PHS.

"Omigod! My dad's photographer friend said she has cellulite," said Sara.

"*Ewwww!*" said Manda and Bridget in unison.

"Yeah, he said they call her *quote* Stucco Butt *unquote* behind her back."

Sara all too frequently utters the phrases "Omigod!" and "quote, unquote." To her credit, Sara has stopped making the double-finger-bending gesture that traditionally accompanies the latter. She loves the sound of her own voice, one of dulled consonants and nasal vowels, as though her whole cranium is clogged with a bizillion pounds or gallons or whatever unit measures mucus. Her father, Wally D'Abruzzi, owns Winning Wally's Arcade, Wally D's Sweet Treat Shoppe, and other boardwalk gold mines, so she is also the most moneyed chick at Pineville High. This isn't such a feat in our middle-/working-class district. She could go to some pricey private school, but she begged her parents to let her go public. Here, her family's extra buckage gives her some social leverage. At a super chi-chi school full of bizillionaires, she knows she'd be a scrub.

I glanced at the covercow in question. She wasn't skinny, but she definitely wasn't fat. She looked curvy. Sexy. Strong. I thought about Sabrina, without eyelashes, in a turtleneck. I decided to come to the model's defense.

"I bet the editors put her on the cover to make us feel good about ourselves. To show that you don't have to be perfect to be pretty . . ."

"Puh-leeze, Jess," Manda said, pushing her glasses past the bridge of her nose so she could look down at me over the rims. "Stop being so Naomi Wolf, already."

Manda thinks that reading feminist manifestos makes up for her borderline ho-bag behavior. I'm pretty sure that's why she wears Poindexter glasses instead of contacts, so she seems less sexual and more intellectual. She's not fooling anyone, though. Hope and I called her The Kissing Slut because she'd made out with thirty-one different guys by her fifteenth birthday. That's when she decided it was time to move on to manual stimulation, so we christened her Lend-A-Hand-A-Manda. And when she turned sixteen, well, let's just say she earned the title The Headmaster.

Manda calls herself an "extreme" virgin and intends on keeping it that way until she finds someone who meets all her criteria: six feet tall; drives a Jeep; lean and cut, but not meathead muscular; blond; surfs in summer, skis in winter; flosses daily. She knows this is a tall order—especially at Pineville—so she settles for messing with one Mr. Wrong after another until Mr. Right comes along.

The Clueless Crew continued flipping through the magazine, taking swigs from their Diet Cokes and passing one-word judgments on the images on each page.

"Nasty."

"Foul."

"Hideola."

Suddenly, Bridget slapped her hand down on a page.

"Now that girl has like, a totally kickin' bod!"

"Totally!" agreed Manda and Sara.

She was a stick figure with balloon boobs—a body that rarely, if ever, occurs in nature.

They complained about how they could do toning exercises until Y3K and they would never, ever look like she did. They discussed their so-called flaws with enthusiasm. Bridget has a covergirl

10

face, but her "huge ass" is holding back her career. (I'd kill for a less bony butt.) Manda "hates" her infamous DD-cup rack. (Yet she continues to show it off in tiny tees and tight sweaters, much to the delight of Pineville's male population.) And let's not forget Sara, whose self-deprecation stems from her belief that she looks like "a butchy softball player instead of a ballerina," an image reinforced by her nickname, "Bruiser." (Her self-esteem has been permanently trashed since her stepmom sent her to fat camp for her fourteenth birthday.)

Finally, Manda said, "Well, Jess would look like that if she got a boob job." And they all looked me up and down.

I would never get a boob job. It's a disgusting procedure—I saw one performed on The Learning Channel. The surgeon went in through the belly button. The belly button! He stretched her skin like it was a wad of Bubble Yum and just pushed and shoved them into place. Ka-Boom: Va-va-va-voom.

"All we're saying is that your abs, ass, and legs are like, totally perfect," Bridget said. "You should take it as a compliment."

I knew where this was headed: a calorie–fat analysis of my lunch followed by a *How-can-you-eat-so-much-and-stay-so-skinny?* interrogation.

"That pepperoni pizza has at least five hundred calories. . . ."

"And twenty-five grams of fat. . . ."

"Not to mention like, two hundred fifty calories' worth of non-diet soda. . . ."

I have pointed out numerous times that while they are doing whatever it is they do after school once cheerleading season is over, I am at track practice. And there, I spend two and a half hours not *sitting* on my ass, daydreaming about how perfect it looks in my bun-hugger uniform, but hauling it around the track. But they refuse to see how all the food I pack in makes it possible for me to do that. So instead of repeating that useless argument, I made a false confession.

"All right. You got me. I'm bulimic."

Manda was unfazed. "Puh-leeze. You're no bulimic. Binge-and-purgers are usually on the chunky side," she paused. "Right, Bruiser?" Manda winked. Sara winced—*almost* imperceptibly—before flipping Manda the bird.

These are supposed to be my friends. But more often than not, I can't stand them.

Well, if I'm not bulimic, why do I have the urge to puke right now?

That's what I should have said. But I didn't. Instead, I just grabbed my backpack and left, without saying a word.

I stood alone in the bathroom until the bell rang. I pressed my forehead against the cool mirror, fogging it up with bursts of hot breath. I drew a smiley face on the mirror with my finger, then wiped it away. Finally, I looked at my reflection and thought, *If Hope had been there, I wouldn't be here.*

the tenth

Earlier tonight Scotty came over to snap me out of my pissy mood at the request of the Clueless Crew. An interwenchion, so to speak. It had taken less than two weeks for them to come to the conclusion that I'm (in their words, via Scotty) "milking the whole Hope-is-gone misery for way too long." This was hilarious, considering how much I've been holding back. They had no idea how much worse I could be.

"They think you need to stop acting like a *gee dee bee* and get over it."

Scotty is the most self-censoring foulmouth I know. Like every other Jock, he worships Opie and Anthony—the afternoon talk-radio duo and misogynistic masterminds behind "Whip 'Em Out Wednesdays" (female motorists are encouraged to titty-flash any male driver with a wow sign on his car) and "Guess What's In My Pants" (a female caller rubs a phone against her most private of areas, and male contestants try to guess whether she's sporting a "Brillo," a "Triangle," a "Hitler," or a "Wood Floor"). Like O and A, Scotty has gotten into the habit of substituting curses with initials. So "a gee dee bee" means "a goddamn bitch." It's kind of endearing in a way, when I'm not in a foul mood. And I've been in a particularly foul mood lately for the obvious reasons, plus a protracted case of PMS that's two weeks in the works.

"What do you think?" I asked.

He hesitated for a second, rubbing his jaw before answering. His jaw is strong and square, like a comic-book hero's.

"I don't think it's a bad idea . . ."

That pissed me off. So I went off on how Hope is not so easily forgotten because I'd have more fun with her pinkie toe than with anyone else because it alone had more kick-ass qualities than the whole school put together . . .

This made no sense.

But I was too upset to think straight, and even though I knew I was sounding psycho, I resented the idea of having to explain myself. And with Scotty, I always have to explain myself.

My tears came all of a sudden, catching us both off guard. Scotty stood there watching me for a few moments with a panicked look on his face.

"*Muther effer*," he said to himself.

But then he sat next to me until I calmed down. This was better than screwing up the moment by saying something corny.

Despite my antisocial tendencies, I don't want to be the sophomore class pariah. While I'm feeling less than warm and fuzzy about the Clueless Crew, I promise to make an effort. After all, you can only be in a bad mood for so long before you have to face up to the fact that it isn't a bad mood at all. It's just your sucky personality.

I'm grateful to Scotty for helping me come to this conclusion. He means well. I just wish he hadn't told Hope about his feelings for me before she left. He knew she would tell me. And it was so classic Scotty for him to be so serious about it, all, *Now that you're gone, Jess and I will grow closer and she will finally realize that we're meant to be together.* Ack. So every time he does something nice—like come over to my house for the sake of preserving my social status at Pineville High—I think, *You're only doing this because you like me.* That pretty much trashes it.

I have no idea why Scotty insists on carrying a torch for me. I got to know him much too well in middle school for anything to happen between us now. He was my first and only boyfriend. We went out for exactly eleven days in eighth grade. If I had ignored him back then, I might be able to see the bulging biceps of a stud in bloom. But I just see Scotty. I see the chronic bed head that made his black hair branch off his head like a bunch of twigs. And how he would blow his nose and point out all the colors in the tissue. And the hard-ons (!) that used to poke through his sweatpants whenever he saw me in my track-and-field uniform. Jesus Christ!

And then there's the infamous Frenching incident. I can still *feel* that. We were in the parking lot right before the buses were about to pull away and Scotty totally tried to ram-jam his tongue down my throat during an "innocent" good-bye kiss. Thank God the bus driver slid the door shut on me before Scotty swallowed me whole. Up to that point, we had simply pecked good-bye. But without any warning, he decided to put an end to the hassling the basketball team was giving him to "slip me the tongue." I had no idea he was going to do it until I suddenly felt this wet thing flip-flopping around my mouth like a landlocked fish. So saliva-sloppy. And—goddamnthisisgrosserthangross—the scratch of his smudgy, prepubescent mustache on my upper lip. Ew! It was as prickly as a daddy longlegs. I can't imagine kissing him again. No way. Never.

The thing is, I don't want to go out with Scotty just to guarantee that I'll have something to do on Saturday nights now that Hope is gone. Of course, everyone—my mom, my sister, the Clueless Crew, to name a few—thinks I'm insane for not jumping at the chance to become the girlfriend of the future captain of the football, basketball, and baseball teams. He's already made varsity as a sophomore. (Well, baseball season hasn't begun yet, but the varsity coach is already bodychecking Scotty into lockers whenever they meet in the halls. I'm told this is a good sign.) It's a given that when he's a senior he'll be the PHS role model for strength, spirit, and sportsmanlike conduct. And like his predecessors, Scotty is sure to make empty promises about persuading the administration to get rid of our "embarrassing" mascot: The Seagull. (I'm apparently the only athlete who thinks it's hilarious that our founding fathers chose a rat with wings as our school symbol.)

Personally, I find it a bit scary that Scotty is following in the Nike-clad footsteps of Rob Driscoll, his close personal friend and this year's captain of the überjock triumvirate. Rob's recent claim to fame is that he celebrated an away-game victory by persuading a freshman cheerleader to hide under his Seagulls varsity jacket and suck him off in the backseat of the bus. Go team, *go*.

But the biggest reason why I can't go out with Scotty is because I'm way too busy being obsessed with a senior who doesn't know I exist.

Paul Parlipiano and I have spoken exactly once. (He bumped into me on the buffet line at last year's indoor track banquet. He said he was sorry. I giggled like an idiot, then dropped my plate of macaroni and cheese on the floor—too long after for the fumble to be the result of the collision.) Yet, I know he is the only one worthy of my virginity. He's been accepted by early decision to Columbia University, so he's supersmart. And when I see him without a shirt at track practice I'm overwhelmed by the urge to lick the sweat off his six-pack. Yum-yum.

Lately, I've been having a special Sweet Sixteen variation on my standard Paul-Parlipiano-and-I-get-stuck-in-an-enclosed-space-together-and-the-trauma-bonds-us-sexually-and-otherwise daydream. In this one, it's my birthday and Paul Parlipiano and I have gotten locked inside the gym closet. (As always, how we got trapped is inconsequential.) At first, he's none too happy to be in there with me of all people. And though I'm secretly thrilled, I pretend to be totally bummed out because it's my Sweet Sixteen and who would want to spend a Sweet Sixteen trapped in a closet full of athletic equipment?

Eventually, he talks to me because we've been trapped in there for hours, and he's already juggled the soccer ball long enough and there's nothing more for him to do. Paul Parlipiano and I end up having what is the most fun, enlightening, intelligent, and all-around awesome conversation of both of our lives. Then, after a brief silence, he says,

"So is this still the worst birthday you've ever had?"

And I say, "No, not anymore."

And he says, "I can think of one way to make it even better."

And then he slowly walks over to me, cups my (totally zit-free) face in his hands and ever so gently kisses me on the lips. We break away for a brief moment, look each other in the eyes, and smile. We start kissing again, but with more passion. Then we tumble onto the gymnastic mat that is conveniently lying on the floor and have the sweetest sexual experience ever to occur within the hallowed halls of Pineville High.

What's even more twisted is that I believe if I pray, acknowledging that I know it will never happen, it will somehow up the odds that this dream will come to fruition.

I am hopeless. (Ha. In more ways than one.)

But I don't need demented daydreams to tell me that my obsession with Paul Parlipiano has gotten out of control. Today at track practice, I couldn't take my eyes off him. He was jumping over hurdles. He was all smoothness and grace. He made it look easy—a sign of pure genius. OneTwoThreeAIR . . . OneTwoThree-AIR. I got so distracted by his poetry in motion that I wasn't ready when my track teammate Carrie P. came at me in a full-on sprint to hand off the baton. She crashed into me and I dropped it. Coach Kiley was pissed. Thank God Kiley thinks he can't scream at girls, otherwise Paul Parlipiano would have heard his embarrassing *Stop gawking at the guys!* lecture.

Later, in the locker room, Carrie P. brought me back to reality in the straight-talking way that only she can.

16

"Jess, if you keep torturing yourself, I'm gonna kick your fucking ass."

I think maybe she should. Kick my fucking ass, that is. I am hopelessly in love with a guy I barely know. If this doesn't qualify me for an ass-kicking, nothing does. As a senior, Carrie P. has seen this kind of lame behavior a bizillion times before. I suspect that she's figured out how I feel about him even though I've never said a word about it to anyone but Hope. In accordance with alphabetical destiny, Paul Parlipiano and Carrie P. have sat by each other in nearly every class since seventh grade, so I can't ever confirm her suspicions.

"I have no idea what you're talking about," I said.

the eighteenth

I got in trouble today (*technically*, yesterday—but until I fall asleep, my day isn't done). This was a big deal. I can remember every time I've been so much as reprimanded by a teacher.

1. First grade. I'm running back to Miss Moore's class from my accelerated reading group. I'm in a hurry because it's Thanksgiving and we're making mini-turkeys out of apples, toothpicks, marshmallows, and gumdrops. I'm about halfway there when I'm stopped by Mr. Buxton, whose villainous handlebar mustache automatically makes him the meanest teacher in school. He tells me that running isn't allowed and asks for my name. I can barely say it because the snickering sixth-graders are so grown-up and intimidating. He writes my name down on his calendar and tells me that if he stops me again before he turns the page, I will have to take the late bus home. (The late bus is a pretty hefty threat because it's for *bad kids*.)

I cry all the way back to my classroom, where all the kids are making mini-turkeys and singing songs about Pilgrims and Indians. Miss Moore asks me what's wrong and I tell her that I don't like books anymore. For a while after that, I pretend to forget how to read so I won't have to walk all the way to Mrs. Steinbeck's third-grade class and miss out on all the fun my first-grade friends have with Miss Moore.

2. Fifth grade. Someone has written JESS D. IS A BITCH in pencil on the door to the middle stall in the girls' bathroom. This really upsets me. Bridget—who at this point in time is still my best friend and a very reliable source—tells me that it was written by Lisa Caputo. Lisa has been holding a grudge against me ever since I said that I don't like sleeping over at her house because her father doesn't wear any underwear underneath his bathrobe and sits with his legs spread wide apart at breakfast.

So it's recess and my friends and I are hanging out by the back-stop, playing the fortune-telling game MASH like we always do. I've just found out that I'm destined to marry Screech from *Saved by the Bell*, have six kids, drive an olive-green golf cart, and live in a shack when Bridget suddenly grabs Lisa by the arms and says, *Here's your chance to get back at her! Kick her!* I kick her. Lisa screams and then cries, which catches the attention of our teacher, Mrs. Cahill, who tries to get Lisa to tell her who kicked her. She tells her. Then I explain it was because she wrote the "B" word about me in the bathroom. Mrs. Cahill makes us both take the late bus. (The threat finally put into effect.)

My dad is still reconfiguring a network, or whatever he does with computers when he isn't riding his bike. My mom is showing a newly minted Wall Street millionaire a wildly overpriced beach-front property that will bring her a sweet commission. I know I'll get home before either one of them, so I don't worry about their reaction. They never find out about it.

3. Eighth grade. Although I was pissed that we got caught, I never felt bad about anything Hope and I wrote in our Brutal Book.

Thank God our English teacher only lectured us about using our hyperobservant brainpower for good, not evil. Whoo-boy! Imagine the shit that would've gone down if she'd read our character assassinations to the class.

I tended to exaggerate for effect. On Bridget: *Did the orthodontist remove half her brain along with her braces?* On Sara: *She kisses up to Manda and Bridget so much they're crapping strawberry LipSmacker.* But Hope only spoke the ugly truth. On Manda: *If Manda keeps thrusting her ta-tas in Mr. Cole's face, she just might ace Algebra after all.* Observations like that made it clear to me that Bridget ditching me for Burke was the best thing that could have happened to me. Hope was the friend I'd always wanted, but never had.

To add to this list, today's misdemeanor. When I get bored in class, I write sad song lyrics all over my book covers. I'm currently in an eighties phase—no surprise there. My current favorite is featured in *Pretty in Pink*, the third installment of the Molly Ringwald teen-queen trilogy (all of which I've enjoyed over and over again thanks to the programming execs at TNT, who seem to agree with my assertion that any John Hughes flick should be classified as a "new classic"):

Please, please, please . . . let me, let me, let me . . .
Let me get what I want this time.

The Smiths' ode to yearning didn't get me in trouble. In a less musical bad mood, I guess I scribbled: LIFE SUCKS, THEN YOU DIE on the cover of my Chemistry book. I don't even remember doing it. But it raised the unibrow of Mr. Scherzer, who quickly informed my guidance counselor, Mrs. Glick, who called me out of Trig to meet Brandi, the school's pseudo shrink. Her nameplate says "Professional Counselor," which I figure means she's a few credits short of a legit Ph.D. She probably couldn't find enough evidence for her doctoral thesis to prove that hugs are indeed better than drugs.

Brandi is *mean* skinny, the kind that doesn't come naturally and makes her face look all hollow and scary. She tries to make up for this with a bug-eyed bubble and gush that I know better than to trust. She—like me—is a fan of the eighties, but her devotion has tragic consequences: Kentucky-fried bangs and suntan panty hose.

Every inch of space on the counseling office walls is covered with posters that are supposed to stop us from driving drunk, doing drugs, having sex, and sticking our fingers down our throats. Most of them are totally corny: *There once was a girl named Lydia, who had sex and got chlamydia . . .*

Others aim to depress the hell out of you. The best/worst one had a blowup of a girl's yearbook picture. Her name was Lindsey Greenbush and she was pretty in an unimaginative JC Penney catalog sort of way, like Bridget. Underneath her pic is a list of her activities: National Honor Society, Field Hockey, Soccer, Homecoming Committee, French Club. Then underneath that it says in bold print: **Two weeks before her yearbook came out, Lindsey was killed when she got into a car with a drunk driver.**

I have to admit that it made me think about what would happen if I got killed by a drunk driver. I can understand why the Weavers won't fly Hope in for my Bitter Sixteen, but I assume they'd pay for a flight for my funeral. Who else would make sure that my mom buried me in my denim halter dress—especially if I died in winter? I could see my mom arguing that it isn't warm enough for me to wear something sleeveless, you know, because it's very important for dead people not to catch cold.

Plus, I'd want Hope to make the show-stopping speech, "The Jessica You Never Knew." She gave a similar speech at Heath's Mass, so I know she can handle it.

I don't know *how* she handled it, to tell you the truth. Heath's death went *so* public. The Weavers found themselves smack-dab in the middle of a local media feeding frenzy. TEEN'S DEATH EXPOSES TOWN'S SECRET SHAME screamed the headlines of the *Ocean County Observer*. YOUTH OVERDOSES, SHOCKED LOCALS CALL FOR CRACKDOWN shouted the *Asbury Park Press*. In death, Heath became emblematic of the "atypical" heroin user, which sparked a McCarthy-esque paranoia that YOUR CHILD COULD BE NEXT. See, Heath didn't come from a "bad family." Mrs. Weaver was a nurse. Mr. Weaver was an elementary-school teacher and a eucharistic minister at Saint Bernadette's, the Catholic church they attended as a family every Sunday. Both parents were active in the PTA and never missed a back-to-school night or ignored a bad report card. How could such a tragedy happen to such good people? Everyone wanted answers. And the only person who had one was dead.

Quite frankly, I think the reason Heath got high was because he was bored out of his mind. He was a really smart guy, and really smart people in Pineville have it rough. There's *nothing* to do here. His death really made me sad (still does) and not only because it ripped me apart to see Hope cry and wonder *Why?* like everyone else. I had always fantasized that when we got older, Heath would see me as more than his little sister's playmate. Not that I had a crush on him or anything. He seemed like someone who would understand me. I was looking forward to being his equal. His friend.

However, I can't seem to get out of the anger stage of my grief. I can't help but feel like Heath ruined *everything*, not just between us, but between Hope and me.

It was kind of ironic that I was thinking about all this when Brandi told me about what Scherzer saw on my book cover and asked me if I've thought about suicide.

Deep down, I wanted to tell her that I've considered killing myself no more than the average almost-sixteen-year-old honor student with no best friend or boyfriend and bigger bumps on her face than in her bra. But there's no way that Brandi would understand.

Brandi graduated from PHS about fifteen years ago—a fact unearthed by Sara via an uncle who used to "bang" her. (Sara's verb choice.) We found the yearbook from that year in the library and saw firsthand that our Professional Counselor had swept the most crucial Class Character categories: Best Dressed, Best Looking, and Most Popular. She was Upper Crust all the way—or whatever they called the U.C. then.

I wasn't about to confide in her because there's nothing more annoying than an adult who tells me that I will look back on all this and laugh—especially when it comes from an adult who heartily tee-heed all along. This is why I also refuse advice from my mother and my sister.

So I told her that this was all a misunderstanding. "Life Sucks, Then You Die" is not my personal philosophy, no, no, no. Life Sucks, Then You Die (L.S.T.Y.D.) is the name of an indie funk band that I just love, love, *love*. She not only totally bought it, but started acting like she's *heard* of them because she couldn't stand the idea of not being clued in anymore.

"They had one song that got some airplay," I said.

"Right! They did, didn't they? What was the name again?" Her peepers were popping right out of her head at this point.

"'Tongue-Kissing Cousins.'"

"Right!" Brandi starts nearly every sentence with that exclamation. It's a method of positively affirming her mixed-up counselees, something she learned in one of her Professional Counselor classes no doubt. "'Tongue-Kissing Cousins.' That song rocks."

"It's a slow jam."

"That's right! A slow jam."

And so continued our bonding for a minute or two until she deemed me stable enough to let me go with nary a mark on my permanent record.

Then a kind of weird thing happened.

I walked out of her office and nearly tripped over two bare legs covered in scars and scabs. Marcus Flutie was slumped in a chair, stretching his long limbs right in front of the door. Marcus is what we at PHS categorize as a "Dreg." I think he was waiting to meet with his parole officer. Last spring, he got busted for buying or selling or using—I don't know for sure—as part of the town's War on Drugs effort that followed Heath's death. Marcus was four years younger than Heath and his burnout buds, so they made him their marijuana-smoking mascot. (He's a year older than Hope and me, but he's on our grade level because he got left back in elementary school for doing God only knows what.) Of course, marijuana being the gateway drug and all, they moved on to bigger and better mind-altering substances: acid, E, 'shrooms, Special K, heroin, etc.

The other thing about Marcus is that crackheaded girls who don't know any better think he's sexy. I don't see it. He's got dusty reddish dreads that a girl could never run her hands through. His eyes are always half-shut. His lips are usually curled into a semi-smile, like he's in on a big joke that's being played on you but you don't know it yet. He *always* has a girlfriend and he *always* cheats on her. Thus, Marcus is widely known by the moniker "Krispy Kreme" because he's always "burnt to a crisp" and is rumored to have "bought three boxes of donuts." (In PHS lingo, that means he's slept with at least thirty-six girls. A dozen donuts per box—get it?)

In short, Marcus Flutie is precisely the type of "unsavory character" that the Weavers wanted to get Hope away from. This really wasn't necessary because Hope hates Marcus and the rest of Heath's former friends almost as much as she hates drugs and alcohol. She would be profoundly disappointed if I associated with him or his vices, so I walked right past him. My hand was on the doorknob when he called out to me.

"Hey, *Tongue-Kissing Cousin!*"

Though I used to see him sometimes at Hope's house, Marcus and I had never, ever acknowledged each other's existence before. So I froze, not knowing whether I should (a) laugh, (b) say something, or (c) ignore him and keep on walking. I chose a brilliant combo of (a) and (b).

"Uh, yeah. Ha. Ha. Ha."

I turned around and saw that Marcus was smiling at me. It freaked me out. I mean, it wasn't an unfamiliar smile. He smiled like he knew me and was used to looking at me full in the face even though I don't remember him ever giving me so much as a lazy I'm-too-stoned-to-avert-my-eyes look when I walked past his desk in homeroom.

"I almost pissed myself out here," he said.

"Uh, thanks, I guess."

"You're a natural con artist."

He was still looking right at me. I giggled. I always giggle like a girlie-girl when I get nervous. It's my most annoying habit.

"What other secrets are you hiding?"

I chewed on my lip (my second most annoying habit) and flew through the door.

The thing is, he's right. I get going on a lie and I can't stop. This is a largely untapped talent. I could probably talk my way out of a bizillion sticky situations—if I only got myself into them. It was just weird hearing it from someone who doesn't even know me.

the twentieth

My insomnia kicked in three months ago, right after Hope told me she was crossing the Mason-Dixon Line. Since then, I've learned to hate every inch of my body.

I'll be lying here in the dark urging myself to sleep, when I'll suddenly become excruciatingly aware of how sweaty my thighs get when stuck together in the fetal position. So I have to shift them. Then my thighs are okay, but a lock of hair falls across my forehead and I can't stand the weight of it on my brow. So I brush it aside. Then my forehead is okay, but the toes of my right foot get all cramped up. So I have to crack them. Then my toes are okay, but I get an itch on my butt. So I have to scratch it . . .

This goes on for hours with every conceivable combination of body parts and complaints. I've tried warm milk, counting sheep, even the I-dare-myself-to-stay-awake reverse-psychology trick. Nothing works. I've stopped short of Tylenol PM because I don't want to be a person who requires drugs to get in and out of bed. As if Heath weren't enough of a warning, I've seen too many *Behind the Musics* to let that happen.

There is only one good thing about my middle-of-the-night restlessness. I have some crazy-ass dreams that are really easy to remember when I wake up. Take last night's, for example:

I show up at a student council meeting wearing nothing but a pair of polka-dot panties. My nipples are doing a full-on, friendly *How do you do?* to everyone in the room. No one minds, as though I always show up for after-school activities nearly au naturel.

The meeting is just about to get under way when Scotty comes up to me all outraged and yells, "Jess! Why are you showing everyone your tits? Today isn't Whip 'Em Out Wednesday!"

And then Bridget says, "And it's not like she has much to show off."

And then Marcus Flutie says, "But she has a lot to hide on the inside."

Then I announce to them and everyone at the student council meeting that I'm conducting an experiment. I'm testing how comfortable everyone is with the sight of my breasts. The auditorium, which is now standing-room-only because the entire student body is there, bursts into applause.

Then Paul Parlipiano whispers in my ear, "I thought you were being a tease. But now that I know it was an experiment, I admire you."

I could lie and say that's when we have hot-buttered sex right there on the stage in front of 800 screaming students. But unfortunately for me, that's when I woke up. Christ, I can't even touch him in my *dreams*.

Dreams are so weird, aren't they? I mean, you can't control who shows up in them. Like when I saw Marcus Flutie in homeroom today, my stomach bungeed down to my toes, then sprang up into to my throat. I was actually worried that he somehow knew that he was in my dream last night. Of course, he didn't even look up from the notebook he's always scribbling in. He'll never know. But it makes me wonder if I was in anyone's dreams last night.

(No, Scotty's masturbation fantasies don't count.)

February 1st

Hope,

Okay. My Bitter Sixteen is officially over. I've opened up all my birthday presents and your mosaic is still by far the best one. Thankyouthankyouthankyouthankyouthankyou.

My love for your present above all others *isn't* a coincidence. Did you ever notice that how much you dig a gift all depends on the giver? For example, Paul Parlipiano could've given me a filthy wad of gum scraped off the bottom of his shoe and it would've rocked my world. OH MY GOD! YOU SHOULDN'T HAVE GONE TO ALL THIS TROUBLE FOR LITTLE OL' ME. DID THIS GUM COME FROM YOUR VERY OWN MOUTH?

On the other end of the spectrum is Scotty. He gave me a rose before homeroom. Though this was a nice gesture, I didn't feel like carrying it around all day. But I couldn't just stuff it in my locker, so I was forced to field questions from the Clueless Crew all damn day. Who bought you the flower? Why would he buy you a flower if he didn't want to go out? Are you going out? Why aren't you going out?

Maybe I'd be more psyched about the flower if Scotty weren't currently going by the name "Mike Ockenballz." Referring to each other with double-entendred nicknames has replaced Purple Nurple Pursuit as the latest diversion of choice for Scotty and his friends.

Burke Roy is now "Hugh G. Reckshun."
Rob Driscoll is now "Heywood Jablomie."
P. J. Carvello is now "Adolf Oliver Bush."

I'm the only girl who doesn't think this is the cutest thing ever.

As for the rest of my birthday, it came and went, and Paul Parlipiano did not come within 100 yards, let alone share a sweaty 5x5 closet with me. And there was nary a sign of the Breast Fairy. Maybe she's holding out for next year, when the combo of mondo boobage and a driver's license will make me a major man-killer. Figuratively speaking.

No party, either, which was only slightly less depressing than having one would've been. My mom bought a carrot cake from a bakery that made the criminal mistake of using plain-vanilla frosting instead of the cream-cheese kind. I wanted to go off on how it would be nice if even the

smallest thing went right for me. Cream-cheese frosting could have easily met that need. That isn't too much to ask for, is it?

But then I saw the way my mom was looking at me. She was feeling
sorry for me. I was her *lame-ass, loser* daughter, whose birthday would
never be as sweet as her own sixteenth, or Bethany's—both of which
were celebrated with a *huge* catered party for a few dozen of their nearest and dearest friends. What can be more pathetic than that?

I lost the nerve to say something snotty. She and my dad sang "Happy
Birthday" and I blew out my candles. I opened up my presents (some
CDs, a girlie-girl dress I'm returning, and a new pair of running shoes
from Dad). I ate a big piece of that cake and pretended to enjoy it. Then I
went to my room and cried as quietly as I could.

By the way, the Clueless Crew gave me a silver charm bracelet. A "16"
dangles from one of the links. I guess the idea is that I'll look down at
my wrist and always remember this as the time of my life. That is, unless
Brandi was right and I slit it first.

I'm kidding . . .

Long Duck Dongly Yours, J.

february

the fifth

I f Bethany had gone to high school with me, I would've hated her, and to her, I would've been the dweeby sibling she was too cool to acknowledge in the halls. Thus, our eleven-year age gap is a blessing.

I spent the whole day at the dress shop trying on this satin monstrosity for her wedding. Brides are evil. They are so hell-bent on looking better than everyone else that they pick out brides-maids' dresses that no one could possibly look good in. The one I have to wear is yellow (*"Maize!"* as my sister and mother corrected me at least a bizillion times), strapless, and straight to the floor. I look like a banana in it. Bridesmaid bonus: Once the alterations are done, I'll have enough leftover material from the bust to make not only a matching handbag, but a whole set of luggage!

So I'm standing in the shop in all my Chiquita splendor when Bethany starts telling me that she doesn't want me to get my hair cut before the wedding because she wants it to be long enough to put up in some elaborate whoop-de 'do.

"But I *never* wear my hair up," I protested.

"You will for the wedding," Bethany said.

"But I don't look good with my hair up."

"Well, that's too bad because all the bridesmaids are wearing their hair up."

"Why do we all have to wear our hair the same way?"

She sighed heavily. "Because it will look better in the pictures."

"But why do we all have to look the same to look good?"

At this point she did the sigh-and-eye-rolling double whammy. "Mother?!"

So my mom intervened.

"When it's your big day you can tell your bridesmaids to wear their hair however you want. But since it's not, listen to your sister."

I said that considering I couldn't even get a *date* to the wedding, I doubted I'd be planning my own any time soon. Bad move on my part.

That's when my mom and Bethany tag teamed me about Scotty—how I'm so stupid not to invite him to the wedding because he's good-looking and sweet, and how I'm really going to regret it when he gets another girlfriend. Then they stopped talking *at* me and started talking *about* me like I wasn't even there.

"I don't understand her, Bethie. Your sister would rather mope away her teenage years than go out with such a catch."

"She likes to wallow, Mother. She needs to lighten up."

"You know what she really needs?"

"What, Mother?"

"She needs a little perspective."

"Yes, she does."

"I mean, when the worst thing in your life is trying to decide whether you should take a cute football player to your sister's wedding . . ."

I realized long ago that my mom and Bethany have a blonde bond that I can't bust into. I'm better off not even bothering to try.

"Jesus Christ! The wedding is four months away," I screeched. "Did you ever think that I might get a real boyfriend before then?"

Their identical icy-blue glares told me that they hadn't.

The ancient woman doing the alterations kept right on pulling and pinning the fabric around my body. I bet she's heard far worse in this dressing room: a bride in for her first fitting, tearfully confessing that she's pregnant with the best man's baby; bitchy bridesmaids betting how long it will be before the divorce; a mother-of-the-groom who suspects her son may be gay.

Am I the only creature with a vagina who thinks that weddings are ridiculous? I'm going to elope. Just me, my hubby, and a minister on a beach in Jamaica. That's better than Bethany asking a church full of people to pretend that she's a virgin and having my father "give her away" like she's a garbage bag of Goodwill clothes. As the Maid of Dubious Honor, I can't just be bored in the background. I'm there front and center for the entire spectacle.

Honestly, I don't get what Bethany and her fiancé, Grant, see in each other. Big whoop: They're virtually indistinguishable from a Barbie and Ken wedding-cake topper. And he turned new money into even newer money with some Wall Street wheeling-dealing. (Hence his nickname, G-Money.) He's jetted between Silicon Valley, California, and Silicon Alley, New York, for a few years. After the wedding, the happy couple will follow the Techie gold rush and settle for good in the Bay area, ground zero for venture capitalists.

I guess there are worse reasons to get married. After all, my parents have been together twenty-eight years simply because Dad was "Dar the Star," All-County point guard for the basketball team, and Mom was the captain of the rah-rah squad. Ack.

What Bethany and G-Money really lack is *oomph*. I see zero passion. I don't mean that they should have their tongues down each others' throats 24-7. But as a couple, they don't add anything when they enter a room. I've never heard them have anything other than a mind-numbingly inane conversation.

Bethany: *I hope this beautiful weather lasts all day.*
G-Money: *Me, too.*
Bethany: *I don't want it to get too hot.*
G-Money: *Me either.*

And since they got engaged two and a half years ago, they don't even discuss current events anymore. All they talk about is the wedding.

Bethany: *I hope we have beautiful weather on our wedding day.*
G-Money: *Me, too.*
Bethany: *I don't want it to get too hot.*
G-Money: *Me either.*

If I get a husband—hell, if I get a *boyfriend*—I never want to have a conversation like this. This is why I will never date Scotty. I need my boyfriend to be the male equivalent of Hope. My best friend. If I could have the same relationship with my boyfriend that I have with Hope *and* have deep, meaningful sex—well, that would be perfect. Whether it's possible, I have no idea.

"Regardless of who you invite," Bethany said, breaking the silence, "You should be more concerned about the part in your hair than you are about wearing it up."

"What do you mean? My part is just fine," I said, immediately looking in the mirror for a confirmation. My hair was tucked back, curling just under my earlobes, with a silver barrette clipped to the right side of my head to keep my bangs from falling into my eyes. Same as always.

"Well, sure, it looks fine in the *mirror*."

"And that's fine because that's what I look like."

"No it isn't," she laughed.

Then she sprung the bit of big sister torture she's probably been saving for years.

I knew that numbers and letters were backward in the mirror, but I never thought the same principle could apply to *faces*. I never realized that what I see in the mirror is my *reverse* image. Bethany positioned me in front of a set of mirrors that bounced off each other in a way that let me see the *reverse* of my reverse image— which is what I *really* look like.

What a shock. Bethany was right. I *do* part my hair on the wrong side. But that wasn't the worst of it. Suddenly, the unevenness of my nostrils jumped out at me: The left one kind of comes from the front, while the right one sort of comes from the side. I always thought that I didn't photograph well, but it turns out *that's* how I appear to others.

I tried holding my hand mirror up to the bathroom mirror so I can get ready for school with my real face in mind. There's nothing I can do about my nostrils. But I've been trying to use styling goop, a paddle brush, and a hair-dryer to train my part to hang a left instead of a right, but it's just not working. The part is already sixteen years in the making.

the eighth

We have a new girl in the honors track. Her name is Hyacinth Wallace. She told us to call her "Hy." Every teacher thought it was positively hysterical when he or she said, "Well, hi, Hy!"

Everyone is all freaked out about her. First, she's from New York City, which is about as exotic as you can get at PHS. Second, she is gorgeous in a dark-eyed, olive-skinned, nonsuburban way that intimidates males and females alike. Third, she seems older than us, an image enhanced by her raspy, two-pack-a-day alto. Fourth, and most significant, everyone thinks it's too *X-Files* that a girl with the initials "H.W." moves in just over a month after a girl with the initials "H.W." moved out. Naturally, everyone thinks that she is destined to be my new best friend.

Scotty believes this is a great opportunity for me to try out my new-and-improved attitude. He resorted to pimping.

"Hy seems really cool."

"Yeah, I guess," I said.

"She seems really nice."

"Yeah, I guess."

"You should go out of your way to be nice to her."

"Well, I won't go out of my way to be *mean* to her."

"Maybe you should invite her over to your house or something."

I don't invite my so-called friends over to my house, let alone perfect strangers. I told Scotty I would get to know her before I extended any invitations.

Besides, the Clueless Crew had already taken Hy under their collective wing—she didn't need any extra-special-wecial attention from me. Hy's short black hair is chopped in complicated chunks and streaked with spicy shades of red: ginger, cinnamon, chili. Add that to a deconstructed Run-DMC T-shirt that's been cropped and covered with sequins, an ankle-length patchwork denim skirt with a generous front slit, and knee-high lace-up jack boots, and Hy was clearly a beauty and fashion force to be reckoned with. One the Clueless Crew, who are identical from their plastic mini-butterfly clips down to their platform Mary Janes, transparently wanted to tap into.

"You'd better sit with us, since you don't know like, the safe areas of the cafeteria," urged Bridget.

"What *safe areas?*" asked Hy. An obvious question for the uninitiated.

While we got on line for our food (she eats—good sign), I explained Pineville High's social zoning laws and their origins:

The Upper Crusters are at long tables by the windows because, well, it's the best spot in the cafeteria and why the hell shouldn't they be there? They're surrounded on all sides by the Hangers-On, the popular juniors who will sit at the U.C. table when they rule the school as seniors. Jocks (separated by sport) sit front and center, symbolic of their importance in the minds of 99.9 percent of the student body, flanked by Groupies (the Jocks' girlfriends or, more often, those who are dying to be). Dregs are way in the back by the emergency exit, so they can sneak out to get high. 404s (an ironic twist on the techie put-down for idiot users, derived from the Web error message "404 Not Found") are in the back on the opposite side, hovered over their laptops, hoping to avoid humiliation at the hands of the Jocks or the occasional mean-spirited Upper Cruster. IQs sit up front and close to the doors so they can make it to their next class on time. Over by the vending machines, Double As (ebony) and Wiggaz (ivory) live together in hip-hop harmony, the former outnumbered by the latter five to one. (Which isn't bad, considering whites outnumber blacks thirty to one in the PHS population at large. Latino and Asian communities consist of a token representative or two in each grade. "Hey, Alice," I said to Hy, "welcome to Wonderbreadland.") Finally, because most of their counterparts leave PHS before lunch to take beauty culture or mechanics classes at the vocational school, Hoochies and Hicks are in small clusters throughout the cafeteria.

"These are just the main categories," I said. "There are too many subdivisions to mention."

"Where do you sit?"

"We're on the boundary between the Hangers-On and the IQs. It's decent real estate for sophomores."

"So what happens to border-jumpers?" Hy asked. Again, a good question.

"Well, the IQs wouldn't care. But if you had the nerve to take a Hangers-On table, you'd be pelted with the more aerodynamic components of the vegetable medley."

"That would be ironic," she said.

"What?"

"Girl, I left the city to get away from real gangs," she said. "Then I come to New Jersey and get caught up in a turf war."

I thought that was pretty funny.

That was the high point of lunch. I had wanted to ask Hy if she was serious about the gangs, but when we got back to the table, the Clueless Crew hounded her with questions for the next sixteen minutes and I couldn't get a word in edgewise. Here's the gist:

Q. Where did you get your T-shirt? (A. *A friend attending the Fashion Institute of Technology made it for her.*)

Q. Where did you get your skirt? (A. *At a vintage clothing store in the Village—that's Greenwich Village to you and me.*)

Q. Where did you get your boots? (A. *From "the world's best" Salvation Army.*)

By the end of the interrogation, Bridget, Manda, and Sara were swearing off the Ocean County Mall.

Oh. There was one crucial non-wardrobe-related question:

Q. Do you have a boyfriend?

I must admit that I too breathed a sigh of relief when the answer was "Yes." No competition. He's a nineteen-year-old DJ she met at a rave. His name is—get this—Fly. Fly and Hy. I think this is hilarious.

I doubt I'll ask Hy over to my house. Don't get me wrong, I think she's cool. But Hy is way too happening to cozy up to a suburban loser like me. I'd constantly be looking over my shoulder for the cooler friends she'd ditch me for.

the tenth

Tonight was the indoor track awards dinner. Girls' team only. The boys decided to have a separate banquet, so I didn't have the pleasure of having my second mortifying "conversation" with Paul Parlipiano.

I got the Scholar Athlete Award. My GPA has risen to 99.66. The crazy thing is, the higher my GPA gets, the more I realize that high school is useless. I'm serious. I forget everything I'm supposed to have learned immediately after the test. For example, I got back a Chemistry quiz I took last week. I nailed a 95. But when I looked over the formulas today, they meant nothing to me.

All subjects are the same. I memorize notes for a test, spew it, ace it, then forget it. What makes this scary for the future of our country is that I'm in the tip-top percentile on every standardized test. I'm a model student with a very crappy attitude about learning.

It's a good thing I'm smart. My parents won't let me know just how smart I am, though. I had my IQ tested in first grade but they would never tell me what the number was. I assume it's because they found out I was smarter than they were. I know this because I overheard my mom saying to my dad, "How are we supposed to feel knowing our kid is smarter than we are?" (I knew they weren't talking about Bethany—a straight B-minus student who only applied to bantamweight state schools and had the good fortune of getting hit on by G-Money at the Bamboo Bar in the summer of 1993, an event that guaranteed she'd never work a steady job in her life.)

My parents aren't dumb. My dad is a high-school network administrator (not at PHS, thank God), so he knows a ton of I.T. mumbo jumbo. And my mom was the top broker associate at Century 21 last year. But still I wonder where I inherited my overactive brain. They think about things waaaaaay less than I do. Their boring suburbanness doesn't cause *them* any existential angst that keeps them awake at night. Nope, they do their jobs, come home, eat dinner, drink a few glasses of wine, watch whatever is on TV from eight P.M. until midnight, go to sleep, and wake up at six A.M. to do it all over again. The most exciting things going on in their lives aren't even going on in *their* lives. My mom lives for Bethany's wedding appointments. My dad lives for my meets. And that seems to be okey-dokey to them.

I can't settle for such a lackluster life. Which is why it bothers me that this award was no big deal. Or that the whole indoor track season was no big deal. Maybe I feel this way because I'm naturally good at it. I work hard at practice and all, but I don't put in any superhuman effort to be the top distance runner on the team. I just am. Scotty has told me that he isn't a natural athlete. But he's gotten so good because he puts his mind, body, and spirit into every workout. There's a history of hard work behind every touchdown, every basket, every run, and that's why sports give him a rush.

But I can't think of anything (track, student council, Key Club, and so on) that gets me as psyched as that. Or as giddy as the Clueless Crew gets from organizing a pep rally or decorating the Jocks' lockers before a big game. I wish I were artistic, like Hope. That's passion. That's something to get excited about. I do everything I do because it will look good on my college applications. Depressing, isn't it?

the fourteenth

Valentine's Day. Excruciating.

The torture started at lunch. It took every ounce of my energy to restrain myself from throttling Bridget and Manda. (This is part of my ongoing effort to avoid turning into a social outcast.) All they did was complain about how their boyfriends didn't put as much effort into this mushy, Blue Mountain Arts watercolor holiday as they did. They made the classic mistake that all cupid-stupid girlfriends make: They assumed guys give a damn about V-Day.

"I bought Burke a card. And a teddy bear. And a bag of Hershey's Kisses," Bridget said, seething. "All he bought me was a cruddy carnation that's like, sold by the Key Club."

"Well, at least Burke bought you something. I got squat," Manda whined. Then she paused for effect. "After this weekend, Bernie should've gotten me something *really* nice. *If you know what I mean.*"

The Headmaster's wink-wink, nudge-nudge aside was totally unnecessary. Even Hy is hip to Manda's reputation, and she's only been here for a little over a week. A few days ago Manda was wearing what Hope and I call the "infamous booty skirt." This inspired Burke and P.J. to whisper about how hypocritical it was that Manda wouldn't hook up with the coolest sophomores or juniors but would happily do total dorks just because they're *seniors.*

Hy overheard this convo and pulled me aside in between classes.

"Is Manda a skank or what?"

Hy can be pretty blunt.

"What's your definition of skank?" I asked.

Hy didn't hesitate. "A skank fucks skeezas she barely knows."

"Well, then Manda isn't a skank."

Then I explained Manda's Clintonian philosophy: *100 percent pure until penetration.*

Hy thought about this for a moment.

"She may not be a skank," she said. "But girl, she's skanky for real."

I had to agree.

Manda's latest conquest is Bernie Hufnagel. I remember the day she decided Bernie was cute. She spotted him across the crowded cafeteria, putting one of his fellow wrestlers in a headlock, and said, "Bernie Hufnagel is cute." Less than a week later, they were swapping spit outside the boys' locker room before his wrestling match.

I've got to give that girl props. Manda is only okay-looking: Her full lips and lush lashes are the best features on an otherwise flat face. Yet she makes the most of what she's got. She starts pouting and fluttering—not to mention flaunting her huge hooters—and she can get anyone she wants. If she wanted to, she'd be in Paul Parlipiano's pants by the end of the day. And that's a power I can't help but envy.

She's only been "dating" Bernie for a week and it's highly unlikely he'll make it to March. (Although they do have something in common: He's always trying to make weight, so he never eats either.) So it was incredibly annoying to have to listen to her gripe about his insensitivity on this, a day devoted to all things lovey-dovey.

What was worse, however, was hearing Hy go on about how she and Fly don't celebrate V-Day because they think it's more important to show love for each other *every* day, and not get all artificially mushy on February fourteenth.

"That's deep," said Manda.

"Yeah," said Bridget.

Sara, who celebrates this holiday by quadrupling the number of *Omigod!-I'm-so-fat-I'll-never-get-a-boyfriends*, just sighed into her Diet Coke.

Jesus Christ. I hate Valentine's Day. It goes back to that elementary-school tradition of collecting all the valentines in one big cardboard box o'love and the teacher handing them out one by one in front of the entire class. This was fine and dandy in first and second grade when Valentine's Day was an equal-opportunity holiday and everyone gave valentines to everyone else. This lovely little practice made the sentiment completely meaningless because it didn't discriminate.

By third grade, Pineville Elementary School's reigning prepubescent bitch realized that Valentine's Day could serve as a sadistic competition. Nadine LaDieu declared that she was only giving Valentines to *boys*. Not just any boys, mind you, but only the ones she considered cute and/or cool enough to be part of the elementary-school elite. All the girls agreed to do the same, my Smuckers-spined self included. Then she made all the boys promise that they would only give valentines to the girls they thought were cute and/or cool enough.

I gave one to Len Levy. This is when he was still fairly popular, before he developed a case of socially crippling purple-all-over acne.

I went home empty-handed. And brokenhearted.

It's gotten worse as we've gotten older. On no other day does the world find as much delight in reminding those of us not fortunate enough to be getting down with a significant other on a regular basis just how pathetic and undesirable we really are.

I thought Scotty might give me an ironic V-Day gift, like those chalky candies with messages like HOT STUFF and SWEET LIPS on them. He could have given them to me as a friend, for laughs. But deep down I would've known that the effort involved meant it wasn't a joke at all. But he didn't. And I can't blame him. Especially after my lukewarm reaction to the birthday rose. Not to mention that most *boyfriends* fail to deliver what girls want on V-Day. And Scotty is not my boyfriend.

The only person who showed any romantic interest in me was this tiny black kid who sits in front of me in French class. Even *I* outweigh him—he wrestles in the 103-pound weight class. For the past few weeks he's been giving me these goofy, googly-eyed grins or turning around at random intervals to say, *Bonjour, mon amie.* Today he asked me a bizillion times if I had a Valentine. Conclusion: He has a huge Pepe Le Pew–like crush on me. I don't know how this is possible because he's one of those freshmen who looks too young to have a working set of nads. (Though, with my menstrual cycle MIA, I'm one to talk.)

Of course, I bitched and moaned about my bad luck. Why would this half-pint choose me as the object of his affection? The only info he has on me is what he's found out via our forced French I Q&A sessions: _Je m'appelle Jessica. J'ai seize ans. J'aime courir._ (My name is Jessica. I'm sixteen years old. I like to run.) That's what I get for wanting to be trilingual and taking an academic elective with freshmen.

By the time eighth period rolled around, I was more depressed about my loser love life than ever. I decided to cheer myself up by watching Paul Parlipiano leave his AP Physics class. As he glided out of the lab, I thought about how perfect he looked in his khakis and plaid button-down shirt. He was laughing, so I wondered what he thought was so funny. I saw ink scrawled all over his book covers and wanted to read what it said. I fantasized about what it would feel like if I wrapped one of his sandy blond curls around my pinky finger. At that moment, what I wanted most in the world—more than world peace, more than a cure for cancer, even more than Hope moving back to Pineville—was for Paul Parlipiano to smile at me and say, _Hey, Jessica. What's up?_

Then it hit me: _I'm Paul Parlipiano's Pepe Le Pew._

That was my Valentine's Day epiphany.

the twenty-fifth

I'm pretty sure I'm losing my mind.

I forgot my locker combination today. This wouldn't be so weird if I had just returned from vacation. But today is _Friday._ I opened my locker twenty times this week with no problem. However, when I got to my locker this morning before homeroom, my hand had no clue what to do. My mind was blank. Left *nothing*, right *nothing*, left *nothing*.

I turned the knob, hoping that my subconscious would kick in and instinctively stop on the correct numbers. It didn't. Then I furiously tugged on the lock, hoping that it would miraculously pop open. It didn't. I got all panicky when the warning bell rang and I wasn't any closer to getting it open. My ears got red-hot and I could feel the sweat trickling into my bra crevice. In desperation, I started spinning out random combinations that *seemed* like they could work: left 38, right 13, left 9 . . . left 42, right 23, left 2 . . . I stopped only when Mr. "Rico Suave" Ricardo popped his head out the door and asked, "Well, Miss Darling, are you going to join the rest of the Ds-through-the-Fs for homeroom this morning?"

I went to homeroom and proceeded to have a quiet connip-tion. The only other person who knows my combination is Hope. Not much help.

So I tried to visualize then analyze the particular situation I was in each time I opened my locker. Was there a pattern? Did I usually carry on a conversation while I turned the knob? Or did I open it in silent concentration? Was my backpack on my shoulders or off?

By the time homeroom was over, I was out of my head. Not because I couldn't get my books, but because it was my very own brain malfunction that was preventing me from doing so. We learned in Psych that the "breakdown in selective attention" is one of the first signs of schizophrenia. Does this qualify?

Then again, menopausal women are known to go a little wacko, so maybe the fact that I haven't menstruated in almost two months is having a similarly psychotic effect. I'm waaaay late. However, there's no possible way that I'm pregnant unless (a) I got knocked up by daydreaming about a very naked Paul Parlipiano while I was sitting on the toilet or (b) I've been chosen for the Immaculate Conception Part Two: Electric Boog-a-loo.

Ha. Ha. Ha. Funny.

This is my attempt at being blasé. I can't get too freaked about my non-period because stress is probably responsible for it's tardiness to begin with. But every time I go to the bathroom, I silently pray for a smudge of blood on my skivvies, only to be let down. I feel like I'm in ninth grade again, when I was the last girl I knew waiting for menarche to open the door to the *wonderful world of womanhood*. Ack.

Still, if I keep getting more and more bizarre, I don't think I can blame it all on PMS. I'll have to persuade my parents to take me to a doc who can give me the get-right-in-the-head meds I need.

Schizophrenia or no, I needed my books. I had to go down to the office and have the secretary look up the number for me. No way would I admit that I'd forgotten it, though. Not seven months into the school year. On a Friday. I'd rather lie. I'd say that I hadn't used my locker in ages because it was so far away from all my classes and I hated being tardy. Scotty (it's always good to name-drop a fellow scholar/athlete in these situations) was nice enough to share his with me, even though it was *technically* against school rules. But now I needed to get a pair of running shoes (again, evoking the scholar/athlete thing) that I'd stuffed in there during cross-country season . . .

I had the lie set up by the time I got to the office.

"Well if it isn't Jess Darling!" chirped Mrs. Newman. "We don't see your face around here very often."

School secretaries are always thrilled to see me. It's the last-name thing. They assume I'm way nicer than I really am.

"Hi, Mrs. Newman."

"What can I do you for?"

Is hokeyness a prerequisite for high-school secretaries?

"Well, it's a long story, but I need my locker combination . . ."

"Jess, say no more." She started clicking away at the nearest computer.

"Uh, you don't need to know why?" I asked. I was a little disappointed. I had my faux facts in order.

She just kept right on smiling. "Not from *you* I don't."

Even though I didn't have to, I gave her the whole bogus story anyway. Her only response? "That Scotty Glazer is a nice boy, isn't he?"

She wrote the numbers down on a slip of paper and handed them to me. (For future reference: left 45, right 17, left 5.) Then I turned to leave without looking up from the paper and crashed right into . . . Marcus Flutie! He had just gotten up from the bench behind me. He had been there the whole time. *Again.*

"Ain't you Jess Darlin'?" Marcus drawled, mocking Mrs. Newman. But it came out sounding like a Bible-belting, Ritz-cracker-casserole-making housewife's comment about a poodle wearing a crocheted sweater: *Ain't you jus' darlin'!*

Mrs. Newman's smile disappeared. Marcus ignored her.

"I know where your locker is, Miss Darlin'," he singsonged, which was true because his is located only about a half-dozen or so away from mine. He knew I had lied. He gave me the two-fingered *tsk-tsk*. I froze.

"Leave her alone. Don't you have enough problems of your own?"

While Mrs. Newman lectured, Marcus brushed my hair back with his hand, leaned in, and whispered, "I won't narc on you, Cuz."

He smelled sweet and woodsy, like cedar shavings. I felt his hand on my neck and his breath on my cheek. Suddenly, I was rubbery and red.

I stumbled out of there. And when I did, I found myself face-to-face with the last person I wanted to see after something like this happens: Sara. Oh, she would just love to be the one to tell everyone about me and Marcus. Not that there *is* a *Me and Marcus*, mind you. But whatever almost-nonexistent thing that exists between us would be too much for Pineville High to handle. That's exactly why this next scene was so painful:

Me: [Trying to sound cool.] *Oh, hey, Bruiser. What's up?*

Sara: I'm *fine. But what's up with you? Are you feeling okay? Omigod! You're bright red. And sweating. And you're out of breath.*

[She's viciously suspicious. She searches for clues.]

Me: *Oh, no. I'm fine. I just ran down here to get . . . uh . . . something.
I . . . uh . . . got a little winded.*

Sara: *The track star got winded running to the office?*

[Sara shakes her head and purses her lips. She's onto me.]

Me: *Uh . . . I . . . uh . . .*

[Marcus strolls out of the office and stands between Sara and me.]

Marcus: *Let's hear you sling the bullshit.*

Me: *Uh . . . I . . .*

[Marcus crosses his arms, covering up the five smiling faces of the
Backstreet Boys, whose images and silver-glitter BSB logo are
emblazoned across his chest. He risks ridicule whenever he wears
this teenybopper T-shirt, which is quite often. Most people don't
get the joke. I do. In a world where Marilyn Manson can't shock
anyone anymore, Marcus knows that wearing the Backstreet Boys
T-shirt is one of the most subversive things that he—being "Krispy
Kreme," after all—can do. He thinks it's funny. It *is*.]

Sara: [Shoots Marcus a withering glance.] *Omigod! Ugh. Stop bothering us.*

Marcus: [Looking at me.] *I'm not bothering you, am I?*

[The T-shirt cotton is thin. The ink-black Chinese character band
tattooed around Marcus's bicep shows through, needing translation,
needing to be understood.]

Me: *Uh . . .*

[Marcus walks away, laughing.]

Sara: *Omigod! What was that all about?*

Me: *That freak? I have no idea. He must be high.*

Fortunately, when Sara recounts this strange story—this iso-
lated, unprovoked incident—to everyone we know, she puts herself
in a role that is equal to mine.

"Can you believe that *quote* Krispy Kreme *unquote* came up to
us all high to spout off some weird-ass shit?" she asks. "Like we care."

Us. We. Both innocent.

The thing is, *I* do care. I don't know why. But with the Marcus–
Heath history and all, I simply can't tell Hope about what happened
today. Not the truth anyway. And that makes me a horrible friend.

47

March 1st

Hope,

Sorry you always have to go through my mom or dad to get to me. I'm phone phobic since you left. I never pick it up anymore. The reason I don't pick it up is because the very idea of having a conversation sucks all the life right out of me. It really does. Besides you, I resent *everyone* who barges in on the few precious hours of downtime I have between track practice and tossing and turning all night.

Well, tonight that person was none other than Hy. I shouldn't have been so shocked. I was the one who gave her my phone number.

To be honest, I was thinking more about *you* than her when I did it. See, I was thinking about you at your new school and how hard it's been for you to make new friends. And how you said you were grateful whenever anyone went out of her way to be nice to you.

So we talked. She told me all about the circumstances that got her exiled to Pineville. Apparently, Hy used to go to some hoity-toity private school in Manhattan. ("You needed mad bank or mad brains to get in—I had the brains," said Hy.) Midway through her fall term the dean sent a letter saying that the school no longer had funding to continue her scholarship. ("They had to bounce the riffraff to make way for more trustafarians," Hy said.) Her mom couldn't afford the tuition for the spring term. ("I never knew my dad," said Hy.) But there was no way she was going to put Hy in New York City's public school system. ("With the chickenheads and thugs," Hy said.) So until her mom transfers to her company's Jersey branch, Hy is living with her aunt and enrolled at PHS. ("With the Hoochies, Wiggaz, and Hicks," I said.)

Our convo wasn't bad or anything. Hy's history was fairly interesting. But the whole time I was talking to her, I was thinking about how sweet it would be when the clock read 9:27 P.M., which meant twenty minutes were up and I could end the conversation without seeming rude and I could try to get some sleep.

This is my new hobby. I watch my life depart minute by minute. I anticipate the end of everything and anything—a conversation, a class, track practice, darkness—only to be left with more clock-watching to take its place. I'm continually waiting for something better that never comes. Maybe it would help if I knew what I wanted.

Until I figure that out, I guess I'm waiting for the end of my sophomore year so summer can start, so I can wait for that to end so I can go back to school and do the waiting game for another two years until I graduate and finally escape to college, where I'm hoping to begin my "real life." Whatever that is.

I didn't do this as much when you were here.

I really missed you tonight. I miss talking to you. Knowing that you get me. And every time I talk to someone else it just reminds me how much they don't.

Tick-tockingly yours, J.

march

the fourth

My first spring track meet isn't for another four weeks and already I wish the whole goddamn season were over.

Today I snuck out of the house so I could do my four-mile loop around the neighborhood all alone. When I'm out running by myself, without Kiley yelling out splits, or Paul Parlipiano distracting me with his God-like grace, my mind quiets. Clears.

Forgetting my locker combination was unsettling, sure. And I'm more than a little freaked about my non-period. But the whole Marcus incident had messed with my mind royally. I couldn't stop thinking about him and what would happen if Sara started making her famous insinuations. *You know, I think there's something going on between—omigod!—Krispy Kreme and the Class Brainiac . . .*

I really needed a half hour of not thinking about anything.

My father must have planted a homing device in the soles of my Sauconys because I was no farther than a half-mile from the house when I heard the whizzing wheels of his ten-speed. I should have known. My dad is always in one of two places: In front of his computer or on his bike. And when he's not off on his solo Lance Armstrong adventures, he's tailing me.

"Pick up the pace, Notso!" he yelled. "You think Alexis Ford runs this slow?"

Alexis Ford goes to Eastland High School. She beat me by four-tenths of a second in the 1600 meters at the freshman championships last year. My father analyzes the video of that race more than the Feds did the Zapruder film when Kennedy was shot. I'm not kidding. It usually goes like this:

"You lost the race right there," he says.

"Dad, the gun just went off. We weren't even twenty-five meters into it."

Dad rewinds and freezes the tape. "Look right there," he says, pointing at the screen. "See how you had to go all the way into the third lane to get around that girl from Lacey? That was a waste of energy. Energy you needed for the sprint in the final straightaway. That's why Alexis Ford beat you by four-tenths of a second."

A few weeks ago Dad spliced together an entire tape of these race-breaking moments to create a video montage I like to call "Notso Darling's Agony of Defeat, Volume One." I'm supposed to watch and learn and never let them happen again.

"Look right there," he says. "See how your arms are swinging all over the place? See how you got boxed in?"

All his coaching is lost on me. The way I see it, there's only one racing strategy that matters. It's the one I run by: *Get in the lead and don't let anyone pass you.*

I know that my dad is just excited to have an athlete in the family. Bethany never broke a bead of sweat in her life. And he's relieved I'm not one of those chunky girls who lumber around the track, hoping to break an eight-minute mile. I'm actually good. That almost makes up for the Little League games and Pee-Wee Basketball tournaments he thought he would attend but never got the chance to.

He sees these father–daughter jaunts as a way for us to bond, but I resent the interruption. As soon as he starts in, the blank-slate state of my brain gets all mucked up.

It got so bad today that I had this psycho fantasy: I wished he'd hit me with his bike. I imagined him losing control for a split second, the wheel clipping my leg hard enough to make me lose balance, and me smacking the asphalt. I'd roll into a ball of pain and fury, my hands and legs a mess of blood, skin, and gravel. I'd scream, "WHAT THE HELL WERE YOU THINKING RIDING SO CLOSE? THIS IS ALL YOUR FAULT! WHY CAN'T YOU JUST LEAVE ME ALONE?" Maybe I'd break a leg or arm. Maybe I'd be out the whole season and my dad would feel too bad to be mad.

I got so excited by the idea of getting injured that I decided I couldn't wait for fate. I'd carefully orchestrate the crash. Yes. I'd fake the fall, confident that he wouldn't ride right over my body, crushing and killing me. No, just a brush, a bump, enough to make him *leave me alone*. My adrenaline cranked up and I started running faster at the thought of it. And that's when my dad said, "That's more like it, Notso!" Instead of making me feel better, like I knew he wanted it to, his praise made me feel worse. And more than ever I wanted him to hit me and end my running career altogether. I knew there were bumpy tree roots up ahead bursting out of the asphalt, so I could logically trip over them and ("That's it. Keep it up, Notso! You're flying!") fall into his path and he would hit me. I wouldn't have to run anymore and hear about Alexis Ford and swinging arms and the Agony of Defeat. I knew it was now or never so I stepped on the sticky-outiest root. My arms flailed and I felt like I was falling in slow motion, all the while anticipating the sting of rubber tire treading ("No!") on my ankle, my shin, my thigh. I was waiting to scream, to yell, to vent, to blame.

But my dad instinctively swerved out of the way.

Later, when I was applying hydrogen peroxide to my bloody, banged-up knee and shredded palm, my dad stood in the doorway and lectured me about being more careful.

"You could have ended the season right there," he said.

"Yes," I sighed. "But I didn't."

My skin still stings.

the tenth

A bunch of us went to the annual PHS talent show tonight. We needed a break from the weekend-in-Pineville monotony of hitting the multiplex, chowing at Helga's Diner, or vegging at Scotty's. Plus, we needed to give Hy a tasty slice of Pineville culture.

"I dare you to find a better freak show for a five-dollar admission," I said.

"Girl, I'm from the city, where the freak shows are free," she said.

"Wait and see."

At the end of the night, Hy agreed with me. Neither one of us could understand what compelled these people to willingly humiliate themselves in front of their peers.

I'll give you a brief review.

The show opened with a band rather narcissistically named The Len Levy Four. It was fronted by none other than Len Levy, the boy who broke my eight-year-old heart. He wore about six inches of pancake makeup, as though the audience would be tricked into thinking that somehow the spotlight, or perhaps the very aura of rap/metal greatness itself, had erased the purple lesions from his face. I say this with all bitterness aside, of course.

So The Len Levy Four launched into a Rage Against the Machine rip-off song. I have to admit that the band itself was pretty tight. But Len was frightening. He's pretty stiff and robotic in everyday life. Well, jack that up on crack and you've got Len's idea of stage presence. PHS's answer to Zack de la Rocha marched around his cohorts like a short-circuited cyborg, so fast that the spotlight couldn't keep up with him.

Len wasn't even halfway through the first verse when he yelled, "Pineville!" and attempted a stage dive. Talk about premature ejaculation. Everyone was still sitting in their seats. There wasn't anyone to catch him. He landed right on his feet and just kind of stood there, stunned that he was on the ground instead of surfing the crowd.

So then he went the audience-participation route.

"Pineville!" he yelled into the microphone.

Then he held it out for the audience to respond in kind. Silence.

"*Pineville!*" he yelled even louder.

This time he was met with howling laughter. The song ended not long thereafter with Len Levy throwing down the mike with a deafening squeal of feedback and storming out of the auditorium.

Rock and roll.

Next up was Dori Sipowitz, a die-hard Britney Spears fan if there ever was one. Much like the genuine Lolita diva, Dori's act was heavy on the choreography and light on the singing, relying on prerecorded vocals and lip-synching. Dori's mother was sitting right in front of us and screamed, "*Sexy, baby! Sexy, sexy, sexy!*" as her daughter writhed and gyrated in a pink, sequined catsuit with a belly-baring cutout.

I don't even need to tell you how completely sick and inappropriate that is.

She was followed by a trio of Hoochie hip-hop dancers who should've known better than to wear white spandex. (They put the "boom" in *boom-shaka-laka-shaka-laka-shaka-laka*.) A posse of Wiggaz rapped about *da thug life* outfitted in the bangingest, bling-blingingest ghetto superstar gear available at the Ocean County Mall. There was also a juggler and a Grateful Dead cover band named Long Strange Trip.

There were a few more acts but I've blocked them out. No emotion is more squirmy than feeling embarrassed for someone else.

The final act was Percy Floyd, a Double-A Elvis impersonator. After thirty seconds of anticipation-building Vegas-style vamping and spotlight swirling, The Black Elvis took the stage like a tornado. Like all Elvis impersonators worth their Quaaludes and fried peanut butter and banana sandwiches, he chose to give homage to the jelly-bellied, sideburned, rhinestone-jumpsuited Elvis, the one who sadly lost the vote for the commemorative stamp.

The audience went nuts.

I was laughing and clapping and cheering along with the rest of the audience as The Black Elvis crooned his way through "Suspicious Minds." It was only when he whipped off his huge tinted sunglasses to wipe his brow with a red scarf that I discovered the shocking identity of The Black Elvis. I nearly fainted in the aisle— which would've been a nice dramatic touch.

"Holy shit!" I screamed. "I know that kid!"

"Who is he?" yelled Hy.

"He's Pepe Le Pew!"

"Who?"

"Pepe. Pierre. This kid in my French class who has a crush on me."

Pepe must have stuffed his jumpsuit with about a dozen pillows. But fake fat aside, he was pure King. He did mock karate chops. He even had two burly "bodyguards" come out and throw a cape over him. The final touch? An announcement over the loudspeaker that *Elvis had left the building*.

I was so proud of him when he won.

I don't know how I didn't recognize him instantly. While a few hundred Wiggaz front like boyz and girlz in da hood, there are only twenty-five real black students at PHS. And there's only *one* black kid in my French class who has a crush on me, for Christ's sake. Maybe the reason I didn't immediately recognize Pepe is because he's such a gifted chameleon. I've been observing him lately. He's one of the few kids at PHS who defies categorization. He wins the talent show *and* wrestling matches. He speaks English, French, *and* Ebonics. He hangs with Double-As *and* Wiggaz, 404s *and* Dregs, Jocks *and* I.Q.s. I wish I felt as comfy with *one* clique as he seems to be with them all.

the seventeenth

Things are getting really weird.

Greg Mahoney was shot at a kegger last night. Greg is a Dreg–Hick hybrid, a burnout who blasts country music and decorates his pickup truck with a Confederate flag and an I'M A PINEY, FROM MY HEAD DOWN TO MY HEINIE bumper sticker. (Translation: I'm proud to live off a dirt road in the middle of the woods.) Anyway, this wasn't another tragic teenage rampage. No one had a gun. Greg found some loose bullets in his truck that, for reasons that remain unclear, he drunkenly decided to throw into the bonfire. The bullets exploded and shot up Greg's ass.

I heard about it in homeroom from Sara, who just loves sharing gossip like this.

"Omigod! Only a total idiot would try to, *quote* make fuckin' fireworks *unquote*."

"That's why he did it?"

"That's what I heard."

"I bet there wasn't any thinking involved at all," I said. "Greg did it because that's what Dregs do. It's his contribution to society."

Then I heard a voice say, "Excuse me, Miss Don't-Get-High-and-Mighty . . ."

I didn't have to look up to know who it was. And when I did look up and saw him zooming in on me from two rows over, I was proven right.

"What's *your* contribution to society?" Marcus asked.

I giggled. Jesus Christ, that's annoying.

"Omigod! Ugh. Mind your own fucking business," Sara said.

"Why don't *you* mind your own fucking business?" Marcus countered. "You weren't at the party, were you?"

And that's when our homeroom teacher, Rico Suave, got involved.

"What's my rule about foul language in this room?"

"Well, if you're going to bust me, bust her, too," he said, pointing at Sara. "She said 'fucking' before I did."

Before Sara even had a chance to protest, Rico Suave said, "I didn't hear her. I only heard you. Out."

"You've got to be kidding me," laughed Marcus.

"Out!"

It wasn't fair. It really wasn't fair.

Marcus didn't take his eyes off me as he gathered his stuff to go down to the principal's office. That's when I realized that Sara and I hadn't been talking that loud. Marcus had been listening to our conversation on purpose. And he wanted me to know it.

Why? He had pretty much ignored me since the office incident. And I had done my best to ignore him, too. I don't know what he's doing with me, but he definitely did it again. Now I can't stop thinking about it.

the nineteenth

Sara and Manda undoubtedly killed time on their flight to Mexico today by (a) analyzing Marcus's outburst and (b) hypothesizing about my role in it. I'm telling myself that there's nothing I can do to stop this, so there's no point in getting all hung up on it. I'm doing an okay-to-sucky job.

Only two thirds of the Clueless Crew are spending spring break in Cancún. (All expenses paid for by Wally D.) Sara and Manda tried to keep it a secret from me via a half-assed hush-hush that I can only compare to a stage whisper. *DON'T LET JESS FIND OUT ABOUT OUR TRIP.* They thought I'd be crushed when I found out they were bonding without me.

Uh, *no.*

Ironically, once they found out that I had found out, they had no problem dishing about their trip in front of Bridget. Bridget masked her pain for thirty seconds before she lost it.

"How come I didn't get invited?!"

"We assumed you wanted to spend all of your time with Burke," said Manda.

"Yeah!" said Sara.

"We can't help it if you're lucky enough to have a great boyfriend to spend spring break with and we don't," said Manda, who conveniently dumped Bernie as soon as Sara offered her the trip.

"Yeah!" said Sara.

I guess Bridget decided that she was indeed the lucky one. So she forgave them and there were hugs all around. Typical Clueless Crew conflict resolution.

Spring break is stressful. All that freedom freaks me out. It's like I'm expected to do something cool with all this free time. Maybe that's why I slept in until 3:37 P.M., throwing my sleeping schedule even more out of whack. But no matter how bored I get, it's better than being in school.

the twentieth

$\mathbf{M}$y mom came home from work last night and asked how my day was.

"Amaya is boiling bunnies over Colin . . ."

"Who? What?!"

"And Ruthie is an alkie in denial. And Justin . . ."

"Jessie! What are you talking about? Who are these people? Are they friends of yours?"

"Uh, not really," I said. "They're from *The Real World*."

My mom sighed and said, "Jessie, I asked you how *your* day was."

That's when I realized I had gotten too attached to the TV.

When Scotty invited me over to his house today, I thought, *Okay. Here's my chance to be social.* I rode my bike over. When I arrived, I rang the bell and waited for someone to come to the door. No one did. I could hear noises coming from inside, so I knew they were in there. I rang a few more times before I just let myself in.

Shouts led me to the basement. Besides Scotty, Bridget and Burke were there, and Scotty's baseball buddy P.J. The guys were huddled around the TV, playing a wrestling videogame. Bridget was standing over Burke's shoulder, watching intently.

"Hey, guys!" I shouted.

"Waaaaazzzzzzuuuuup!" shouted Scotty.

"Smackdown!" shouted P.J.

"Three sixteen! Three sixteen!" shouted B. and B.

I tried talking to Bridget, thinking she might be grateful for the arrival of someone without a Y chromosome. But she gave me one-word answers, eyes superglued to the screen.

I can't believe we used to be best friends.

The Royal Rumble went on for ten more minutes before Burke "Stone Cold" Roy was declared the winner. Only then did they acknowledge my presence.

"Hey Jess, did you see how I made Glazer my bitch?"

"*Bee ess*! Don't believe that *muther effing see* sucker."

"You got spanked! You pussy!"

And then Scotty twisted P.J.'s arms around his neck and made him beg for mercy.

I was stupid to think that they would turn off the game and—I don't know—*talk* or something. Instead, they just popped in another game. This one involved riding on skateboards and blowing each other up. I was used to this for an hour or two on Saturday nights. But I realized that they were going to do this *all day*. Girls will get together just to get together. Guys need an activity as an excuse. Otherwise it's too homo for them to handle.

Just then, I heard a toilet flush—not with a *whoosh*, but with a long, labored belch. Rob emerged from the bathroom, zipping up his fly, Lysol in hand.

"Dude, I just destroyed your shitter," he said with scatological pride.

Rob's assplosion was, literally, the final blow, so I said good-bye. Scotty handed his controller off to Bridget—who squealed "I can't play this!"—and walked me out to the driveway.

"Sucked for you, huh?" he said.

"Not really."

"Yeah, right."

Pause.

"What are you gonna do now?"

I didn't know. But I didn't want to come right out and say I didn't know.

"I think I might go over to Hy's for a while," I lied.

"You two are becoming pretty good friends, huh?"

"I guess."

"Sorry it sucked for you."

"Yeah, me too."

And I meant it. Things would be a lot easier if it hadn't.

the twenty-second

I made the mistake of promising my mom that I'd help her and Bethany prepare invitations for *the big day*. This is how desperate I was for things to do.

At first, my mom and my sister did what they do best: Torture me about Scotty.

"So are you taking Scotty to the wedding?" my sister asked.

"Uh, I don't know yet."

Her nostrils flared with a sharp, annoyed exhalation of air. "You don't know?" she asked. "Mother?!"

My mom intervened.

"Jessie, when are you planning to ask him?"

"I don't know," I said. "The wedding *is* still three months away."

My sister was about to pop a blood vessel.

"What do you think we're doing right now? We're preparing invitations. How can I know whether to send him one if you haven't decided if you're taking him?"

"He won't care if he doesn't get an invitation," I said.

"I don't care if he doesn't care," snorted my sister. "It's the proper thing to do."

I'm sure this would have gone on for hours if my sister hadn't picked up an invitation to wave in my face. Before she put it back

63

on the pile, she glanced at the writing. That's when the blonde bond broke down and things got ugly. I mean *really* ugly, to the point where it wasn't even fun to watch them go at each other.

"You call that calligraphy, Mother?"

"What do you mean?"

"The addresses are all running downhill!"

"No one is going to notice."

"*Everyone* is going to notice! I only let you do it because you promised it would look professional!"

"You think I enjoy doing this? If Grant didn't insist on inviting three hundred people, we might have been able to afford professional calligraphy."

"Don't blame Grant."

"Well, his family is twice as large and has ten times more money than we do. It would be nice if they helped out a little."

"That's not the groom's responsibility, Mother."

"This is the twenty-first century; it's time for traditions to change. The bride's family shouldn't have to pay for everything anymore."

"Well it's just too bad you don't have a boy . . ."

Matthew Michael Darling. Born August 16. Died September 1.

I don't know what fell faster, my sister's face or my mom's tears. Mom ran out of the room but my sister stayed put, knowing there wasn't anything she could do or say that could take it back.

"You are such a bitch," I said in that quiet, calm way that makes vicious words sound even worse.

Bethany's mouth went slack. She couldn't believe what I had said.

I couldn't believe it myself. I'd never said anything like that to anyone in my family before. I got up and went to my room before I found out what would happen. No way could I stay there, though, sticking LOVE stamps on the envelopes.

About a half hour later, my mom came up and told me that what I had said to my sister was totally inappropriate. Her eyes were rimmed red.

"And like what *she* said wasn't?"

"She's got a lot on her mind," my mom said, running her finger along the dust on my dresser. "She didn't mean what she said. *You* did. Which is why I want you to apologize."

"You're right, I did mean it," I said, bitterly. "But I'm not going to apologize. No way. I'm not sorry. I wouldn't expect you to understand."

"And why not?"

I wanted to say, *Because you're exactly like her.*

"Because Hope is the only one who understands."

Then my mom did her combination *There's no use talking to you–Stop moping over Hope* speech and told me I wasn't allowed out for the rest of the night, which, of course, was a blessing in disguise.

the twenty-fifth

I had to get away from my mom. So today I gave hanging out with Hy a try.

"I'm amped that you called," she said. "I was supposed to chill with my girls, but my aunt is being a *bizotch* and won't drive me to the bus station. So I'm stuck here."

"Sorry," I said. "I'll be right over."

Hy's aunt lives on the far side of Hope's old neighborhood. Her house is the same model as Hope's except all the rooms are on the opposite side: Hope's kitchen is on the left, Hy's kitchen is on the right; Hope's living room is on the right, Hy's is on the left.

You get the idea.

Anyway, I had such a feeling of topsy-turvy déjà-vu that I thought, *Omigod! Maybe Hy is destined to be my best friend. Maybe she's the Bizarro Hope.* Then I started collecting supporting evidence:

Hope has natural red hair.
Hy has black hair with (currently) artificial blue streaks.
Hope is 5 feet 11 inches tall.
Hy is 5 feet 1 inch tall.
Hope used to play the baritone horn.
Hy used to play the flute.

I just about had myself convinced. But then, in a perfect example of how I can make the ludicrous legit, I thought, *Wait—if she were Bizarro Hope, her initials would be W.H., not H.W.*

And that ended that.

I kind of enjoy going over to someone's house for the first time because I can check out her or his bedroom. A bedroom reveals a lot about what's important to a person.

Bridget's room: Highlighted newspaper clippings, mushy greeting cards (on the inside of every one: To B., Love Ya, B.), and dried carnations tacked to a bulletin board. Football practice jersey (ROY 33) hanging on the back of her door. Countless couple pics in frames, wedged in her mirror, loose and waiting to be put in a photo album, including: B. and B. at homecoming, B. and B. in front of a Christmas tree, and B. and B. in the black-and-white photo booth on the boardwalk.
Conclusion: We're *all* in trouble when B. and B. break up.

Manda's room: Millions of tiny holes in the walls, the only sign that they used to be covered with tons of kissable pics of hot hunks, gorgeous guys, and studly celebs torn out of *Bop* and *Sixteen* magazines. These fantasy photos have been replaced with wallet-size school pictures of all her past boyfriends. They look like mug shots. She's not in any of them. Above her bed? A poster: WELL-BEHAVED WOMEN RARELY MAKE HISTORY.
Conclusion: Boys, boys, boys and Women's Lib—perfect together.

Sara's room: Crucial communication devices (cell phone, headset phone, two-way pager, Palm Pilot, laptop) within reach of her bed—a queen-size model with a white- and gold-flecked marble frame, scalloped seashell headboard, and a black velvet duvet. *YM, Twist, Seventeen, CosmoGirl!, Cosmopolitan, Vogue, Entertain-*

ment *Weekly, People, National Enquirer,* and many other mags and rags sink into the ankle-deep crimson carpet. A professionally framed collage of skeletal models and actresses is the only wall hanging that doesn't fit in with the die-hard faux-rococo décor favored by her stepmother, Shelly.

Conclusion: Poor little rich Eye-talian girl wants to be a size zero—and will gripe about that or gossip about anything else to anyone who will listen.

My room: Walls the color of a week-old bruise from when Hope and I tried to slap gray over the hot pink paint my parents picked when I was a baby. Dozens of dusty plaques, trophies, and ribbons unceremoniously toppling over each other on a shelf in the far corner. Several "new classics" movie posters (*Sixteen Candles, Stand by Me, Say Anything*). Mind-blowing mosaic of two smiling friends.

Conclusion: Obviously on the brink of schizophrenia.

Hope's (old) room: Girlie flowered wallpaper covered up by dozens of paintings, sketches, and works in progress. Framed snapshot of a little boy with a crew cut, wearing overalls, struggling to carry a crying baby with flame-red hair, a funeral mass card for Heath Allen Weaver tucked into the corner. Small bookcase, packed with art books of Monet, Picasso, Warhol.

Conclusion: I'll never know her new room as well as the old one.

I got only the briefest glimpse inside Hy's psyche. She's staying in her aunt's guest bedroom until her mom's transfer, so her room isn't really *her* room. (**Her aunt's guest room:** Page 12 from the Pottery Barn catalog—from the trundle bed to the brass curtain tiebacks, from the area rug to the arrangement of fresh lilies in the vase. **Conclusion:** She makes a decent amount of money, but doesn't have a lot of time or imagination.)

The only personal items on display were a Sony VAIO laptop and a few pictures in silver frames. I picked up one of Hy hugging a wiry guy in phat pantz and a white sleeveless T-shirt with the words WHY TOO KAY? in all caps across his chest. His close-cropped hair was dyed yellow-bronze so it would glow under the strobes. Tattoo script crawled up his arm: P L U R. Peace Love Unity Respect. The Raver Mantra.

"That's Fly," she said with an uncharacteristically giddy lift to her voice. "Raves are wack, but I love him anyway. You can see why my 'rents don't."

I could see that. Then I thought about what she'd just said. Parents. Plural. She'd told me she never knew her father, so I assumed she lived alone with her mom. Maybe there's a stepfather. I didn't want to brave the tangled branches of her family tree, so I let it drop.

There was another photo of Hy wearing a slinky black dress lined up with six other girls in similar slinky black dresses. They were all hiking up their skirts to show off their legs. Hy's hair had berry-colored tips that matched her lips.

If I'm using Hy as a Hope substitute, it's clear that she's subbing me for a whole clique. After spending the afternoon with her at her house, I now understand why Hy was so pissed about PHS's anti-cell/pager legislation—she's got a lot of friends to stay connected to. In three hours, Hy got no fewer than twelve pages. ("Beeps from my peeps," she said after every one.)

"Was it hard leaving your friends?" I asked after number eight.

"Not really," she said with a shrug. "It's not like this is permanent."

She lost me there. And she must have realized it because she quickly spun around and explained that what she meant was that she'd be seeing a lot more of them once school got out.

I should have figured as much. She's fortunate to still live close enough to her friends to be able to do that. If I could visit Hope, you can bet that I wouldn't have been hanging out at Hy's house.

"Wanna Red Bull?" she asked, changing the subject.

"Huh?"

"Red Bull. You've never heard of it?"

"Uh, no."

"No surprise. I just got a few cases from the city. I should've known they wouldn't have it at the *Pineville Super-Foodtown*."

Those last words were oozing with a skull-and-crossbone toxicity that I resented. Openly expressing disgust for Pineville should be a privilege for people who've been stuck here their entire lives— not a measly two months.

"It's an energy drink," she continued. "Like crank in your soda, but legal."

"I don't think I need to be any more cranked that I am."

No, I need a drink that's the liquid equivalent of one of Mr. "Bee Gee" Gleason's boring-as-hell history lectures. As if I don't have enough sources of paranoia, I've been extra edgy about my no-show menstrual cycle. What if there's something seriously wrong with me? What if I picked up an as-of-yet undiscovered crazy cow virus by eating an undercooked cheeseburger? What if I'm a bizarro, *Ripley's Believe It or Not!* girl–boy hybrid, mere moments away from popping a set of nads between my legs? What if I'm a genetically mutated by-product of an intergalactic liaison between my mother and an alien's proboscis? (That would explain *a lot*, not just my wayward period.)

"Ain't no thing," said Hy.

Most of the afternoon was spent answering questions about life at Pineville High and watching Hy search through stacks of CDs. She's got more than 500: Everything from Acid House to Zydeco, in no order whatsoever. So it took a while to find the one she was looking for. It's called *Kind of Blue*, and according to Hy it's *the* essential jazz recording.

"Girl, you sweatin' Scotty or what?" Hy asked.

"Me and Scotty? We're just friends."

"But he's so *hunky* . . . so *beefcake*," said Hy, putting her hand over her heart and pretending to swoon. "Do you know how many chickenheads at school wanna piece of that?"

"I know," I admitted. "I just don't see myself with him."

"Why not?"

I wasn't comfy sharing my passion for Paul Parlipiano. I launched into excuse number two.

"Because I'm not Pineville's typical Groupie. I'm not a cheerleader. I hate pep rallies. I don't have fun at football games—or *any* games for that matter. And I'm bad at booting-and-rallying . . ."

She sighed. "Just because you date a Jock doesn't mean you have to be a Groupie. Scotty's been scopin' you forever. Shouldn't he know that you're not Groupie material?"

Jesus Christ. Was this a conspiracy?

"Are you trying to get me to go out with Scotty?"

Hy laughed. "Girl, I'm not trying to get you to do anything. I'm just saying that you going with Scotty could be *the* thing that throws off Pineville High's hierarchy."

Hy is the only person I know who could turn a routine question about Scotty into a rallying cry for the oppressed teen proletariat.

"You could be model girlfriend for 2G, setting the standard for the rest of the millennium," she said.

"Oh, yeah," I snorted. "Boobless, neurotic, PMS-y . . ."

"All I'm saying is that you could revolutionize the notion of popularity."

"Because I'm not the typical Groupie," I said.

"Word."

I got it. Me going out with Scotty was subversive in the same way that Marcus wearing the Backstreet Boys T-shirt was subversive: We messed with mainstream culture simply by embracing it. It was genius in theory, sure. But did it change the fact that I couldn't imagine actually kissing Scotty and performing uh, other girl-friendly duties?

"But what if I totally immersed myself in the culture of football games and keggers and turned into a bubble-gum bimbo?" I asked.

"Hmmmm . . ."

"Hmmm . . . *what?*"

"If you wanna come correct, why are you slummin' with Bridget, Manda, and Sara?"

"What do you mean?" I asked, even though I knew.

"You hate them."

Another one of Hy's humdinger zingers.

I laughed. "It's that obvious, huh?"

"You can't play me," she said, shaking a Wu-Tang CD at me for emphasis. "You're rollin' with girls you hate because you're afraid of being alone."

I started getting really sad. If Hope were still here, I wouldn't have had to make that choice. Together, we would've broken free from the Clueless Crew. But without her . . .

"Is that it?"

There was only one answer to that. And if I'd said it out loud I swear I would've lost it right then and there. Hy didn't make me.

"Girl, stop trippin'. You're dope despite being born and raised here. You'd be down with me and my peeps."

I considered this for a moment, long enough to stop feeling sad and ensure that my words wouldn't come out choked and teary.

"Bubble-gum bimbos," Hy said, laughing. "That's the *shiznit*. You and I are better than that. And though I don't know him, Scotty sees something in you, which might mean that he's not an assembly-line meatballer."

"Maybe you're right."

I had to say I found this conversation very encouraging and empowering. To hear Hy not only accepting me but aligning herself with me boosted my ego quite a bit. Maybe we will be friends after all. And I'm trying not to feel guilty about it. Being friends with her doesn't make me any less of a friend to Hope, does it?

the twenty-eighth

I dreaded going back to school today, fearing Marcus Flutie fallout. But nothing happened. Marcus didn't even sneeze in my direction. I've decided that his erratic attention means that he doesn't have a malicious motive. His taunts didn't have anything to do with me. He could've done it to anyone. I could've been anyone.

Anyway, Sara had more important things on her mind.

"Omigod!" she whispered with glee. "I had sex in Cancún!"

Marcus was a long-forgotten memory.

Hy and I got the lowdown at lunch. Apparently Sara and Manda spent the whole week lying about their age and getting inebriated college guys to buy them margaritas. I can't go into all the dirty details of their seven-day ho-down because it's too disturbing.

Here's all I can say about our fair Sara's deflowering: It took place on day six of their trip in Room 203 of La Casa de la Playa, an establishment that Sara's and Manda's frat-boy friends in a fit of cleverness renamed "La Casa de la Cucaracha." He was a Kappa Sigma at some school in Arizona and went by the last name of Bender. (Bruiser 'N' Bender. Isn't that precious?) He wore a condom. Upon climaxing, he paid homage to one of Mexico's finest actors by yelling ¡Arriba! ¡Arriba! This tribute to Speedy Gonzalez was appropriate since the whole messy act took no more than two minutes.

Wait, it gets even more repulsive. Manda could corroborate Sara's story because she was in the room throwing a freaky-deaky fiesta with Bender's frat-boy buddy, Sherm "The Worm." (Insert tequila shot/oral sex joke here.)

They both think this is the coolest thing ever.

What's truly pathetic is that Sara actually thinks that Bender is now her boyfriend or something. She *knows* he's going to keep in touch with her. Manda isn't helping matters by encouraging this fantasy.

"Why else would he have asked for Bruiser's E-mail address?"

Hy and I couldn't believe that they could be so oblivious to this, the most basic of post-one-night-stand face-savers. Then Hy decided to stir up some controversy by asking provocative questions. This is her most endearing quality.

"So does Bender know that you're only sixteen?"

"Fifteen," corrected Sara.

"Fifteen," amended Hy.

"No," said Sara. "I figured I'd tell him the truth later."

"Hmmmm . . ."

"Hmmmm . . . *what?*" asked Sara.

"Well, technically, he raped you."

"WHAT?!"

"He was twenty-one. You were fifteen. That's statutory rape."

"Omigod! No it's not! I was drunk off my ass, but I wanted to do it."

"Doesn't matter," said Hy. "The law's the law."

I wondered about jurisdiction—whether he could be prose-cuted in the United States for a crime that occurred south-of-the-border. (Ha. In more ways than one.) But Hy was so matter-of-fact about it that Sara's face was turning all sorts of colors. It kind of reminded me of a Mexican sunset. Or a tequila sunrise.

"Well, I wouldn't press charges anyway," said Sara.

"Oh, I didn't think you would." Hy glanced at me as she casu-ally sipped her Red Bull. For the first time, I read her mind.

"Your parents might," I said, picking up where Hy left off. "You know, if you got knocked up or diseased or something."

"Omigod! So now *you're* going to start in on me too?"

"What about Fly?" attacked Manda. "He's nineteen. Rape. Right?"

Sara smiled at Manda for coming to her defense, then shot Hy a *So, there!* look.

"Who says Fly and I are having sex?"

There was an awkward moment of silence. Then Sara turned her attention to Bridget.

"And what are you going to do when Burke turns eighteen, Bridge?"

Bridget had been sidelining this whole conversation. Her pretty face squished with annoyance for being dragged into it against her will.

"Who says Burke and I are like, having sex?"

I just about fell down with shock. Bridget's devirginization was a foregone conclusion in my mind, and apparently everyone else's. I figured Bridget had been giving Manda and Sara the passion play-by-play all along. I was wrong. Their suntans drained from their faces.

Unfortunately, *La Aventura Mexicana de Manda y Sara* was still open for discussion. As if the blow-by-blow (pun intended) account of their trip weren't bad enough, our Spanish teacher was so eager to hear about their journey to her homeland that she let them take up class time to tell us all about it. Of course, Señora Vega got the censored version.

"The Mexican people are so welcoming of Americans," said Manda.

"*Sí!*" said Sara.

"And their culture is so rich with tradition," said Manda.

"*Sí!*" said Sara.

How they managed to keep a straight face is beyond me.

In the middle of all this, Scotty passed me a note saying: *They party for a week and we have to sit here and listen to them talk about culture? B.S.!* I turned and mouthed, "I know!"

This was a breakthrough for Scotty and me. He usually doesn't stoop to my cynical level. Maybe I never paid enough attention before.

Still, no one missed me more than Pepe. I've forgiven him for that brief period when he was too busy basking in the post-talent-show glow to toss one *Bonjour!* my way. Today he couldn't stop spinning around in his seat to smile at me. Madame Rogan got tired of shouting, "*Tournez-vous, Pierre!*" ("Turn around, Pierre!") and moved him a few rows away from me. He waved good-bye and dramatically said, "*Je suis triste. Au revoir.*" ("I'm sad. Good-bye.") Everyone laughed, but not in a mean-spirited way because Pepe gets away with stuff like that. It was funny. But I felt like I was going to cry.

April 1st

Hope,

   Just to reinforce the lessons learned in our last phone call: Sara is a skank. Bridget is still a virgin. Manda is too, but she might as well not be because—in my totally unsubstantiated opinion—oral is way more inti-mate than real sex.

   Did I mention that Hy hasn't done it either? It's more than a little unbelievable, but why would she lie? I'll take her word because knowing such a hip virgin makes me feel like less of a leper for being one too.

   I like Hy. But she always refers to NYC as "the city," as if it were the only metropolis on earth. And to further show off her cosmopolitan superiority, she tries too hard to be both "street" and "elite." She doesn't pull off either one. Hy was the poorest student at her private school, but she clearly picked up the POVs of her high-society schoolmates. She's got an opinion on everything and she just *has* to share them.

   Pineville doesn't have Latin classes? How do they expect you to rock the SAT verbal section without Latin? There's no girl's lacrosse team here? It doesn't mat-ter if there's zero interest. Two words: Title IX. This year's school musical is South Pacific? Damn. That's wack. Last year we put on an original musical written and directed by a senior who's now at Juilliard. It was called Rotten Apple and was about Lilith, you know, the first woman bounced out of Eden. You've never heard of Lilith?! Where do you think the name for Lilith Fair came from? You've really got to wise up to feminist theory . . .

   No fear. Hy and I will never be more than casual confidants.

   While I'm off the subject of virginities and lack thereof, how do you feel about me getting together with Scotty? I'll let you decide whether that's an April Fools' joke.

Cryptically yours, J.

april

the sixth

Prom fever has already hit PHS with a vengeance. I will lose it if I hear one more chirpy voice say, *It's pink, and it's cut down to here, with a layer of chiffon that starts about here, and goes just a squinch above the knee . . .*

As a sophomore, I shouldn't be forced to listen to this talk about the junior–senior prom. I certainly shouldn't be forced to feel bad about it. But enough girls in honors are going with upperclassmen that I feel like a loser because no junior or senior boy wants to get me drunk off Boone's Strawberry Hill so he can cop easy sex off me in the backseat of his parents' SUV.

Jesus Christ. What's wrong with me?

Rob asked Hy. She said yes, then took it back when she found out from Sara that he was suspended for jerking off into a Milky Way wrapper during study hall last year. Hy's refusal shocked everyone but me. If anyone has the guts to dis the captain of the überjock triumvirate on account of his sexually deviant behavior, it's Hy.

A few days later she was asked by a junior in her Economics class. Once she did a background check ("Okay. Has he waxed his jimmie in public?"), she surprised *all* of us by saying yes. Especially me.

"Won't Fly get jealous?" asked Bridget.

"Nah, he knows he's more dope than any high-school shorty."

"What I really want to know," I said, "Is why an NYC club queen would want to go to Pineville's lame-ass prom."

"I wanna see what a Pineville throw-down is like. Is that okay?" She sounded a wee bit annoyed.

"Hey. Fine by me," I shrugged. "But you're the one always dissing Pineville's social activities."

"That's because I haven't given them a chance yet." Hy slowly broke out into a smile. She has very white, very even, very perfect teeth. "Besides, I missed a lot of my friends' Sweet Sixteens and need to do some flossin'. I wanna rock a new dress."

The Clueless Crew loved that one because it's exactly the type of thing they would say, minus vocab cribbed from *The Source*. It was very weird. Is this what promaganda does to people? Makes them think it's perfectly normal to wear a corsage or a *crinoline*?

Bridget is going with Burke. Yes, they're still together, uniting daily before Chem for a pre-third-period dry-hump against Burke's locker.

I can't believe they haven't had sex yet. But I've known Bridget since birth, and she has *never* told a lie. Whenever we committed a kiddie caper—like plucking all the American Beauties off old Miss Weinmaker's prized rosebushes, or scarfing a box of Thin Mints that we were supposed to deliver to the Girl Scouts supporter who rightfully bought it—she always copped to the truth before I could even begin to launch into our (false) alibi. I'm not kidding. I think lying would complicate things too much for Bridget. She wouldn't be able to keep her stories straight.

Anyway, because the prom is a special occasion, Manda is breaking her "Seniors Only" rule by agreeing to go with Vinnie Carvello, a junior who just happens to be P.J.'s older brother. This nearly drove the younger Carvello to commit hari-kari with a bottle opener. ("Oh, *now* she decides to freely give out hummers?") Manda is also going to Eastland's senior prom with some guy she's "known forever," which probably means she let him feel her up under the boardwalk last summer. Manda is a pathological prom goer. These will be her fourth and fifth. Promming for her is like low-level prostitution. She gets all dressed up. They pay for everything. She gets them off.

Even *Scotty* is going to the prom. He was asked by Kelsey Barney. She's a senior, the manager of the baseball team. Scotty said she's going to some small college in North Carolina that I've never heard of. I don't think she's too smart. She's got big crunchy hair. Borderline Hoochie. In my unbiased opinion, he could do so much better.

Sara and I are the only ones with nothing to do on prom night. Fortunately, right now she's so heartbroken about hearing nada from her Kappa Sigma soulmate that she can't even muster enough sorrow to get depressed about the prom. So I have some time before I need to come up with some excuse as to why we can't wallow in our loneliness together.

the tenth

A day of high highs and low lows.

I had a track meet this afternoon. It started almost an hour and a half late because the visitors' bus broke down or something. I easily won my first two races, but that's not important to this story.

Because their away meet started on time, the boys' team returned to the school just as the 4 × 400 relay—the last event— was getting under way. Now, in a tense meet situation, I wouldn't run this event because I'd have to do the Triple Threat: 800 meters, 1600 meters, and 3200 meters. But since we had already scored twenty points more than we needed to lock in the win, Coach decided not to kill me today and put me in the relay to help me build up my sprinting strength. (A strategy wholeheartedly supported by my unofficial coach in the bleachers.)

The point is, under normal circumstances, Paul Parlipiano would not have been there to see me run. And not only did he see me run, he actually cheered me on. *Me!* As I came around the far turn by the flagpole I heard him yell, "Go Pineville! You're kicking her butt!" Which I was. And I was going so fast that I didn't even see him. I just heard that voice and knew. Once I passed the baton, I looked back just to confirm that I hadn't made up the moment. He was still there, leaning on the fence. It really was him.

Thanks to my enormous lead, the next three runners would've

had to have been struck down by polio to blow the race. It was a totally insignificant victory in the grand scheme of things, but for me, it was one of the greatest triumphs of my life. Paul Parlipiano had noticed me, and I hadn't totally blown it by collapsing at the sound of his voice. I was positively flying.

A half hour later, I came crashing down.

I was getting my stuff out of the locker room while a group of juniors and seniors were talking about (what else?) the prom. I heard Carrie P. mention Paul Parlipiano's name. I could hear his name if it were whispered in a football stadium filled with 10,000 screaming fans. I was feeling gutsier than usual, so I asked, "What about Paul Parlipiano?"

"He's taking Monica Jennings. They're sitting at our table."

From blue skies to *splat!* Just like that.

"You're not gonna get all fucking depressed now, are you?"

"No," I lied.

Monica Jennings isn't that blond, big-boobed bitch you love to hate in the movies. She's sometimes pretty, sometimes plain. She's in Honors, but isn't ranked in the top five in her class. She's on the tennis team, but isn't the captain. She's friends with members of the Upper Crust, but isn't invited to all their private parties. She's a totally normal girl.

And that makes this hard for me to take. It means that there's no reason why *I* couldn't go to the prom with Paul Parlipiano—other than the fact that to him I'm just another girl in a Pineville uniform, one who has never said as much as *Bonjour, mon ami* to him.

the twelfth

Marcus and his latest ho-bagity Hoochie girlfriend were kissing each other by his locker this morning. I don't know her name. I saw her from behind, so I don't know what she looks like exactly.

But like most Hoochies, she has over-dyed, over-everythinged hair. She's also a size twelve who thinks she's a size six.

I had to walk past them to get to homeroom and I was trying to avert my eyes. Just as I got within a few feet of the couple, Marcus took his hands off her big ol' Lycra/spandexed butt and waved at me. His eyes were on mine, but his mouth never stopped moving in and out and around hers.

When he passed my desk two minutes later, I didn't exist.

This has got to stop.

the sixteenth

It was 4:20 A.M. and I was buzzing as usual. It was really warm out. Practically 50 degrees. I started thinking about how stupid it was that I was stuck in my room, 100 percent awake, waiting for the sun to come up to start my day. Why can't I start my day when it's still dark out?

I decided to listen to the message my twitchy muscles were trying to tell me: *Let's go running.* Right then. My dad was guaranteed not to follow me. I threw on shorts and a T-shirt and laced up my shoes. I crept to the kitchen and wrote a note: I COULDN'T SLEEP. I WENT RUNNING. 4 A.M. DON'T GET MAD. JESS.

I tiptoed out the back door and stretched on the patio. The air smelled like wet grass. Crickets chirped. Leaves rustled in the breeze. The moon was a sliver short of being full, so I didn't have to worry about lunatics.

I ran.

Everything was different in the dark. My neighborhood's bi-level, split-level, bi-level, split-level scheme seemed so safe and predictable in daylight. But at night, these same houses were secret and mysterious. Especially the ones that had a single light on. All the nights that I've been alone and awake in my bedroom, I never stopped to think about all the other people who might be tossing and turning too.

After I don't know how many miles, I stopped thinking. I know this sounds all Oprah–Chopra, but everything got in synch: the beat of my breath, the flow of my feet, the rhythm of the road, the bursts of color blurring by. I was running so effortlessly that I didn't stop when I finished my loop. I kept right on running, as though my body made the decision before my brain had a chance to shoot it down.

By the time I got back to the house, the sun was coming up all pink and orange over the horizon. It was a little past 5:45 A.M. I had run for a little over an hour, and for some strange reason, I wasn't the least bit tired. More important, my mind had kept quiet for the first time in a long while. For more than an hour, I didn't think about prom, or Paul Parlipiano, or my non-period, or anything.

And that includes Marcus Flutie.

My heart was pumping and I was intensely aware of being alive. Amazing. I wish life could be like that all the time, or that I could will it that way whenever I wanted. When my worries shut up, everything just feels right.

I was feeling so optimistic that I made a vow to myself then and there: *I will be normal.* I will accept that Hope is gone. I will not be afraid of being friends with Hy. I will face up to the fact that Paul Parlipiano will not deviginize me. I will stop thinking that Marcus Flutie is trying to corrupt me. *I will be normal.*

The first logical step in becoming a normal high school sophomore?

Asking Scotty to my sister's wedding.

It made perfect sense. Scotty is normal. Scotty has fun. Scotty can sleep at night. I've been in public school too long to totally buy into Hy's theory of revolution, but maybe she's partly right. If I hang with him, some of his positive vibes might rub off on me. Maybe I can be normal—perhaps even *popular*—without losing myself in the process. I'll never know unless I try.

Just so I wouldn't lose my nerve, I biked to Scotty's house to ask him in person, as soon as I cleaned myself up after my cathartic run.

When I arrived, there was an unfamiliar car parked in the driveway. By the time I figured out who it belonged to and had the impulse to hop on my bike and ride home, it was already too late. I'd been spotted by Scotty and his cradle-robbing prom date.

"Oh hey, Jess," called Scotty from the screened-in porch. "You know Kelsey Barney, right?"

I said "yes" and smiled and she said "hi" and smiled and all three of us stood there and smiled and everything was swell.

"She drove me home from this morning's crack-of-dawn practice," he explained.

"It's on my way home," she said.

"Buttcrack," I said.

"Huh?"

"Buttcrack-of-dawn practice," I explained.

"Huh?"

"Buttcrack . . . uh, because it sucks to get up so early."

"Oh."

This was not what I had in mind at all. *Not at all.* My first step to being a normal high-school sophomore was down a manhole, on a land mine, off a cliff, Wile E. Coyote–style.

"Do you want to come in?" asked Scotty

I was still on the opposite side of the screen.

"Uh, sure," I said.

"I was about to get going anyway," said Kelsey.

Scotty got up and swung the door open. He let her out and me in.

"See ya," Kelsey said.

"See ya," Scotty said.

"Good-bye," I said.

Scotty and I didn't say anything until after Kelsey started her car, pulled out of the driveway, and drove off with a honk and a wave. He sat down next to me on the porch swing.

"So what's up?"

"Are you guys going out, or what?"

He looked shocked. "Who, me and Kelsey? No. No way!" he said, as if he had honestly never considered it. "We're just friends."

"That's not how she sees it."

"Stop being an *a hole*. No way."

Guys are total morons.

"Scotty, she wants you."

"Well, I don't want her," he said matter-of-factly.

"Fine."

"Fine."

I pushed the swing back and forth with my foot.

"So why did you come over here?" he asked.

Why did I come over here? Oh, yeah.

"Are you *sure* you guys aren't going out?" I asked.

He laughed. "I think I would know if we were going out."

Valid point. I took a deep breath. "Well, you know Bethany is getting married, right?"

"Is that thing finally happening?"

"Yeah. The thing is, I kind of need a date because I'm the Maid of Dubious Honor . . ."

"Huh?"

"Maid of Honor," I corrected, opting not to explain the joke. "It's kind of a high-profile position, I guess. And if I go alone Bethany and my mom said it will look 'conspicuous,' whatever the hell that means. So I was wondering . . ."

"Are you asking me if I'll be your date to your sister's wedding?"

"Well, not my *daaaaaate*," I said, feigning grade-school disgust. "The guy I go with."

"Well, when you put it that way, how can I resist?"

"You know what I mean."

He stopped the swing. "So it's like a prom. Only with free booze."

"Yeah. And I'll be wearing a really ugly yellow dress."

"*Ooooooh*, now you're talking all sexy."

I like that Scotty and I can joke like this. Scotty is the only boy my parents let me hang out with in my bedroom. Alone, with the door closed. Not that I have tested this by bringing many strange boys home. But one time P.J. came over to work with me on a science project and my parents insisted that he stay in the kitchen. It's almost as though my parents *want* me and Scotty to have sex because then they could catch me and punish me for a *normal* teenagery reason instead of for my vaguely misanthropic behavior.

"Sure, I'll go with you."

And we hugged. I was happy. And I was still happy when I called my sister to tell her the news. She was nicer to me than I can ever remember her being. Amazing, considering I called her a bitch the last time we spoke. And when I told my mom, she just about burst out of her twinset with excitement.

Everything is going to be okay. Normal.

the twenty-first

I wasn't surprised that the Clueless Crew was beyond thrilled that I had asked Scotty to the wedding.

"Omigod! You must tell me everything!" said Sara.

"That's what I like to see, a woman taking control!" said Manda.

"We can double date!" said Bridget.

"*¡Viva la revolución!*" joked Hy, to the collective confusion of the Clueless Crew.

And for a few days, I felt like I belonged. That's why what happened today sucker-punched me in the gut.

"When is your track season over?" asked Manda after home-room this morning.

"Not until June."

"And you have games every Saturday, right?"

"*Meets*," I corrected.

"Meets, games, whatever," said Manda, waving away the mistake mindlessly with her hand. She was clearly tired of this conversation, and no wonder. I had explained the intricacies of my track schedule whenever a crucial social opportunity popped up.

"Do you have one this Saturday?"

"Yes. I have two duals a week, plus a relay, invitational, or championship meet every Saturday."

"Oh," Manda said, glancing at Hy.

"Why?"

"Well, I'm taking them shopping in the city this Saturday . . ." Hy explained.

"To look for prom dresses . . ." said Manda.

"And other stuff," said Sara, defensively.

I couldn't believe it. After all the smack-talk about the Clueless Crew, Hy was willingly hanging out with them? And without my sane brain to bounce off of? Sure, I talked about the Clueless Crew behind their backs and then went out with them on weekends, but that's because I've got history with them. I *have* to. But Hy is under no such obligation.

At first, I was cool with it. *You don't even like shopping, remember? And New York City is a dirty, disgusting, dangerous place.* But as soon as we got to history class and I saw them going over the New Jersey Transit bus schedule, I felt sick to my stomach. I told Bee Gee that I had to go to the girls' room, giving him the conspiratorial raising of the eyebrows that implies "feminine problems." The teacher gave me a pass, no questions asked.

I sprinted to the bathroom. I was so upset, I forgot to give the code as I burst through the door. Uh-oh. When I hit the tiles, I saw three Hoochies slicing up a cloud of cigarette smoke with their pastel-painted talons. One of them was Marcus's girlfriend, whose synthetic pants were *obscenely* tight in the crotch.

"Fuck! It's just an IQ," grunted Camel Toe when she saw me.

"Fuck! I just lit that cigarette," griped her friend.

"What the fuck?" asked the third, murdering me with her black-lined eyes. "Why didn't you give the fuckin' code?"

I apologized for forgetting to say "It's cool" as I walked in. *The code.* The fuckin' code.

"You better be fuckin' sorry," said Camel Toe. "You made me waste a fuckin' cigarette."

I wasn't sure where wasting a fuckin' cigarette fell on the Hoochie brawling scale, but I wasn't about to find out.

"I'm sorry," I said as I quickly hightailed it out of there.

Their whoops and cackles echoed off the walls, loud enough that I could still hear them as I headed back to history class.

I never get to be alone when I want to.

A period later, I was still fuming. So I decided to confront Hy. I followed her to her locker, and tried to get some answers as she applied her lip gloss.

"What's going on?"

"What do you mean?"

"You knew I had a meet and planned the trip anyway . . ."

"Girl, I must have been trippin'," she said in between puckers. "You're not mad at me are you? Ain't no thing."

I *was* mad. And hurt. And confused. Since when did I become "no thing" in Hy's eyes? Since when did I even care?

"I'm not mad."

"You better not be. That's some triflin' shit."

I watched her looking at herself in the mirror and a strange feeling passed over me. Stranger than I already felt.

"What is it?" Hy asked.

I said the first thing that came to mind.

"Did you know that when you look in the mirror, that's not what you really look like? Your image is actually reversed."

Hy laughed, but it wasn't a legit ha-ha funny laugh. "Girl, you don't even know the half of it," she said softly, almost to herself.

the twenty-fourth

Scotty called me tonight. We've been talking to each other a lot more on the phone since I asked him to the wedding. But tonight's phone call was different.

"I think you're right," he said. "I think Kelsey likes me."

No kidding. Jesus Christ, I was tired.

"She booked a room at the Surfside Hotel for post-prom . . ."

This was one ballsy phone call. I know that he likes me. So was I still expected to take this conversation at platonic-female-friend face value? I don't think so. He was doing this just to make me jealous. I have to admit, it was working.

"She wants to devirginize you, huh?"

"*Gee dee*, yeah. I guess."

I was so tired—of this and everything else.

"Are you going to let her pop your cherry? Oh, wait. Guys don't have cherries. Traditionally, it's the guy who is the popp*er*, not the pop*ee*. So what do you a call it when a guy gets *touched for the very first time?*" I sang the last six words, of course.

"You make it sound like I'm gonna *eff* the *ess* out of her."

"Well, aren't you?"

"I told you I don't like her."

"Mutual like isn't always a prerequisite for fucking the shit out of someone."

"*Gee dee*, Jess. Why do you have to put it like that?"

"You said it, not me."

"That's not how I said it."

"Fine. I guess if you can't say it, you can't do it."

Scotty sighed. "You're doing this on purpose."

"I'm not doing anything." My dulcet voice, innocent.

"Yes you are. You're pissing me off on purpose."

"Me? No, *you're* doing this on purpose."

"Doing what?"

Here it was. My chance to get this thing—this *us* thing—out in the open. "Trying to make me jealous."

He sputtered into the receiver. "W-w-why would I try to make you jealous?"

Get ready. Here it comes. "Because you like me. Because you want me to be your girlfriend again."

Silence.

"Did you really think Hope wasn't going to tell me?"

More silence. A barely-there groan, maybe.

"You give me an *effing* headache. Good night." Scotty hung up the phone.

And I was tired, tired, tired, tired.

the twenty-ninth

Today was Hy's trip to N.Y.C. with the Clueless Crew. Big whoop.

It turned out that I didn't have a meet. Coach Kiley pulled us from today's relays to rest us up for the more important meets coming up. I didn't intentionally lie to them. But once I realized my mistake, I didn't correct it either. Too demoralizing.

So I could've been on a bus to N.Y.C. this morning. Instead, I was downing coffee and Cap'n Crunch while my mother yapped about making table favors for *the big day*. But I was too tired for tulle talk.

"Spare me, Mom."

"I am sick of your bad moods," she said.

"It's not *my* fault I've been PMS-ing for five months."

"What?!"

I informed her that I hadn't had my period since December. And that's when she freaked out. Her eyes immediately shot down to my abdomen, looking for signs of life.

I laughed out loud. "Mom! There is no possible way I'm pregnant."

Mom wanted me to go to the gyno but I told her I wasn't getting in the stirrups until I was eighteen or sexually active—and let's face it, we know which one of those is going to come first. So she called up our family doc, Dr. Hayden. To tell you the truth, I was incredibly relieved. It was about time I found out what was wrong with me.

As soon as I got there, I remembered why I'd held off. I hate waiting rooms in doctors' offices. First of all, they're full of sick people, spreading their germs all over the place. I found this particularly annoying today because I wasn't sick. I was *getting* all the contamination without giving any. Secondly, the magazines suck. I guess they figure *Highlights* will appeal to both ends of the drooling spectrum: children and senile senior citizens. Everyone in between can just die of boredom, or of whatever disease you're at the doctor's office for, since they make you sit there so damn long.

After an eternal wait, I was finally called into the examining room.

"Do you want me to go with you?" my mom asked.

"No."

First I got measured (5 feet 5 inches) and weighed (105 pounds in my clothes). Then I put on the gown and got my blood pressure and temp taken. The nurse drew some blood. I gave a urine sample.

Then I waited for another twenty-five excruciating minutes.

Dr. Hayden finally came bustling into the room and got right down to business.

"So Jessica, what's the problem?"

"Well, let's just start off with the one that brought me here. I haven't gotten my period in five months."

"I see. Jessica, I'm going to ask you some sensitive questions that I need to know the answers to. You can be sure I won't tell your mother."

"I'm not sexually active, if that's what you want to know."

"Yes, that's one thing I wanted to know."

He looked over my chart. "You're very thin. Are you familiar with the female athlete triad?"

Jesus Christ! My own doctor thinks I'm anorexic.

"Perhaps you don't eat enough and exercise too much, which contributes to the absence of the menstrual period. . . ."

"Amenorrhea," I said.

"Amenorrhea," he repeated, surprised that I knew the technical term. "Which, over time, leads to a third problem. . . ."

"Osteoporosis."

"Correct!" His enthusiastic affirmation reminded me of a combo of my professional counselor, Brandi, and Regis in the $32,000 round of *Millionaire*. "So you're familiar with it?"

"Yes, I'm familiar with it. Not only have I had months to think about this, but my coach has warned us all about it around a bizillion times. But I know that's not the problem because I eat more food than any girl I know."

"I see."

"And I don't vomit it up either, which is more than I can say about the girls I eat lunch with every day. Only they don't eat. They sit there and worship anorexic models in magazines."

"I see."

"I hate them."

"Who? The models in magazines?"

"No," I said, picking at the fresh Band-Aid the nurse had just stuck on the crook of my arm. "My friends."

As I sat there with my butt hanging out of the paper gown, I told him about how I stopped sleeping when Hope moved away. Then I told him all about how Hy and the Clueless Crew were blowing a bundle in the Village. Next I was revealing how my dad is obsessed with my running career and the pressure he puts on me to win every race and *Notso Darling's Agony of Defeat, Volume One*. Then I exposed my mom's obsession with my sister's wedding. It got even more personal as I went on and on about asking Scotty to the reception, and how Kelsey is closing in on him, and to top it off, how I don't have a boyfriend, probably because I'm too busy being in love with a guy who doesn't know my name.

But for some reason, I stopped short of telling him about the Marcus Flutie situation. I guess at the time I thought that would've been a bit too much information. I already knew that it was kind of needy and desperate and insane that I was spilling my guts to my doctor. But he was the first adult to treat me like I was one, too. Unlike my parents, he didn't trivialize my feelings by trying to talk me out of them. He just sat there silently and let me go off, which I really appreciated. It was all very weird.

Afterward, Dr. Hayden called my mom into his office so they could talk privately about me, which was very annoying. But I knew he couldn't go into the details because of doctor-patient privilege and all. Five minutes later, my mom came out with a very tight smile.

"Let's go," she said through clenched teeth.

"Bye, Jessica," Dr. Hayden said. "Have a great season. I'll be looking for your name in the sports pages."

I said good-bye. Then I asked my mom what he had said about me.

"Nothing."

"Isn't it illegal to talk about my medical problems without me in the room? Don't I have a right to know?"

My mom sighed. "Not until you're eighteen."

"So you're not going to tell me what's wrong until I'm eighteen?"

"No, I'm going to tell you what's wrong right now," she said.

I have to say, I was looking forward to this. I had my amateur opinion—that my mental instability was pushing me toward a nervous breakdown—but I wanted to hear what a pro thought was wrong with me.

"Dr. Hayden thinks you could benefit from taking a multivitamin."

What a disappointment. I thought he had really listened to me. Adults suck.

"He also thinks I should consider taking you to a psychologist."

Hallelujah! Now we were getting somewhere.

"Does he think I'm borderline schizophrenic?"

"No," she said. "He says you worry too much. Put on your seat belt."

"I worry too much? I've *always* worried too much," I said. "That's the best diagnosis we could get for a hundred dollars?"

"He says stress is taking a toll on your health. That's why you're not sleeping and probably why you're not getting your period. Put on your seat belt."

"I will gladly live without my period . . ."

"*Put on your seat belt.*"

I put on my seat belt.

Dr. Hayden had given her the name of a good child/adolescent psychologist. If I were a legitimate wack-job, sure I'd hit the couch. But I told her there was no way I was going to see a shrink just to mellow out.

"Is there anything you want to tell me?" she asked, very earnestly.

Is there anything I want to tell her? Sure. There are a bizillion things that I *want* to tell her. If I could talk to her, I wouldn't have had to spill my guts to poor Dr. Hayden, now would I? But as much as Mom would love a touching mother–daughter moment, she can't suddenly become my bestest bud just because she stopped thinking about *the big day* for the two seconds it took her to ask the question. I wouldn't give her the satisfaction.

"No."

She sighed for about ten minutes.

"I'm not going to tell your father about this. It will only upset him, too," she said, picking up speed on the highway. "What I don't understand is what you have to be so worried about in the first place. And why you feel the need to take it out on us . . ."

I love that she twisted this around to make it about them and not me. That's when I zoned out, listening to the hum of the tires. Staring at the yellow dashes on the road, I reveled in my contentment and my decision to keep my mouth shut from now on.

May 6th

Hope,

Period Watch 2000 continues. Of course, my amenorrhea anxiety has reached an all-time high ever since I found out that there's no legit diagnosis.

So it's no coincidence that my tolerance for the Clueless Crew has hit a new low. I'll spare you a torturous travelogue of that shopping trip I told you about. Suffice it to say that Mr. D'Abruzzi's credit card got quite a workout; the four of them have been sporting new gear and makeup all week. Blatant buddy-buying at its best. Or worst.

And now Hy is the ringleader. She knew Wally D would pay up if Sara told him she'd been crying all the time because she was the only one left out on all the prom-related fun. No one noticed or cared that I wasn't going to the prom. They were so completely suspended in their own collective delusional reality that they were oblivious to the fact that they'd left *me* out of their prom-related fun, and that the real reason Sara had been crying was because she thought she'd gotten knocked up. In one of her first acts of solidarity, Hy had rechristened Sara's devirginizer That Frat-Boy Fuckhead.

Hy now jokes with them like she enjoys it. As I've said many times, she wasn't best-friend material for me. But I was cool with that as long as she wasn't best-friend material for the Clueless Crew either. Hy changes personas as often as she changes the color of her highlights (currently shades of purple). Maybe she never was who I thought.

Oh, and Scotty still isn't talking to me. Combine all this with about three minutes of sleep each night, and the fact that prom hysteria is at its shrieky peak, and you'll understand why I'm feeling psycho and not at all ready to run in the qualifying time trials for the state sectionals this afternoon. Hopefully, I'll be cured before our next convo.

Schizophrenically yours, J.

_may

the fourteenth

This is how I spent my Saturday, instead of running in the state sectionals or participating in all-day prom prep:

I woke up at 1:45 P.M. The only reason why my eyes opened is because my mother tore into my bedroom, whipped up the shades, and yelled, "It's one-forty-five p.m.—well past time to wake up!" before swirling out the door in a blur of pastel and perfume. My tongue was too weighed down by nocturnal mouth muck to give her the lashing she deserved for destroying my slumber. Unfortunately, I couldn't pretend that she was just a cheerfully terrifying nightmare. Once I'm up, I'm up.

So I got out of bed. I looked out the window. The sun was shining and it was seventy-one degrees—perfect for prom photos. And track meets. I put on a pair of board shorts and a tank top and twisted my hair back into two lopsided pigtails. Then I grabbed a hand mirror and bounced my real reflection off the full-length mirror on my door.

All of this took about forty-five minutes.

"Jessica Lynn Darling! Are you up yet?"

I went down to the kitchen.

"Nice of you to join us," my mom said as she sorted through the Accepts and Declines, with regrets that arrived in today's mail.

My dad, who was still mad about me blowing my race last week, just grunted and pretended to read a computer magazine. I mumbled some sort of greeting and poured a mammoth breakfast-and-lunch-size bowl of Cap'n Crunch.

"Maybe if you had a better diet you wouldn't be so tired all the time," my dad said, eyeing my bowl.

"Very subtle, Dad," I said. I knew this would provoke him. I wanted to provoke him. For the past 168 hours he'd been either grunting at me or ignoring me altogether, and I couldn't take it anymore.

"What does that mean?"

"You were *obviously* referring to my race," I said.

And we were off.

"That wasn't a race. It was the furthest thing from a race I've seen out of you all year." The words came pouring out, as though he'd been sitting there all morning, waiting for me to wake up. "You beat three of those girls during dual meets this year. How could you lose to them? I never thought you wouldn't qualify for the sectionals."

"I had a bad day."

"That's all you can say?" he said. "You had a bad day?"

My mom finally looked up. "Dar, take it easy on her. She had a bad day."

"Back when I was playing ball, there was no such thing as a bad day, Helen. I worked through my pain. I gutted it out," he was really getting on a roll. "I wouldn't be so upset if she had been outclassed by superior runners. I don't know what was wrong with her. I know she's a girl, but she's got to get tough."

And that's when *I* lost it.

"STOP TALKING ABOUT ME LIKE I'M NOT EVEN HERE! I AM SO SICK OF BOTH OF YOU! JUST LEAVE ME THE HELL ALONE!"

I sprinted out the back door before they could react. I hung out at the playground about a half-mile away from my house, hoping that there'd be a bunch of rugrats running around and doing cute kid-like things. Yet even though it was a gorgeous day, I was the only one there.

When I came home a few hours later, my parents went ballistic. They had put up with my outbursts in the past because they knew I was upset about Hope. But they could *tolerate my tongue no longer*. They revoked my phone and computer privileges for two weeks, which completely and royally sucks because keeping in touch with Hope is the only thing that prevents me from completely losing it. And I told them that. So, being the totally unfair, tyrannical assholes that they are, they added another week. I didn't want to go for a month, so I grunted that I understood and went upstairs to my bedroom.

How I spent the rest of my day is just too depressing to write about. But maybe I'll write about it another day. When I'm extraordinarily happy. After Paul Parlipiano has pledged his undying love. Or when Hope has moved back to Pineville. Or I've gotten a perfect score on my SATs and can go to any college in the country, particularly those far, far away from here. When I'm so bursting with joy that I simply can't believe that pathetic girl crying at the kiddie park and me are the same person. A day when writing about today doesn't make me ache.

Until then, I'd rather just forget it.

the seventeenth

I spent the rest of the weekend and all day Monday in bed. I told my parents I'd been feeling flu-ey for awhile and they were happy to let me stay home because my illness provided them with a reasonable excuse for last week's bad race and my even worse mood.

Point being—I hadn't talked to anyone since the prom.

I was at my locker before homeroom this morning when Scotty came up to me. This wasn't weird, mostly because he's been coming up to me before homeroom to say hi since the invite. What was weird was the look on his face.

"You look beat," I said. "Don't tell me you're still recovering from the prom?"

"Yeah. Sorta."

Right then, three baseball players came over and pummeled him.

"Stud!"

"Home run!"

"You better score this easily in today's game!"

Scotty laughed weakly, threw a few punches, and they went away.

"What was that all about?" I asked.

"Why haven't you called me back? I wanted to tell you . . ."

"I'm grounded. Tell me *what?*"

Scotty motioned for me to come closer and create the illusion of privacy in the middle of the packed hallway. He looked scared. Then he said the words that just about knocked me over.

"Kelsey and I had sex after the prom."

"WHAT?!"

"We did it."

I couldn't believe it. I really couldn't believe it. I know we had joked about it and everything, but I didn't think he would actually do it. *Scotty.* My Scotty.

"We did it," he repeated. He wasn't bragging about it. He was merely reinforcing the truth, perhaps for his own benefit as much as mine. I don't think *he* believed it—and he'd had two days to get used to the idea. Virgin no more.

"But you aren't even going out with her!"

I white-knuckled my World History book.

"I know," he said with a hush. "But I think we are now."

"You *think* you are?"

"I'm pretty sure we are."

"Well are you or aren't you?"

He paused for a moment, then looked down at his Nikes. He breathed in again and said, "We are."

Another baseball player slapped Scotty on the back. Scotty ignored him.

"So, I can't go to the wedding with you."

I was feeling too much to think—humiliated to find this out in the middle of the hall before homeroom; betrayed because I had always thought Scotty would never settle for anyone but me; disgusted because Scotty had acted just like the rest of the bootyhounding Jocks; and most of all, angry at my mom and my sister for possibly being right about Scotty, and how I'd regret not going out with him when I had the chance.

Before I could respond to his bombshell, Kelsey ran up to us, put her hands around Scotty's eyes, and cooed, *"Guess who?!"* Then she spun him around, gave him a loud smacking kiss on the mouth, and yanked him down the hall by his arm.

It happened in a flash. In less than five seconds, I was alone.

the eighteenth

The human instinct for survival is nothing short of amazing. In life-or-death situations, ordinary people can be empowered with superheroic abilities. For instance, the housewife who lifts a bus off her baby.

Luckily for me, my instincts kicked in just in time for me to cope with the endless post-prom talk. I entered an alternate stage of consciousness—one in which my body would respond to what Hy and the Clueless Crew were saying with the appropriate nods and smiles and *uh-huhs*, without actually having to process the message in my brain.

All day their mouths hummed white-noise nonsense. Only occasionally would words break through the static, like a local radio station that wasn't quite tuned in to the right frequency. *Bzzzzzzzzzzzzzzzzzstraplesszzzzzzzzzzzzzzzzzzzzzzzqueenzzzzzzzzzzzzzz zzzzzzzzzzzzzzzzzzzzzzzzzzzzzzzzzzzzzzzzzzzzzzzzzzzzzzzzzzzlimozzzzzzz zzzzzzzzzzzzzzzzzdjzzzzzzzzzzzzzzzzzzzzzzzzzzzzzzzzzzzzzzhilariouszzz zzzbruiserzzzzztequilazzzzzzbootyzzzzzvideozzzzzzho . . .*

I snapped out of my walking coma. "What did you just say?"

"I said, it was hilarious when Bruiser downed three shots of tequila and danced like a big booty video ho," said Manda.

"Our girl Bruiser was toe-up," laughed Hy.

"But Sara wasn't at the prom," I said.

There was a pause. They all looked at each other with an expression that I can only describe as *oops*.

"She hooked up with us at the Surfside party," Hy said finally.

"We would've invited you," said Sara.

"But we thought you had a track meet on Sunday," said Manda.

"I've never had a track meet on a Sunday," I said with a meekness so unlike my normal voice that it depressed me.

"Oh," they all said, in unison.

This was no oversight. This was an intentional slight. It was official. The Clueless Crew had ousted me in favor of a new member.

I didn't want to give them the satisfaction of a hasty retreat. So I sat there for the rest of lunch, trying to get back into the zone. No success. I heard every word.

Since I'm already depressed, I might as well say one more thing about the prom. Then I will never mention it again. Ever.

Carrie P. showed me her pics. In one five-by-seven: her table. Number 18. Paul Parlipiano and Monica Jennings are one of four other couples. He's wearing a classic black tux with a silver satin tie and vest. Those pink lips in a broad smile. Flushed cheeks. Dimples. Hair flopping into big brown eyes. Hands resting gently on Monica's sun-kissed shoulders, leaving fingerprints behind in the body glitter.

His hands belong there.

the twentieth

The Senior Class Last Will and Testament was published in today's school paper.

I, Paul Parlipiano, do hereby leave to Chris, a Thanksgiving
feast during the drum solo; to Carrie, pimp lessons from Pinky
La Rue; to Monster, a dozen Nutcrackers; to Gibbs, The Waif
on the left (loser) side; to Ry, a Mr. Tapeworm bootleg; to Fitz
I and II, a last-chance powerdrive; to Nancy, *Angela's Ashes*
dentistry; to Jeannie, a rock-star kit; to Erika, an impromptu
disco dance party; to Katy, eleventh-row memories; to Laurie,
Victor/Victoria and *Some Like It Hot*; to T. J., "Studs I Have
Known."

Inside jokes, obviously. But they sound witty and wise and
wonderful. Like him.

But that's not why I've been reading it over and over again.
Okay, this is a bit twisted. I keep reading his will because I want so
badly to understand what it all means. I'm hoping that if I analyze
it enough, it will suddenly make perfect sense. I'll be able to crack
the complex master code that spells out a message just for me—the
secret info I need to unlock Paul Parlipiano's heart.

Incidentally, Kelsey left Scotty a "tongue twister." I don't even
want to know how to translate that.

No one left me anything.

the thirtieth

I didn't buy a yearbook, which is a criminal offense at PHS. This
is all I've been hearing: *Sign my yearbook. Don't you want me to sign
your yearbook? Why didn't you get a yearbook? Everyone gets a yearbook.*

No. Not everyone gets a yearbook. We're all coming back
next year. And the year after that. Do I really need to spend
seventy-five dollars to be wished a "kick-ass summer" by people I'm

going to spend June through August trying to forget? The unfair thing about this is that I'm expected to exhaust what energy I have trying to come up with nice things to write in everyone's books, when I don't get to suck the life out of them in return.

So I came up with a handy list of all-purpose archetypes that could get me out of awkward signing situations.

jessica darling's guide to yearbook clichés

Opener	Body	Closer
This year went by so fast!	*Our times in (fill-in-the-blank) class were the best.*	*Have a kick-ass summer!*
Whoo-hoo! We're halfway through.	*I hope you always remember (fill-in-the-blank).*	*See ya next year!*

Just mix and match from each column and I had the perfectly sincere-sounding sentiment suitable for just about anyone. And I didn't feel bad about using them. That is, until Pepe came up to me.

"Would you sign my yearbook, *ma belle?*"

That took guts. I mean, you don't see me going up to Paul Parlipiano and asking him to sign my hypothetical yearbook, do you? So I wrote:

Pierre,
I've always admired your ability to conjugate a verb. And I'll never forget the night I found out the true identity of The Black Elvis. See you in French II.

A *bientôt,*
Jessica

The grin on his face was a mile wide. It was as if I had written:

Pierre,
I've always admired your ability to fill out a pair of tightie-

106

whities. And I'll never forget the night I found out that you know your way around a clitoris. See you in my wettest, wildest dreams.

Voulez-vous coucher avec moi ce soir?

Jessica

I wanted to write more, about how I respected that he did his own thing and how I wish I were able to blur boundaries as easily as he did, but I thought that might be too weird. Besides, what I wrote was sufficient. Pepe's gratitude was the highlight of a hellacious past few weeks. My morose mood is exacerbated by the fact that the four members of Clueless Crew are even chummier than usual. It's a blitzkrieg bond-a-thon: shopping, trips to the beach, weekend keggers. Jesus Christ, why do I even care?

And as I walked home today, I caught Scotty and Kelsey kissing each other in her car at a stoplight. I passed right by them in the crosswalk and he didn't even see me. It wouldn't have mattered if he had. We don't talk anymore anyway. According to Sara, via God only knows, Kelsey is threatened by me.

That's a laugh riot. I'm weaker than I've ever been.

June 1st

Hope,

My parents suck ass. Banning me from the phone and restricting my computer privileges are *the most assholic parental gestures* I can think of. Don't they realize that you're the only person who keeps me sane?

No. They don't. That's the problem.

I don't see how things could get any worse. After seeing my attempts at normalcy blow up in my face, I'm less motivated to fit in than ever.

But I still fake it.

Everyone is obsessing about all the graduation blowouts. I bitch about having to miss them because they're the same weekend as Bethany's wedding. *Of course* I'm relieved. Not hitting the party circuit because I have something else to do is socially acceptable. However, not hitting the party circuit because I'd rather sit at home and squeeze all the gunk out of the humongous pores in my nose, well, *isn't*.

I don't think I'm fooling anyone, though.

Congrats on getting that job at the visual arts camp. Sounds cool. Maybe we'll get to see each other when it's over, before school starts up again. But I can't think that far ahead right now.

Take care of yourself.

Morbidly yours, J.

june

the second

My Psych book says that prolonged lack of sleep *will* drive a person insane. I am living proof. What else could've made me risk ruining my reputation? My life?

From the beginning:

We had a substitute in French today, which meant that we were going to waste the period watching a subtitled Gérard Depardieu video. No way I was going to miss this opportunity to steal some sleep. So I faked a cramp and got a pass to the nurse's office.

Nurse Payne wanted to soothe my ovaries with an electric heating pad, but I insisted that all I needed was to lie down and wait for the PMS pain reliever to kick in. She didn't argue because a Hick-on-Wigga brawl had just been broken up and she had minor abrasions and lacerations to treat.

She hurried me to the private recovery room. I had it totally to myself! For forty-five minutes! I fell asleep within two seconds of crashing on the cot.

The next thing I knew, I felt a soft tickle on my cheek. Someone was whispering, "Wake up, sleepyhead . . ."

Whoever it was flipped the light switch, blinding me with florescence. As my eyes adjusted to the light, I saw a dark figure in the shape of a person . . . then a male figure . . . then a male figure in a *Dawson's Creek* T-shirt . . . then Marcus Flutie.

Marcus Flutie!

I went from REM to ready-for-action in a millisecond.

"What are you doing in here?"

"Hey, Cuz," he said. "I need to ask you for a favor."

He needed a favor. *Marcus Flutie* needed a favor from me. Why did Marcus Flutie need a favor from me?

"A favor? Why do you need a favor?"

He bent over and looked like he was going to tie his shoe.

Instead, he unrolled the six-inch cuff in his jeans and pulled out a plastic Dannon yogurt container. Vanilla.

"Is that how you always carry your lunch?" I giggled. Damn. I chewed on my bottom lip. Double damn.

He took the top off the yogurt. It was empty inside. Then Marcus made what is without a doubt the most bizarre request that has ever been made of me.

"I need you to piss in this."

"What?!"

He said it again. "I need you to piss in this."

I said it again. "What?!"

He sat down next to me, much closer than was necessary.

"My parole officer showed up for a surprise urine test," he said. "I know you think that I'm a Dreg, a worthless piece of garbage who deserves to be busted. But besides a few blunts and a few hits of E . . ."

"You want me to fake your drug test? Are you insane? I don't even know you!"

"I know *you* better than you think."

I snorted. "How do you know me?"

He answered by putting his hand on my knee.

I freaked out. I was sure that if the nurse came in and saw Marcus and me just sitting next to each other on the cot with his hand on my knee and that grin on his face, that alone would be enough to get us detention, or suspended, or something worse.

"Wait a sec. Isn't this a violation of your constitutional rights?"

"As a minor *and* a repeat offender, I have no rights," he said, snickering. "Call the ACLU."

I looked at the yogurt container, then the clock on the wall. Tick-tock. Tick-tock.

"Payne will be back here any second. If you don't do this, I'll get kicked out of school for good."

Couldn't he make this argument without his hand on my knee?

"You'll be keeping me off the streets."

Shouldn't I shake it off?

"You'll be saving my life. I'll owe you a favor, and I never renege on a promise."

Wouldn't they be able to tell that the pee came out of a girl?

"I can't," I said, looking away.

Marcus got up and walked to the door. But before he left, he turned and said the most infuriating thing.

"I knew you wouldn't do it."

I can't even describe the fiery rage that came over me.

I was so tired of everyone telling me what I would and should and could do and not do. My parents. The Clueless Crew. Hy. And now Marcus. Anger that had been simmering inside me for months, years, my whole life, boiled over and spilled out all over Marcus.

"How do you know what I'll do?"

The next thing I knew I was grabbing the yogurt container out of his hand and heading to the private bathroom to pee in it. And I did. Then I handed the warm cup back to him. He was standing there, silenced by this unexpected turn of events, not knowing what to do. Finally, he said, "I won't narc on you."

Then, without saying another word, he walked out. I hyperventilated on the cot for the next twenty minutes, until the bell rang. When I walked into the main room of the nurse's office, Marcus was nowhere to be seen.

I spent the rest of the day in a daze, worrying about whatever was going to happen to him—to me. I wondered how long it took to get results from a urine test. Maybe he peed on a stick and it instantly turned purple for pot, like a home pregnancy kit.

I waited for the cop cars to pull up in the parking lot, sirens wailing. I waited to see Marcus cuffed and kicking and screaming as they threw him in the back of the squad car to haul him off to Middlebury Clinic, one of the state's best in-patient detox/treatment centers. I waited for everyone in the school to hear him screaming, *"Don't worry, Cuz! I won't narc on you."* For weeks, everyone would wonder who "Cuz" was.

But nothing happened.

I can still feel the heat of his hand on my knee.

the fifth

If it weren't for this dream, I would've sworn I was wide awake all weekend.

I'm in the recovery room of the nurse's office, sleeping on the cot. Only this time, I've left the light on. So when the door opens, I can see right away that it's Paul Parlipiano.

He sits down next to me and says, "I need your help."

I say, "My help? Why do you need my help?"

Then he pulls a yogurt container out of the cuff of his khakis.

He says, "I need you to piss in this."

And I say, "No problem. I'll do it."

Then he says, "If you do it, I promise to have sex with you."

Then I say, "No problem. I'll do it."

And he says, "And I never renege on a promise."

So I say, "No problem. I'll do it."

And though I don't see myself do it, I guess I go for it.

Then Paul Parlipiano says, "Thanks. Now I'll have sex with you," and he turns off the lights.

Then I guess we start having sex, though I don't actually see us having sex.

A moment later, I hear a girl's giggle and the sound of the doorknob turning. The lights flash on.

It's Kelsey, laughing and pulling Scotty into the room by his hand. Though they don't say it, I just know they were going in there to have sex.

Scotty sees me having sex and yells, "How could you screw Marcus Flutie?"

I scream, "But it's Paul!"

Then I look into Paul Parlipiano's face, only it isn't Paul Parlipiano anymore. Scotty's right. It's Marcus Flutie.

Now that's what I call a mindfuck.

Needless to say, I was a walking anxiety attack when I got to school. I'd had all weekend to worry about the Marcus thing and I was on the brink of a breakdown. I prayed that Marcus would show up in homeroom, because that meant that everything had worked out and that I wouldn't get caught. Then I could finally stop feeling so psychotic.

An armada could've set sail on my sigh of relief when Marcus strolled past my desk in homeroom this morning.

Throughout the Pledge of Allegiance, attendance, and PA announcements, I looked over at him, hoping he'd make eye contact with me. But he just kept his head bent over his notebook until the bell rang. Marcus was playing it smart. He knew any out-of-the-ordinary behavior on either of our parts would arouse suspicion.

As I was walked into the hall, I felt a gentle shove from behind. I looked back, and for the first time I wasn't surprised to see Marcus. He apologized with that grin of his, pressing one hand into the small of my back and the other on my waist to "steady" himself. Before I even had a _chance_ to ask what had happened (not that I would have) he passed me by, a gleam in his eye, leaving behind his sweet, woodsy smell.

"Omigod! He's so messed up, he can't even walk in a straight line," snapped Sara.

You have no idea how much I wanted to tell her to—omigod!—shut the fuck up.

I'd only taken a few steps when I felt a bulge in my back pocket. Fortunately, Sara saw the Clueless Crew down the hall and ran to catch up with them. In those split seconds of solitude, I reached back and sure enough, there was a piece of notebook paper, folded into an intricate origami square that opened and closed like a flower. Or a mouth.

Marcus! I was dying to open it.

But at that moment the Clueless Crew were coming right at me from the other end of the hall. Damn them! I stuffed Marcus's present back into my jeans. I needed privacy for whatever he wanted to tell me.

The huge irony of ironies is this: For someone who feels so alone, I couldn't get a moment by myself all damn day. Every time I tried to slip away—to my locker, to the bathroom, to a shower stall before gym—someone would find it absolutely crucial to strike up a conversation with me. That note burned a hole in my back pocket for almost six hours. I was in such anticipatory agony that I didn't even change back into my school clothes after last-period gym class—I ran straight home and up to my room.

"Jessie, I want to talk to you," my mom said as I dashed up the stairs.

"Give me a minute!" I yelled back as I locked the door.

I opened up my backpack and pulled out my jeans. I stuck my hand into the back pocket and pulled out . . . lint.

"Jessie?" my mom called from the kitchen.

I quickly shook out the other pockets, though I knew I hadn't stuffed Marcus's note in any of them. Then I rifled through my backpack, eventually dumping out its entire contents onto the floor.

"Jessica!" my mom yelled.

Now I started to panic. My ears got hot and I started to sweat. Where could it be? Whose hands could it have fallen into? I got on my knees and picked through every object on the floor: jeans; striped V-neck tank; bra; Chucks; *The Catcher in the Rye*; two spiral notebooks; Chem book; Student Council schedule; three Baby Ruth wrappers; calculator; highlighter; stick deodorant; Carmex; brush; an assortment of pens.

No origami mouth from Marcus.

"Jessica Lynn Darling, get down here!"

I went downstairs, clutching my stomach—this time for real. A ball of anxiety was bouncing up and down inside my body, but I lied and said it was my period. Mom was so relieved by this news that she let me go without a struggle when I asked to be excused to my room. Here, I have rifled through the aforementioned objects approximately a bizillion times for the past ten hours.

How could I have possibly lost the most important thing that has ever been given to me? The only logical explanation is this: There never *was* an origami mouth from Marcus. I made it all up just to drive myself crazy. In fact, I made this whole thing up. I never peed in the cup. No way. Not me. Why would I do something as totally insane as that?

Maybe if I keep telling myself this long enough, I'll believe it.

the sixth

I arrived at school today with a mission: To find out the message inside the origami mouth. I knew there was no hope in retrieving it, so there was only one option left. An option simultaneously terrifying and titillating.

I'd ask Marcus what it said.

This would be a big deal for all the obvious reasons (I'm me, he's Marcus Flutie. . . . It could draw unwanted attention to my crime. . . .) plus one more. See, this would mark a dramatic departure from our previous exchanges. Up to this point, he had initiated all contact between us. But today I would be the one to decide that it was time to talk. I would be the one in the powerful position.

If I didn't projectile-vomit all over him.

So I lingered outside the door to homeroom, hoping to catch him as he walked in. I waited through the five-minute bell. I waited through the warning bell. At the final bell, I went to my seat. I told myself that it wasn't uncommon for him to shuffle to his seat a minute or two late. But by the time we got to the pledge, I'd lost all hope.

Marcus never showed up for homeroom. Maybe I would've known that if I hadn't lost the mouth.

Of course, it was Sara who broke the news.

"Omigod! Did you hear about Kripsy Kreme? He got some girl to fake his drug test last week!"

I almost launched my Cap'n Crunch.

It turns out that there *was* a way for the docs to tell that the pee came out of a girl and not a guy—a hormonal thing. It took them a few days to get tipped off. Marcus must have been called down to the office right after he gave me the origami mouth. There, his parole officer, Principal Masters, and good ol' Brandi confronted him about the faked sample. They knew it wasn't his, but they wouldn't know who it came from unless he told them.

"So far Marcus has refused to tell who he got it from," said Sara, positively beside herself with this juicy gossip. "They threatened him for hours, supposedly. But he wouldn't cave."

"How do you know all this?"

"My dad went golfing with Principal Masters."

"Oh."

"And he asked me for ideas on who it could be, you know, since I'm a fountain of information."

Jesus Christ.

"I suggested his girlfriends, the ones I could remember," Sara continued. "It's probably not any of them, though."

"Why?"

"Because the faked sample was drug-free."

"Really?"

"Which means his partner in crime was someone like *you* . . ." She paused, for approximately a half hour. "Or me."

At that moment, I knew that I was going to get caught. And my life was going to be destroyed. And for what? To prove to everyone they were wrong about me? Brilliant. But I wasn't ready to fess up. Not yet.

It took every ounce of strength that I had to act normal and respond to conversation about this subject as though I were a totally uninvolved observer.

"What kind of chickenhead would help him pass his drug test?" said Hy.

"An insecure one," I said.

"He must be really good in bed," said Manda.

"I doubt he promised sex," I said.

"Burke says that he's seen Marcus in the locker room and that he's got like, ten inches of New Jersey Whitesnake," said Bridget.

"What?" all four of us asked.

"He's got a huge penis."

"Oh," said Hy.

"Oh!" said Manda.

"Oh?" said Sara.

"Whoa," said I.

It was exhausting.

The Clueless Crew aren't the only ones talking about it. Everyone has theories on what Marcus said to the secret donor— that he promised her drugs, or a date. Of course, I didn't correct them. I didn't tell them that I know he wouldn't be so crude. That he just *asked* her in a way that only Marcus could ask. Putting his hand on her knee. Promising to return the favor. Grinning.

the ninth

I have survived the most nerve-racking five minutes of my life.

I had gotten used to acting innocent around the Clueless Crew and everyone else. It was as easy as breathing.

Then I got called out of class.

"Could you send Jess Darling down to Principal Masters's office immediately?" said the fuzzy, disembodied voice of Mrs. Newman over the PA system.

The whole class looked at me with wonder. I made a big deal out of shrugging and wearing a *What's this all about?* expression.

119

On the walk to the office, I kept hearing Marcus's words over and over again: *I won't narc on you. I won't narc on you. I won't narc on you. . . .*

When I got to the office, Principal Masters was waiting for me. He greeted me with a smile and a "So sorry to pull you out of class." But I knew from watching enough interrogation scenes on TV cop shows that his warm countenance could be a setup.

"I'm sure you've heard about this incident with Marcus Flutie, correct?" Principal Masters asked as soon as I sat down.

"Yes."

That's good. Keep it simple. Don't elaborate.

"Nurse Payne says that you were in the recovery room that afternoon."

"Yes."

Good. Simple. Good.

"What were you doing there?"

"Oh. I had some, uh . . . feminine problems . . ."

"Oh!" he exclaimed, looking embarrassed. "Sorry."

He shifted in his creaky leather chair and stroked his bushy gray beard. His ample stomach strained against his cheap brown polyester suit.

My life is about to be destroyed by a fat man in a cheap brown polyester suit.

"The reason I've asked you here is because you were the only one in there about the time that Marcus was called down for his test . . ."

Here it comes. He's moving in for the kill. I'm dead. Done. Toast.

"Did you see him with anyone? Don't be afraid to tell me."

What?

"I know that these troublemakers might have put pressure on you . . ."

Is he suggesting what I think he—

"They might have even threatened you physically . . ."

Hallelujah! He didn't suspect me at all. Once I understood the goal of our meeting—to rat out the troublemaker who did this—I was able to speak more freely. I told him that no one had threatened me. I was asleep the whole time. I hadn't seen Marcus or anyone else.

"I wish I had, so I could help you out," I said.

"I wish you had, too," he said.

My cutesy last name and straight As had saved me again.

the thirteenth

My conversation with Principal Masters had calmed me down quite a bit. But I knew that until they found the culprit, I'd never be completely off the hook.

Today, they got one. And no one was more stunned than I was.

"They found out who peed in the cup!" Sara cried in homeroom.

"They did?"

"Yeah. A total nobody named Taryn Baker."

Taryn Baker is a dweeby freshman, so desperate for notoriety that she voluntarily confessed to the crime that she didn't commit. At band practice yesterday, she bragged to a bunch of her fellow clarinet players that *she* was the one who had peed in the cup. They turned her in because they were sick of her ego trip. Band nerd betrayal.

The administration is so thrilled to have a guilty party that they aren't even checking out her story. Marcus didn't confirm or deny it. Of course, poor, insecure Taryn couldn't help but do whatever the cold, calculating Marcus told her to do, so she's getting off relatively unscathed: suspension for the rest of the year. While I certainly appreciate her voluntary scapegoating, I can't help but pity her. Doesn't she know about Pineville's short-term memory? That the name she's making for herself today will be forgotten when she comes back next year?

The evil Marcus, on the other hand, is being sent to Middle-bury. Word is he won't be coming back. His parents are send-ing him to military school. I know I'll never hear from him. He's too smart to trust the confidentiality of *any* form of correspon-dence.

I keep telling myself that even if I had had nothing to do with this, the end result would've been the same. He would've ended up in rehab. I wish I knew that was the best thing for him. I can't help but think about what happened to Heath. Getting kicked out of school didn't help him. That special high school for "high-risk" students didn't straighten Heath out or keep him off the streets. Or even save his life.

The phone ban has been lifted. But I still can't tell Hope about any of this. How can I possibly tell her that I helped one of the people she hates most in the world get away with one of the sins she hates most in the world? I can't afford to lose her friend-ship over something as insanely stupid as this.

So all I can do is vent here.

Who is this for, anyway? Who are you? Who actually found this notebook and cares enough to read it? You must have little to do. Wait. Are you *me* twenty-five years from now? Too weird. Stop thinking, Jessica. Stop getting so ahead of yourself. Just stop.

the sixteenth

At 1:42 A.M. I heard some cracking noises at my window. I was awake, so it didn't take me long to react. I opened the window and leaned out to take a look.

"You're awake!"

It was Scotty with a handful of pebbles.

"I'm always awake. What do you want?"

"I need to talk to you. Can you come out?"

I knew it must be major. Scotty and I hadn't said more than *Hey* to each other since he hooked up with Kelsey. Anyway, I had been too distracted by the whole Marcus thing to care.

"*Shhhhh* . . . I'll be right down."

I was already dressed for a middle-of-the-night run, so I met him in the front yard in less than a minute. I made a slashing motion across my throat to silence him before he spoke up and woke my parents.

"Do you do this a lot?" Scotty asked.

"What?"

"Sneak out."

"Why?"

"It was like you were expecting me."

"Oh. No." I explained how I go running at night.

"I never knew that about you," he said.

"How would you know if I never told you?"

We reached the kiddie park and I headed straight for the swings. The swings have always been my favorite. There's a secret game that I have played on that playground's swings for as long as I can remember: I swing higher and higher and try to hit the leaves on the oak tree with my feet. It's impossible—the leaves are about twenty-five feet up. Even now, I still try in the dark. But I didn't do that with Scotty there. I just sat and swayed.

"So what's up?"

Scotty sighed. "I broke up with Kelsey."

I tried to look surprised.

"Are you upset?" I asked.

"Not really."

"Then why the nine one one?"

"She's really p.o.'ed at you and I wanted you to know before school tomorrow."

"Why is she pissed at me? I've barely talked to you."

"I know," he said, drawing lines in the dirt with a stick. "I kind of missed talking to you and it caused a problem." He snubbed out the lines with his sneaker. "I thought she deserved to know the truth. That my friendship with you is more important than her."

There was a time when I would've thought that was just about the sweetest thing I'd ever heard in my life. But not anymore. Now, Scotty's words only came off as cinematically sweet. Molly-Ringwald-movie sweet. And while I love *watching* those flicks, *living* one was all a bit too contrived for me.

"I sound like a total fag, but it's true," he said.

Scotty was pulling out all the stops to get back in my good graces. How many sixteen-year-old guys would forsake sex for friendship? Now I know that the reality is far less monklike because Scotty is ultimately hoping that this will help him have sex with *me*. Still, it's fairly impressive, even if the more accurate question is: *How many sixteen-year-old guys would give up today's booty for a between-the-sheets uncertainty?*

Somehow, it just wasn't enough.

"I feel bad about dissing you right before your sister's wedding and all."

"Uh-huh."

"And I could still go with you."

"Uh-huh."

"If you still want me to."

That was funny. I never really wanted to go with him in the first place. Everyone else wanted me to. No way was I going to give them all the satisfaction for a second time.

"You know what, Scotty? It's too late."

"Oh."

Of course, it wasn't too late at all. My sister could've accommodated him, no problem. It was just too late for *me*.

"Sorry you came out here for no reason," I said.

"Hey," Scotty replied, "no big fucking deal."

the twenty-second

Today was the last day of school. Sophomore no more.

As usual, PHS held its annual awards assembly today. I think it's supposed to give us incentive to show up. The obvious flaw in this logic is that the Hicks, Hoochies, Wiggaz, Dregs, and miscellaneous PHS bottom-dwellers who would be naturally inclined to skip aren't going to be tricked into showing up by the promise of engraved plaques that will never be theirs. And those of us getting awards would show up anyway.

I usually rack up the plaques. Last year, for example, all the individual subject awards were divided evenly between me and Len Levy—four each. But this year I only got the sophomore English award and the French I award. It's not fair for me to get the latter since I'm a year older than everyone else in the class. Pepe was robbed.

As much as I don't give a crap about these things, I was shocked to be shut out of the rest of the awards. I was beat out by lesser brains. Plus, for the first time ever, Len Levy nudged me out of the top GPA award with 99.02. Apparently, my less-than-stellar performance on my finals (all taken during the Marcus brouhaha) dropped my GPA down to 97.98. That's a two-point drop in less than a marking period. It doesn't sound like a lot, but it is.

I'm slipping.

Hy wasn't at our school long enough to earn any awards. But she came up to me in the auditorium and congratulated me as I gathered up mine. I thanked her, wondering if she still thought I was as smart as the girls at her private school.

Then she opened her mouth like she was about to say something else, but changed her mind. This was weird, because Hy usually says what's on her mind.

"What?" I asked.

"Girl," she said. "Don't take anything I do personally."

What a bizarre thing to say out of nowhere like that. I really wanted to say something snotty to put Hy in her place and vent some pent-up resentment. But I was so drained by the Marcus thing that I didn't really give a damn.

"Ain't no thing, Hy," I said, using her own words against her. "Ain't no thing."

When I got home, I dumped my unimpressive awards into the corner with the rest of them. They're such a given, my parents don't even ask to see them anymore, let alone ooh and ahh over them.

Then I fell asleep for five minutes. Long enough to have a dream about an origami mouth trying to swallow me up.

the twenty-fifth

THE BIG DAY.

Bethany is no longer Miss Bethany Shannon Darling. She's Mrs. Grant Doczylkowski, which is about as bad a new name as you can get.

My primary duty for *the big day* was to fluff Bethany's train and hold her cathedral-length veil so it didn't drag all over the floor. My secondary duty was to tell her how beautiful she looked. Which, of course, she did. But it got annoying having to reassure her.

"How does my makeup look? Not too much, is it? I don't want to scare Grant when I walk down the aisle."

"It looks beautiful."

"How does my dress look? It isn't too tight, is it? I don't want to look like a whale when I walk down the aisle."

"It looks beautiful."

"How does my hair look? It's not too poufy, is it? I don't want to scream Jersey when I walk down the aisle."

"Your bangs are a bit mallratty."

"WHAT?!"

"I'm kidding. I swear. It looks beautiful."

Ad nauseum.

The universe gets so ga-ga about weddings that I expected sentimentality to sneak up on me and make me a mushy mess. But it didn't. Bethany's and G-Money's vows left me unmoved.

Here's what I remember about the ceremony: I sat with my arms folded tightly across my chest, trying to keep warm in the overenthusiastically air-conditioned church. The setting sun through the stained-glass windows turned my yellow ("*Maize!*") dress into a muted tie-dye. My strapless bra was cutting off my circulation, and I couldn't help but think it would have a long-term breast-stunting effect.

The real action was at the reception.

As the Maid of Dubious Honor, I automatically got paired up with the Best Man all day. We walked down the aisle together. We posed for pictures together. We made our entrance into the reception hall together.

The bad news: *G-Money's best man, Tad, is thirty years old and resembles a bloated manatee after a beer bender.*

The better news: *Tad introduced me to his nineteen-year-old brother, Cal. Cal is one tasty morsel in a clean-cut, Abercrombie-ish kind of way.*

The best news: *Cal is a computer genius who pissed off his parents by dropping out of MIT this year to be a whiz-kid consultant for an up-and-coming software company.*

The supa-dupa stupendous news: *When Cal shook my hand he said, "I told my bro I had to meet the girl who made that butt-ugly dress look so damn good."*

Paul Parlipiano, *who?*

"Let's make our getting-to-know-you banter more challenging," he said.

"Okay."

"We'll only discuss subjects most commonly known by abbreviations."

Cal was odd. But I liked it. I asked for an example.

"TRL," he said. "MTV democracy at it's best? Or pitiful battleground for boy bands?"

"WWF," I said. "Harmless white-trash fun? Or the low point in America's cultural landscape?"

And so we went on to discuss: MP3, PBS, IPO, and YMCA.

"Everything a man can enjoy? Or where you hang out with all the bo—?"

Cal interrupted me as the guitar player strummed the opening riff to Kool and the Gang's classic, "Celebration." "*We're gonna have a good time tonight*," Cal spoke the lyrics, straight-faced and very, very serious.

"*Let's celebrate*," I replied, imitating his uptight tone, trying not to smile.

"*It's all right*," he said, grabbing my hand and pulling me onto the dance floor.

And at that moment, I really did feel like everything was going to be all right.

Cal didn't bust the most impressive move, but he had two crucial things that most male dancers don't have: a) rhythm and b) enthusiasm. So we danced our asses off. "I Will Survive." "Twist and Shout." "Everlasting Love." What I liked most about Cal was that he clearly had an off-the-chart IQ, but he didn't E=MC^2 it in my face. He knew how to shut down his brain and have fun. I don't know what I wanted more: to be with him or to *be* him.

Not thirty seconds after we left the dance floor, my dad's eighty-nine-year-old mother, Gladdie, was hobbling toward us at a pretty impressive clip for someone with two artificial hips. She used her Wedding Walker, specially decorated for the occasion with white ribbons and silk flowers. I didn't have a chance to warn Cal that she's a wack-job.

"Jessie, you look *bee-yoo-ti-full*," hollered Gladdie.

I wasn't sure about bee-yoo-ti-full, but I looked better than usual, which was a start. Despite its hideous cut and color, I didn't look so bad in my dress once the seamstress built in artificial boobage. And thanks to a professional makeup job (Bethany, the Nuptials Nazi, wanted to guarantee perfect pictures), my skin looked radiant and unblemished as it has never appeared post-puberty. I'd never admit this to my sister, but I even liked how the artificial bun pinned to my head made me look older and more sophisticated.

Then Gladdie turned her attention to Cal. She let loose a long wolf whistle through her teeth. "Whatta hunka man!" she brayed. "When you two gettin' hitched?"

Cal nearly spit his drink in her face. My face was on fire.

"Gladdie, I'm only sixteen . . ."

"I was only seventeen when I married your grandfather, bless his soul."

"And we just met," I explained.

"Well, you gotta meet your husband sometime. It might as well be tonight," she roared.

The thing is, I was so swoony over Cal at this point that my heart was telling me that Gladdie might be right. We had a con-nection, Cal and me. One that would've never been made if I had brought Scotty like everyone had wanted me to.

"Whoo-wee! He's one fine speci-man," hooted Gladdie. "He really knocks my socks off!" Then she hobbled away, but not before grabbing his butt and giving it a good squeeze.

About ten minutes later, when Cal and I had finally stopped laughing, he said, "And I thought I wasn't going to get lucky tonight," which made us laugh even harder.

Cal and I continued to have corny, Macarena-variety fun throughout the reception. Enough fun that I did something sort of stupid, but it was for a good reason. Cal kept bringing me glasses of champagne, and I conveniently placed them on another table or poured them down the bathroom sink or into the floral centerpiece instead of drinking them. But he thought I drank them all. In fact, I only had two. They made me feel light and giddy, but I pretended to be waaaaaay drunker than I was so I could test out what it was like to kiss him. That way, if our lip-lock was of the daddy longlegs variety—à la Scotty in eighth grade—I could just pretend it had never happened when he called and called and called me all summer long.

So during the cutting of the cake, when I knew all eyes would be on the beautiful bride and groom, I told Cal I wanted to get some air on the golf course. And Cal, who really was as drunk as he seemed to be, gave a thumbs-up and said, "Rock on."

We went outside. The sky was endless with stars and the air was wet with roses. Cal had caddied for his dad here a few times, he said. He knew a great spot. He started running and yelling, "Follow me!" But I couldn't run very far or fast in my banana peel and heels and told him to wait up for me. He doubled back, picked me up, and tossed me over his shoulder. "Light as a feather," he said. I squealed like a girlie girl, in spite of myself.

Cal carried me about a tenth of a mile to a water hazard designed to look like a natural lake. Fuzzy stars rippled in the water. He took off his suit coat and put it on the grass for me to sit on. But sitting was no easy feat in my dress, so I had to lie flat on my back. Cal plopped down beside me, propped on his elbow, his hand holding his head mere inches from mine. I kept my eyes on the sky. I could still hear the band's bass player, thumping and bumping like an irregular heartbeat.

"It's beautiful out here, isn't it?" I said, finally.

Cal inched closer. "Yer *bee-yoo-ti-full*."

I laughed and looked up at the Big Dipper. "Thanks, Gladdie."

"I meannit, yer beautiful," he said softly.

I giggled and bit my lip. All this tension. All this buildup. "You don't have to say that."

"I know," he whispered.

That's when I finally looked at him looking at me. And we

both busted out laughing. Again. When we calmed down, Cal said, "How can I kissya if we keep crackinup?"

I liked that he got it out in the open like that. So I pushed myself up so we were face to face. And then I closed my eyes. Next I felt his mouth on mine. We were kissing.

Kissing him didn't make my skin crawl. I liked it. To be honest, I *really* liked it. I could taste the whiskey on his tongue, and feel the heat of his breath on my face. As our mouths got warmer and wetter, he rolled my body on top of his. His hands in my hair, against the nape of my neck, over my shoulders, on the small of my back . . .

Well, Cal's below-the-belt brain must have picked up on my passion. He suddenly stopped kissing and slurred something in my ear.

"What?" I asked.

"I hafa condom."

"What?!"

Cal just smiled at me.

"Was that what I think it was?"

"Uh?"

"Were you telling me that you have a condom so I could do it with you?"

"Uhhhh . . ."

"So we could have *sex?*"

"Uhhhh . . ."

I pushed him away and straightened up my dress.

"We kiss once and you think you can have sex with me?"

"Uh . . . I thought . . ."

I couldn't believe it! Who did he think I was?

Duh! He knew nothing about me. He didn't know that I cracked 1500 on my PSATs. He didn't know that I run a five-twenty mile. He didn't know that I eat Cap'n Crunch for breakfast, lunch, and dinner. He didn't know that I can't get enough of the "new classics" or *The Real World.* He didn't know that my best friend moved away and I hate everyone else. He didn't know I had only recently made a brief foray into the law-breaking under-world.

No. He didn't know any of these things. As far as he knew, I was just a ho-bag who makes a habit of screwing random guys on golf courses.

"You don't even know me!" I shouted.

He softly stroked the inside of my arm with his fingertips.

"I know 'nuf boutya t'know I wanna know more boutya . . ." he mush-mouthed. He was so drunk he was looking *through* me.

Jesus Christ! Could he be any sleazier? Or cheesier?

I pushed away his hand and stood up.

"I know you're supposed to be a genius and all, but you're a real idiot if you think I'm going to fall for a line like that."

And then I quickly stomped back toward the sounds of fun going on without me, ruining my once-in-a-lifetime shot at losing my virginity at my sister's wedding.

What a nightmare. I guess this is my penance for pushing Scotty away and inviting almost-perfect strangers into my life.

July 4th

Hope,

What better place to celebrate the birth of our nation than the Sleaze-side Heights boardwalk? And what better way to spend this day of Inde-pendence than in minimum-wage slavery, serving artery-clogging confections to fatty boombalatty bennies?

I hate them. Those greasy goombas plunking down an obscene num-ber of quarters to win prizes for their girlfriends—tacky '80s throwbacks whose Aqua Net–shellacked bangs are surpassed in height only by the heels of the Payless pumps that are constantly caught between the wooden planks as they walk. These women cling to their men in never-ending adoration, as if they were cartoon cavemen returning from the hunt. Basking in a blinking neon glow, these outer-borough heroes stalk elusive prey like the overstuffed Squishy Bears that burst their seams and spill their mini Styrofoam guts the moment the victors sling them over their shoulders. If unsuccessful in their quest, they save face with an air-brushed T-shirt, the official sign of guido pre-engagement: GINO 'N' TINA 4-EVA.

When they aren't competing for prizes, or riding one of the Six Flags knockoff rides, they eat food with little or no nutritional value: saltwater taffy, frozen custard, caramel apples, cotton candy. All provided by yours truly at Wally D's Sweet Treat Shoppe.

God Bless America.

To think I actually lowered myself by begging Sara to persuade her dad to hire me despite his having already filled all positions with Europeans with temporary work visas. (They fly in for the summer to take advantage of the typical American teenager's piss-poor work ethic. Only a foreigner would jump at a 100-hour, minimum-wage week. Hurrah for the land of the free! Home of the brave!) But I *had* to get out of the house. My mom was trying way too hard to bond with me, wanting to take me shopping or to the movies or out for lunch and—get this—girl talk. Ack. How transparent can she get? Mom doesn't really want to spend time with me. She just doesn't know what to do with herself now that *the big day* is over and Bethany has moved across the country with G-Money. No way will I ever be a bubble-jet print of my sister.

Anyway, I am not a religious person, but I pray that your job sucks less than mine. And that I actually earn enough to pay for that plane ticket. Until then, you keep right on molding the artistic geniuses of tomorrow at your camp. And I'll do my darndest to make my contribution to the Red-White-and-Blue's obesity epidemic—one sprinkle-covered cone at a time.

Jingoistically yours, J.

july

the twelfth

When you take a summer job in Seaside Heights, New Jersey, the self-proclaimed Home of Sunnin' and Funnin', it pretty much guarantees that you will have no time for either sun or fun. This is particularly frustrating because your sole duty is to serve thousands of ugly urbanites hell-bent on holiday hedonism. (Try telling a bombed-out-of-his-mind Longuylander that you've run out of rainbow sprinkles. It's Armageddon.)

I come home coated in a second skin of funnel-cake grease, chocolate syrup, sea-salt spray, and sweat. My ears ring with buzzers and bells and the *unz unz* beat of the never-ending dance-party mega-mix blasting from Life's a Beach, the clothing store next door that sells T-shirts with slogans like I'M NOT AS THINK AS YOU DRUNK I AM. When I come home, I'm too disgusted with myself to go anywhere or do anything. I'm so tired that I fall asleep as soon as I make contact with the mattress, if you can believe that.

My first few weeks on the job, I bitched and moaned mightily about how catering to these tyrannical tourists guarantees that I'll have little downtime. Not to mention that I spend every shift fending off the advances of my oversexed coworkers. At any moment, an undeodorized, hirsute Hungarian with a no-vowels, unpronounceable name will ask me if I am *spoken for*. (The answer is always *Yes*.)

I almost considered quitting, fully aware that the extra time would leave me no choice but to give in and hang out with my mom, who is more desperate than ever for company. Good thing I stuck it out long enough to enjoy my job's brightest benefit: I have an automatic out from all forms of socialization, without being classified as antisocial.

Practically the entire PHS student body works on the boards. I get face time with people from school without actually having to go through the hassle of hanging out with them. Manda works

137

behind the counter at Winning Wally's Arcade. As far as I can tell, she gets paid to flirt with all the Skee-Ball-loving skater boys who can't handle the complicated mechanics of the change machine, and therefore have no choice but to go to her to get four quarters for a dollar—and her phone number. Scotty takes his life in his hands by working the Beer Bust game (drunken idiots + softballs + beer bottles = certain untimely death) on Funtown Pier. Burke runs the Himalaya roller coaster and drives us all to and from work in exchange for gas money. Sara does not deign to work at any of her dad's boardwalk businesses, but she is there forty hours a week anyway if only to remind us that *we're* working and *she* doesn't have to.

About the only people I haven't seen lately are those lucky enough to escape to more exotic locales for the summer.

Totally out-of-nowhere news: Bridget is staying with her dad in L.A. all summer in the hopes of becoming—get this—an actress. Unreal. Bridget is not fazed by the fact that her acting experience is limited to laughing at jokes I know she doesn't understand.

"Bridge, you haven't even acted in a school play," I pointed out.

"I know," she said. "But how much skill does it take to like, act in a sitcom on the WB?"

Valid point. I decided to drop it. Far be it from me to destroy her dream. I was probably more jealous that she was escaping Pineville for the summer than I was of the possibility of her fame and fortune. (Though, if I'm ever labeled Jessica Darling, Bridget's Childhood Friend on some infotainment cheese-fest, I will kill myself.) I had no clue this was a serious goal of hers. This proves that I am stratospherically out of touch with my former best friend. I assumed that she felt the same way. That's why weirdness-wise, Bridget's West-Coasting doesn't hold a candle to a request she made of me right before she left.

"Jess, I need to ask you for a favor."

Let's see. The last time someone asked me for a favor, I nearly got expelled from school. But I found myself saying "sure" in spite of myself. I was thrown off not only by Bridget's showbiz bombshell, but by the very sight of her standing in the middle of my bedroom. She hadn't been up here for about two years.

"I know Burke is carpooling you guys to the boards all summer and . . ." She hesitated.

"What? What is it?" I was getting antsy already.

She scrunched up her pretty little nose. It's so tiny that I doubt it's functional. No air current could flow in and out of those microscopic nostrils. It's purely for show. I bet it would look damn good on the big screen, though. She's got a pug you could put in an IMAX movie without worrying about the fright factor of redwood-size nostril-hairs.

"Well, you'll get to see him almost every day . . ." Another pause. Pink fireworks exploded all over her fair face and neck. She'd better get through her auditions better than this. "Could you, like, keep an eye on him for me?"

"Huh?"

"This is the first time we've been apart for more than like, three days since I was in seventh grade," she said, tugging her pony-tail. "I'm worried that he like, might . . ."

"Cheat?"

"Yeah."

"Whoa."

"I know."

She nervously twisted her hair around her delicate index finger.

"Do you think there's someone else?" I asked.

"No. I'm just, like, afraid that other girls might take this opportunity to pounce on him. And being a guy and all he won't turn them down . . ."

Why me? Why not Sara? Her sleuthing skills are far superior to mine. And God forbid he actually cheats on her. I've always known that the B. and B. breakup would be a very, very bad one. I sure as hell don't want to be there at ground zero. But if you'd seen Bridget there, all splotchy and jittery, you would've said yes, too. Attractive people are highly persuasive, just by being attractive. It's true. There's research to back me up.

Long story short: My part-time job is eyeballing Burke to make sure he's not balling anyone else. And so far, so good.

If Bridget's ill-conceived stab at fame is the stuff *E! True Hollywood Stories* are made off, then Hy is a *Mysteries and Scandals* in the making. She's as MIA as my menstrual cycle. Seriously. No one has heard from her since the last day of school. I didn't even give it a second thought until Manda and Sara asked me if I had seen or heard from her. I assumed that the three of them had been debauching without me.

At their request, I tried calling Hy at her aunt's house last week. She simply said Hy was vacationing with her family for the summer. I asked her where they went, and she got all flustered and hurried me off the phone with the suspicious "someone's at the front door" routine. As a phone phobic, I saw right through this. Something is up, for sure. I just don't know what. Family problems, I bet. Kids are always sent packing somewhere secret when there are family problems. Or an unplanned pregnancy. Ooooh. What if Fly knocked her up?

Ugh. I sound like Sara.

I can't help but think of the last thing she said: *No matter what I do, don't take it personally*. Maybe she knew then that she was leaving. As much as Hy disappointed me toward the end of school, I hope whatever is going on, it's nothing bad.

Of course, the most conspicuous absentee from my life is Marcus Flutie.

I know he's still at Middlebury, but I can't shake the feeling that I'm going to see him again. The boardwalk is swarming with Marcus mirages. I fall for them every time. I catch split-second glimpses of his dreads, his slouch, and his tattoo. They last long enough for my heart to bang against my insides, like it wants me to expel it from my chest cavity. Every time I think I see Marcus, it turns out to be someone who looks *nothing* like him. One time the Marcus was a black guy. Another time the Marcus was a *girl*. It's like I need to see Marcus so badly that I'm trying to turn him into everyone. And everyone into him.

the twentieth

Still no Marcus. No Hy either.

I'm on Bridget's mass E-mail list, which pisses me off. You would think that after making such an annoying request, she would at least take the time to personalize her correspondence, or at least have the common sense to bcc the other people so I don't know that she's sending the same *I-just-missed-getting-a-tampon-commercial-but-I-saw-Freddie-Prinze-Jr.-at-Trader-Vic's* message to everyone in our class.

I'm still keeping my eye on Burke. The only girls I ever see him talking to are me, Manda, and Sara. He'd better keep it that way.

I see Scotty all the time, but I wish I didn't. It reminds me of the whole Cal thing.

I was seven hours and thirty-eight minutes into my eight-hour shift when I saw Scotty for the bizillionth-or-so time last night. He was standing by a blinking neon sign that persuaded passersby to take ball in hand and WHACK OUR KATS. He was talking to the pruny man who had worked at that boardwalk stand for twenty-five summers and counting.

Scotty lifted his red Funtown Pier employee T-shirt up to his chest hair. There was a girdle binding his newly acquired beer bulge. He's been kicking kegs all summer with the football team. The old man coughed a laugh as Scotty explained the need for the fat-sucking contraption. It was called a Gut Buster, the amazing machine that would sweat his gut away. He seemed okay with the fact that it would take an entire summer of intense weight training and wearing the Gut Buster to undo what it took only opening his mouth and chugging, chugging, chugging to do. The Whack Our Kats man watched and listened and laughed until it was clinically dangerous to laugh any harder.

I knew that this was the story that Scotty was relating. I knew the story because a few days ago, he had acted it out for me. Word for word, gesture for gesture—it was all the same. I had laughed, too. Seeing his repeat performance tonight, however, almost made me cry. Somehow it confirmed what I already knew: I'm no different than the Whack Our Kats man in his eyes.

This is a delayed reaction. I should have had this epiphany three weeks ago, when Scotty stopped carpooling with Burke, Manda, and me and started getting rides from a girl named Becky who goes to Eastland. There was no reason for it to bother me. So it didn't.

Until last night, that is. We were stuck at the sixth of thirteen possible red lights on the route home when I realized that the person in the passenger side of the car directly in front of us was Scotty. I recognized his familiar superhero silhouette. He was violently thrashing up and down to the rap music blasting inside Becky's car.

Becky's dirty-blond braid poked through the back of Scotty's maroon baseball cap, and the sight of it sent my stomach into spasms.

At that moment, I started wondering if Scotty's enlarged gut has in any way affected his back crevice. Scotty had the best back crevice. I saw it whenever Manda rode shotgun and Scotty was stuck in the backseat with me. Scotty would lean toward the front seat to say something to Burke and his shirt would scooch up, revealing the muscular ridge cut from the middle of his back down to the elastic of his underwear.

I was thinking about Scotty and me together on that familiar road.

And I wanted to tell him this.

Suddenly the left-turn signal flashed red in my face. He and Becky were turning onto a road that didn't lead to his house. It's a road I've never been down before. As we passed them on the shoulder, he leaned across Becky to honk the horn with one hand and waved us away with the other. He knew I was behind him all along. More importantly, he knew I would wave back.

I'm being such a girl right now. I have no right to be jealous.

Scotty isn't my boyfriend. I barely let him be my friend, no matter how hard he tried. I guess I just didn't want an in-the-face confirmation that I was right all along: our destinations differed from the get-go. Or perhaps I slammed on the brakes too early.

the twenty-ninth

I really need to get my period. I've got too many hormones stashed in my system. Or not enough. Whatever. All I know is that I'm out-of-control overemotional lately.

This evening's two cases in point:

On my break, I decided to check out how The Geek was doing. The Geek is the main attraction of the skill game called, appropriately, Shoot the Geek. There is always a throng of testosterifically charged-up idiot boys lined up, dollar bills in hand, to fire paintball bazooka guns at The Geek. The Geek's identity has always been anonymous, concealed by camouflage fatigues and an oversize mask in the likeness of the most maligned man of the moment. Past pariahs include Saddam Hussein and Ken Starr. This year The Geek is Bill Gates. For as long as I can remember, even before I started working here, The Geek was universally acknowledged as the most degrading job on the boardwalk.

Until this year.

This summer, The Geek was mesmerizing to watch. He rocked. Seriously. He was lightning quick and dodged those jack-offs' shots with ease. Their inability to blast the hell out of him was an affront to their *muy* macho manhood. They screamed and yelled and pounded their fists in fury. But The Geek wasn't intimidated in the least. In fact, he went out of his way to taunt his tormentors with obscene hand and finger gestures. He totally pissed them off. It was hilarious. The Geek never failed to cheer me up.

Tonight, of course, was the exception.

When I stopped by, The Geek was just *standing* there. He wasn't egging on the enemy by giving them the finger or diving on the ground to dodge their blasts. The Geek just got battered, each hit splattering his camouflage fatigues. Red! Yellow! Blue! I couldn't see his face, but it was clear by the way he slumped and shrugged that The Geek's spirit had been broken. I suppose getting paid five fifty an hour to be pelted by paintballs triggered by attitudinal tourists would do that to the best of us.

I wanted to offer him some encouragement. "C'mon, Geek! Get up! Give 'em hell. You can do it!" This would've been for my benefit as much as his. Yet I kept my mouth shut and moved on.

Then I started thinking. What if this is the best job The Geek can get? That's no joke. What if he's a "lifer" like the Whack Our Kats man? One of those losers who works on the boards between Memorial Day and Labor Day, then collects unemployment the rest of the year? Or what if he's one of the poor Europeans who have to travel thousands of miles just to get a job as sucky as the Geek gig, or serving up greasy eats, for that matter?

I realized that working at Wally D's Sweet Treat Shoppe is probably the worst job I'll ever have. I know I have a bright future ahead of me. But instead of feeling happy about my good fortune, I just felt guilty.

When I went back behind the counter at frozen custard central, I couldn't even engage in my favorite work diversion: making fun of all the customers, the first of which was primo making-fun-of material. If Scotty needs a Gut Buster, this man required a Whole Body Buster. He really pushed the limits of his dishwater-dirty wife-beater T-shirt. When he pounded the counter to get my attention, the pudding flesh on his arm shook, making the tattoo of a top-heavy woman do the hula on his bicep. Scripted letters swayed beneath her tiny feet: SID LOVES MYRNA.

"Wazzat custud?" Sid growled. "Izzat iscream aw smudder shit?"

I understood this language with zero difficulty. This scares me.

"It's richer than ice cream," I replied. "It's made with a heavier cream."

Normally, I would've called him "Sir." See, Sid had several important teeth missing. It usually amuses the hell out of me to call a man with no front teeth, "Sir." But like I said, I was too sad.

Sid leaned into my face, pressing his palms into the cash register. "I wanna chocklit. Lahge. Wit rainbuh sprinkuhs." He then unleashed a long beef burrito belch.

I was repulsed, but somehow I resisted any retaliation. I didn't want him to have a hemorrhage and shoot his sugar-sticky blood all over my counter.

I made his chocolate cone and I got even more depressed than I already was. I mean, it was suddenly pretty depressing to make a large cone for this beyond-obese, toothless guy. I started to wonder about the quality of Sid's life. I wondered if Myrna was a real woman somewhere. Did she love him? I wondered if she left him because he was fat or belched in public. Had her devastating departure left him no choice but to seek solace in cone after chocolate cone?

I handed Sid his treat. He opened up his cavernous mouth and took a huge hunk off the top. Sprinkles that escaped his mouth trickled to the counter. He shoved three pocket-sweaty bills at me and lumbered away, muttering obscenities in between gulps. As I rang up his three dollars and grabbed the nearest rag to wipe the clump of drooly sprinkles off the counter, I tried to shake off my sadness. But I couldn't.

I can't believe people come here to have fun. This is about the least fun place on earth. Besides school, that is. If I get any more depressed about the human condition, I just might feel sorry enough for Tsylt to accept one of his numerous broken-English advances. He's the most persistent of my European suitors, the one I've nicknamed "Woody" for reasons that I don't want or need to explain.

Thank God I'm getting out of here in just a few weeks. I can't believe I'm finally going to see Hope. I'm going to be there for her sixteenth birthday on the twenty-third. I really can't believe it. It's been more than six months. Even though we've been keeping in touch like we promised (with no guilt) I really want to see her surroundings for myself. Maybe seeing her in her element will be the thing that finally convinces me that she isn't coming back.

August 2nd

Hope,

It's not my imagination anymore. For the past week, Burke has started dropping me off before Manda, even though I live closer to him and it makes more geographic sense to take her home first. When I called him on it, he mumbled something about this being the route recommended by Yahoo! Maps. *Bullshitbullshitbullshit.* Then Manda told me that since I didn't even have a learner's permit (like *she* does!) I should just shut up and let him drive. She then proceeded to pat Burke's knee and flutter those goddamn eyelashes of hers as the exclamation point on the insult.

What am I going to tell Bridget? I don't have any hard-core evidence. But I'm not likely to get any. I can't steal their uniforms and test them for DNA, can I?

No. I'm wrong. Waaaaaaay wrong. First of all, the only criterion Burke meets is the fact that he's over six feet tall. Okay. I'll admit. He does have a bod that could best be described as, *foooooooyne.* Maybe he flosses daily— I don't know. But he's not blond, doesn't surf or ski, and drives a Ford Escort, not a jeep.

Plus, Manda wouldn't stoop so low, would she? Flirting with Burke is one thing. Fellating him is another. That's beyond skanky. That would officially make her a full-on skank of the first degree. And surely Burke loves Bridget. He's strong enough not to whip out his junk just because Manda swings her jugs around . . . right? (Please say I'm right.)

There's only one reason why I'm writing about this soap opera instead of *my long overdue visit to see you* in three weeks: I'm afraid that by writing about it, I'll jinx it. And I can't afford to jinx it. I really can't.

Fingers crossingly yours, J.

august

the fifth

JUST EIGHTEEN DAYS UNTIL I SEE HOPE!

Every L.A.me E-mail I get from Bridget, every carnal carpool I share with Manda and Burke, every *quote Omigod! unquote* anecdote I endure from Sara intensifies my need to hang with Hope.

I'm going down there for her birthday. The twenty-third. The fact that she'd still rather celebrate her Sweet Sixteen with me than with anyone she's met down there helps relax the paranoia I have about being replaced.

This worry will only get worse if she gets into the all-girls private school she applied to. It was a last-minute thing; one of her relatives has an in on the board of directors or something. It has an amazing visual arts program that will really help her build the impressive portfolio she needs to get into a first-class college. Great instructors, great facilities, great supplies. She sounded so psyched about it on the phone. More psyched than I have ever sounded about anything in my entire life.

For her birthday, I'm burning her a CD mix. It has to strike the right balance between sincerity and irony. Not too much Beck or too little Duran Duran. Can't go heavy on *South Park* or light on Moby. I will focus all my brainpower on this project until it's done. I need this present to be perfect. Probably more for myself than her. I need to prove that I still know Hope better than anyone else.

the fourteenth

I knew it was too good to be true. I really did. So I wasn't shocked when my plans to see Hope fell through today. But I was shocked (and disgusted) by how I felt about the reason why they fell through.

Hope not only got in to the private school, but nabbed a scholarship. Huge deal.

I know that a true best friend would be happy for her. I know I shouldn't be bothered by the fact that her new school starts two weeks earlier than the public school she would have attended, therefore null-and-voiding my visit. I know I shouldn't be jealous because leaving Pineville may end up being the best thing that ever happened to Hope, while I'm still stuck here doing the same-old, same-old. Going nowhere. I shouldn't be green that Hope is moving on so much better than I am.

But I am.

When I told my mom I wasn't going to spend a week in Tennessee, she gushed, "Great! Now we can spend some quality time together!"

Needless to say, I won't be quitting my job early after all.

I gotta go. I have to mail Hope's present if I want her to still be there when it arrives.

the sixteenth

Matthew Michael Darling would have been twenty today.

As if I weren't depressed enough.

I wonder if things were worse for Hope's parents or mine. Hope told me that in a way, Heath's death was a relief for her parents: They could stop waiting for it happen. My parents never saw it coming. How can you see something like that coming?

I've never been to his grave. My parents have never taken me. Can you imagine how it must have been for them? Instead of picking out stuffed animals they were picking out his burial plot. They do not talk about it. And I know not to acknowledge it.

My mom will be a zombie for the next two weeks. She pops Valiums starting today until September first—the anniversary of his death. Then she stops cold turkey. Mourning over. Supreme self-control.

My dad acts like nothing out of the ordinary is going on. He goes for his three-hour bike rides. He spends hours tinkering with the computer. Our conversations don't go beyond him grilling me about how many miles I've run this week to gear up for cross-country season. Same as usual.

Sometimes I wonder what Matthew would've looked like. Would he be prematurely bald like my dad, or have perfect teeth like my mom? Would he have Bethany's flawless complexion? Or would he be scrawny like me?

I see college guys with Greek letters on their chests and I wonder if he would've celebrated with them. Or would he have celebrated his birthdays alone? Like me.

I know I wasn't planned because Gladdie told me so on my fourteenth birthday. In her uncensored senility, she informed me between bites of Carvel ice-cream cake that I was a "wonderful surprise" for my parents, who never thought they would "have the heart to try again." Of course, this was just a nice way of saying I was a mistake.

I think Bethany always considered me competition. A brother would have been a different deal. Maybe that's why we've never gotten along. But it's safe to say my parents were happy to have me—more so after I made it past the one-month mark. But sometimes, when they go overboard on the groundings and other assholic parental gestures, I can't help but think they're trying to "save" me because they couldn't save Matthew. Maybe that's the real reason why they've been particularly harsh since Heath OD'd. It's not that they were afraid his bad habits had rubbed off on me, as I had thought. No, Heath's death probably reminded them of their own loss, one they don't want to experience again.

I think too goddamn much.

One thing I know for sure, if Matthew had lived, my parents

would've been a lot more vigilant with birth control, thereby elimi-
nating the possibility of a "wonderful surprise" like me. This knowl-
edge comes directly from my mother, who refers to three or more
kids in any family as a "litter." So I'm sort of grateful for Matthew's
death, which is an evil thing. A go-to-hell type of thing, if I
believed in hell.

Right now I feel guilty to be alive. Why? Because I'm wasting
it. I've been given this life and all I do is mope it away.

What's worse is, I am totally aware of how ridiculous I am. It
would be a lot easier if I believed I was the center of the universe,
because then I wouldn't know any better *not* to make a big deal out
of everything. I know how small my problems are, yet that doesn't
stop me from obsessing about them.

I have to stop doing this.

How do other people get happy? I look at people laughing and
smiling and enjoying themselves and try to get inside their heads.
How do Bridget, Manda, and Sara do it? Or Pepe? Or *everyone* but
me?

Why does everything I see bother me? Why can't I just get
over these daily wrongdoings? Why can't I just move on and make
the best of what I've got?

I wish I knew.

the eighteenth

Last night was catastrophic.

Cataclysmically catastrophic.

In fact, the only reason I'm writing about last night at all is
because I think it's important from a purely historical perspective. I
want my descendants to know what event cinched the last strap on
my straightjacket.

About halfway through my shift, Manda came charging up to my stand as fast as her platform sandals would carry her.

"Can you get a ride home tonight?"

"No. Why?"

"Well there's a huge blowout on Carteret Ave. tonight."

"And?"

"*Aaaaaaaand*," she exaggerated, as though my grasp of the English language were worse than Woody's. "We want to go."

"*We* being . . . ?"

"Me," she said.

"And?"

"Sara."

"And?"

"Burke."

"Did you ever think that maybe I might want to go too?"

"Puh-leeze, Jess," she said. "You never want to go *anywhere*."

She was right. I never want to go anywhere. I had avoided going anywhere all summer and look how happy it had made me. I was more depressed than ever. Maybe some good old-fashioned mindless debauchery would do me some good. Liquid lubricant was just the thing to loosen up my torqued-uppedness. I was too uptight about everything. I needed to live a little.

"I want to go."

Manda looked at me, expressionless.

"To the party," I said. "I want to go to the party."

Manda thought this was the funniest thing she had ever heard in her life. She literally bent over and slapped her knees as she laughed, affording Woody and his Hungarian homeboys a golden opportunity to look down her tank top.

"Are you spoken for?" Woody asked Manda.

Manda stopped cackling and started gagging. I ignored him.

"I'll call my parents and tell them I'm sleeping over at Sara's," I said. "They'll be thrilled that I'm out being social."

"You're serious about this?" she asked, as though I were signing away my life, which, as it turned out, wasn't too far from the truth.

"Yes," I said. "I'm ready to par-*tay*."

After work (or nonwork in Sara's case), Burke drove us over to the stretch of beach where the festivities were taking place. We got there around midnight. The fiesta was clearly in its early stages, as there was an even one-to-one ratio of people to beer cans scattered on the sand. Plus, the sexes had yet to mingle. Giggly girls clung in clumps, clutching plastic cups and beer cans kindly provided by members of the opposite sex who wanted to get in their pants. Packs of guys pounded each other in the arm, pointing out the girls whose pants they wanted to get into. We may be in high school, but until everyone is wasted these shindigs are as boy–girl segregated as a kindergarten birthday party. When the sexes interface, that's when you know things are getting really messy.

The "beat of the beach," FM 98.5, blasted a hot weather classic:

Summer summer summertime.
Time to sit back and unwind.

"Still ready to par-*tay*?" yelled Manda over the music.

I had no ride home. No escape.

"I desperately need a beer," I yelled back.

Manda had sent Burke off in search of alcohol. On cue, he returned to us, his arms full of cans of Milwaukee's Best. I really hate the taste of beer. Even *good* beer when it's icy cold, and this "Beast" was neither. But I've learned that once you're buzzed, the foul taste doesn't register anymore. I cracked it open and chugged as much as I could as fast as I could.

"Whoo-hoo!" whooped Manda and Sara. "You go, girl."

I slammed my first beer before the Fresh Prince finished. He was followed by the opening guitar picking of a big Backstreet Boys hit from a couple summers back. Their reign as the undisputed crown princes of teenybopper pop was clearly over because the backlash was immediate: The crowd started booing before BSB began to harmonize. Someone quickly changed the station, but it was too late. I had already started thinking about Marcus Flutie, wondering if he wore that T-shirt at Middlebury. Wondering if anyone got the joke if he did. Wondering if he wondered about me.

I got another beer out of the nearest cooler.

Sara and Manda had barely sipped their beers but were already fronting like they had tied one on.

"Know who I miss?" asked Sara.

"Who do you miss?" asked Manda.

"I miss Hy," said Sara.

"Me, too," said Manda.

I grunted and gulped more beer. I don't know why, but for a split second I thought Sara was going to say, _Hope. I miss Hope._ It's probably because I hadn't really given Hy's disappearance a second thought, while I can't for the life of me forget that Hope is gone. The thing is, if Sara had said, _I miss Hope_, I would have coldcocked her with my beer can.

"Hy was for real, you know?" said Manda.

"Her aunt said she was _quote_ going back to where she belongs _unquote_."

That got my attention.

"What? What does that mean?"

"I think it means she's back in the city," Sara said.

"Why wouldn't she tell us?" I asked.

"Maybe she was embarrassed, you know, after all the bad stuff she said about the stuck-up girls she went to school with," mused Sara. "She didn't want to face us."

I chucked my can into the garbage and grabbed another.

The "conversations" that followed aren't worth going into in detail.

Manda wondered if Bridget would act all stuck up when she got back from L.A. When she went off in search of Burke, I tossed that can away and grabbed another.

Between swigs of Beast, Sara bragged about losing two and a half pounds on the first day of her new lemon-water diet.

I needed to block out what was going on around me.

Another beer.

Then two more.

I was halfway through my sixth when I saw him.

Him.

Paul Parlipiano.

"JESUS CHRIST!" I screamed in Sara's face, the way only an obnoxious boozer can. "IT'S PAUL PARLIPIANO!"

I clamped my hands over my mouth.

"OMIGOD!OMIGOD!OMIGOD! I KNEW IT! I KNEW IT! I KNEW IT!" screamed Sara, blowing my hair back. "YOU'RE IN LOVE WITH HIM!"

I clamped my hands over *her* mouth.

"SHHHHHHHHH . . ." I slurred. "You did not."

"I did too."

"You did not."

"I did too."

This went on in circles for a while, as drunken conversations tend to do.

"I'm just happy you're not a lesbo," she said, finally, bringing the circle to a dead stop.

"You think I'm a lesbian?!"

"Omigod! Not me!"

"Then who? And why?"

"There has been talk, Jess," she said, "I mean, you're a *Jockette*, and you haven't so much as kissed a boy since you went out with Scotty in eighth grade."

"I have too!" I said, reluctantly remembering Cal. "I just didn't tell you about it."

"Let me guess, he lives in Canada, right?" Sara said. "Niagara Falls area. I wouldn't know him."

A nineteen-year-old computer genius/college dropout in Seattle didn't sound much more credible. I didn't even know what to say. I mean, *me?* A *vagitarian?*

"Hey, *I'm* the one who defended your heterosexuality, so don't get pissed at me," Sara said with that all-knowing tone I love to hate. "*I'm the one who pointed out to everyone how you faint dead away whenever someone so much as says the words Paul Parlipiano. So I did too know you were in love with him. I know it just like I knew that Manda and Burke were banging all summer, before I caught them. . . .*"

Then she clamped *her* hands over *her* mouth.

Holy shit!

"Omigod! You can't say anything!" begged Sara.

I was too stunned to say anything. Manda has been banging Burke all summer. Christ. It's one thing to *suspect* the worst about someone. But it's quite another for that low-down dogginess to be confirmed by a very reliable source.

"I promised Manda I wouldn't say anything. And if Bridget finds out . . ." She started to hop up and down in a panic, much like I had moments before. "Omigod! Fuck! Promise you won't tell Bridget! Or Manda! Or anyone! Omigod! Fuck!"

I looked for Paul Parlipiano. He was so beautiful. So pure. So . . . everything.

"Jess! Swear you won't say anything!"

I needed to see him.

"I really don't want to think about this right now," I said, meaning every word with the kind of conviction that only copious amounts of alcohol can bring. "Because Paul Parlipiano and I are at the same party for the first time ever and . . ."

I was silenced by the sight of him. There he was, not ten feet away, sitting cross-legged in the sand, sipping his beer, carrying on what seemed to be a perfectly intelligent convo with a Trekkish geek . . .

YESSSSSSSSS! HE'S NOT WITH A GIRL. Paul Parlipiano is confident enough with his own popularity to hang with a herb. That makes him ever so endearing. And approachable, I thought. Or I might have said this all out loud. I'm not sure. This is where my alcoholic amnesia starts to kick in. All I know is that my beer-buzzed brain started babbling about truths that I would have never believed had

I not been under the influence of mind-altering chemicals. Not that drinking is an excuse for what happened.

Okay. It *is* an excuse. But it's a lame one.

Fate brought me and Paul Parlipiano to the same suck-ass beach party.

He's leaving for college—it's my last chance EVER to tell him how I feel.

If I don't tell him, I will live in agony, then die alone.

I must tell him.

"Excuse me," I said, brushing by Sara, who was still begging. "I have a life to live."

And thus began what is by far the most horrendous chain of events in my young, semitortured life.

I remember checking out my appearance in the side mirror of a car parked nearby.

I remember thinking that as long as my hair looked good, Paul Parlipiano would have no idea that I was blitzed.

I remember thinking that my hair looked good.

I remember stumbling over to Paul Parlipiano and plopping myself down in the sand between him and Trekkie.

I remember saying, *Heeeeeeyyyyy* and Paul Parlipiano saying *Hey* right back and Trekkie saying nothing before getting up and walking away.

I remember him saying, *You're on the track team. Jessica, right?*

I remember bonfire flames lighting up his face.

I remember a lightning bolt shooting straight to my crotch. Sha-ZAM!

I remember telling him about how I admired his smoothness and grace as he jumped over the hurdles OneTwoThreeAIR and the time I heard him cheering for me and how I couldn't believe it because that meant that I existed in his world if only for a short while but it meant so much to me because I respected and yes even loved him even though logic and reason told me I had no business feeling that way about him but I didn't care no I loved him and I wanted him to know it not because I expected him to reciprocate even though I really really wanted him to but because if someone ever loved me in that pure way I would want to know about it. . . .

I remember him smiling an I'm-embarrassed-for-you smile.

I remember acid swirling in my stomach.

I remember him saying words I'll never forget: *You only think you love me. If you knew me, you'd know better.*

Blackout.

I woke up this morning on Sara's bedroom floor with no memory of anything after that. Unfortunately, Sara gleefully filled in the Grand Canyon–size gap in my memory.

All you really need to know is this one horrifying thing:

I puked on Paul Parlipiano's shoes.

After I pledged my love, but before I passed out.

I, Jessica Darling, puked on Paul Parlipiano's shoes.

the nineteenth

I puked on his shoes.

I PUKED ON PAUL PARLIPIANO'S SHOES.

I will be forever immortalized in Paul Parlipiano's mind as The Drunk Girl Who Puked on My Shoes.

I want to die. And not being able to tell Hope makes it even worse. I know she wouldn't approve of my boozy idiocy. And she certainly wouldn't give me the sympathy I need right now.

the twenty-second

Tonight was my last night of work. It rained, so it was dead. I had a lot of time to mull over my mortification in new and creative ways.

Paul Parlipiano is at Columbia now. I will surely be a subject in his can-you-top-this? getting-to-know-you storytelling sessions. I imagine him in his dorm, surrounded by new friends: *You think that's bad? Right before I left for school, this drunk girl I'd never talked to before in my life pledged her undying love, then puked on my shoes. SHE PUKED ON MY SHOES!*

When torturing myself in this manner became exhaustive, I worried about what to tell Bridget about Manda and Burke's Summer of Skankitude (S.O.S.). I still don't know the answer. I don't want to be mixed up in this gruesome mess. Then again, it's my own fault. I could've said no. Instead, I made a promise—albeit reluctantly, and to someone I'm not even that close to anymore—and I feel obligated to follow through on it.

Plus, I think Bridget has a right to know that Manda picked her boyfriend as the lucky winner in the Devirginization Sweepstakes.

I'm seriously sickened by the whole thing. I know this is sexist and totally supports the stud–whore double standard for guys and girls and all, but I'm more mad at Manda than Burke. I mean, it's a *given* that guys don't have as much self-control as girls. They can't help but pop insta-chubbies. But how psychologically messed up is Manda? She refuses to have sex with any of her *own* boyfriends, then snakes her best friend's man? I never liked Manda much, but now I can't look at her without wanting to hose her down with Lysol.

Maybe Burke and Manda will take the high road and tell Bridget themselves. But I think my best bet is Sara: She's never kept a secret before. Why should this one be any different? And there still is the teensy-weensiest chance that Sara got this one wrong. Hey, you never know.

Needless to say, that occupied my mind for a while. When I got too tired to worry about it anymore, I simply stared at the Wacky for Tobacky cigarette stand located right next to mine.

"SMOKE YOUR BRAINS OUT!"

The cigarette-stand crowd never ceases to amaze me. The winners of the packs of their choice jump, holler, and high-five with unparalleled intensity, even by the boardwalk's standards. They seem to forget that for the amount of quarters they bet, they could have purchased a carton, but I guess it was the thrill of victory that had them breaking dollar after dollar for change.

"TEEEEEBAAAAACO! TEEEEEBAAAAACO HEEEEEE-AH!" squawked the boy working the cigarette stand. Tonight he modeled a yellow plastic jacket with a picture of the now-retired phallic Joe Camel printed on the back. It could have melted off his body if the temperature rose above eighty-five degrees. The jacket came up short at his wrists, showing he was at that awkward age when certain body parts grow faster than others. He had the same pathetic smudge of a mustache that Scotty had during our eleven-day relationship. I wanted to tell Cigarette Boy that it was more sickly than sexy and that he should shave it off ASAP.

However, I didn't tell him that, because all of a sudden, I had to know if Cigarette Boy had a girlfriend. I waited for him to start the wheel. It had all the months of the year on it, separated by the four seasons. Winter. Spring. Summer. Fall. It was the best cigarette odds on the boardwalk.

"Hey! At the cigarette stand!" About ten smokers turned away from the wheel to look at me. The boy did not.

"Not *you*. The kid who works it," I yelled above the cacophony.

The smokers turned back to the wheel. The boy looked at me but said nothing. He's not allowed to talk beyond the bark for customers once he's behind the counter.

"Yes. Cigarette Boy. You. Do you have a girlfriend?"

Confusion clouded his face first. Then he started to look smug. It was the smug look of a fourteen-year-old who had an older chick obviously hot for his bod.

"I'm not making the moves on you," I said impatiently.

He slumped.

"Quick. Do you have a girlfriend?"

He nodded.

I thought about me and Scotty, Bridget and Burke, Sid and Myrna, and I grieved for this boy's future. I didn't want to see him several summers from then, with his Myrna tattooed on his arm, mourning his lost love, cone after chocolate cone.

Break up, I wanted to beg. *Before you're in too deep.*

But I couldn't get it out.

The spinner stopped on Fall. The winners rejoiced. The losers slapped down more quarters. They tried again. The years on the wheel whizzed by.

the twenty-third

Today is Hope's birthday. I couldn't contain my excitement when the phone rang. I ran to pick it up because I thought it might be her. Caller ID flashed an UNAVAILABLE warning that I ignored. Thus, the following conversation is my own fault.

"Jayssseeecahhh! Eeet's meee!"

I almost hung up. "Who is this?"

"Eeet's Baythahhhhneeee."

I should have known that after honeymooning in Europe for a month, my sister would adopt some bizarro affected accent.

"How aaahhhrrr yooo?"

Crackly static interrupted me before I could utter a clichéd phrase.

"Saaahhhree. Ahm own mah cehlee."

Her cellie. Of course. I bet she has them in all different colors, to coordinate with her outfits, or her cars. Apparently, the stock-market crash hasn't cramped her style.

"Eeeesss Mowthair thair?"

"Uh, no."

"Whaaahhht ahh peetee."

"Huh?"

"*Whaaahht ahh peetee.*"

What a pity. Jesus Christ. This was worse than Madonna after *Evita*.

"Pleeeze geev hair theees maysaaahhhg."

"Sure," I said. "If I can translate it."

"Whaaahht?"

"Nothing."

"Grahnt ahnd ah cahnnot cohm tooo veeseet forrrrh Labohrrrrrr Dayee."

I personally could care less if G-Money and my sister couldn't make it out for Labor Day. But my mother would be crushed. It's all I've heard about since the wedding.

"No way," I said. "You tell her. She's showing a house right now but should be . . ."

"Nooo caaahhhn doo," she said. "Ahm own mah waaaayeee tooo theee aaahhhrrrpohhhrt. Ah hahv a flaht too [static] . . . Ahm brayking uhp [more static] . . ."

And that was it.

I wouldn't be surprised if the static was fake and she was just making phlegm-hocking noises in the phone just to stop talking to me. I mean, I know she's got eleven years on me, but she's that immature.

When I told my mother the news, she tried to shrug it off—*My daughter, the jet-setter*—but I could tell that she was upset by the way she was violently chopping vegetables for dinner.

"It's okay to get mad," I said.

"Who me, mad?" she said, beheading lettuce. WHACK!

"You seem to have no problem getting mad at me," I said.

"That's because you provoke me on purpose," she said, tearing its leaves, limb by limb.

"I don't provoke you!" I retaliated. "How do *I* provoke *you*?" If anything it was the other way around.

"You provoke me by asking questions like, 'How do I provoke you?'," she said. "Now please stop provoking me and give me some peace and quiet."

As you wish, oh blond one.

By the way, when Hope did call, she said she loves her CD. This does wonders for my psyche. But living in this house, sometimes Hope's phone calls aren't enough to distract me from my self-inflicted misery.

the twenty-ninth

The date of Bridget's return came and went and I didn't hear from her.

Or the next day.

Or the day after that.

Today, Bridget finally called. By then I had already heard via Sara about how her appearance was considered "too apple-pie Americana" and "not edgy enough" by every talent scout in Hollywood, and how her agent wanted her to drop Bridget Milhokovich for a more attention-grabbing stage name like "Bridge Milhouse," "Gette Miller," or "Bebe" (no last name, just Bebe). But I was too pissed off to enjoy a good laugh over any of that. Obviously, confirming Burke's fidelity wasn't as big a priority as I thought it was. All my anxiety was for nothing.

"Hey! I'm back!"

"So I hear."

"Sorry that I haven't called you or anything, but I've been like, way busy, you know unpacking and stuff," she said.

"Uh-huh."

"And I had to like, readjust to East-Coast time."

"Uh-huh."

I was waiting for her to finish making excuses and get down to the real issue at hand: Did Burke bang anyone this summer?

"And you know, Burke and I have been busy," she said. "Like, reuniting."

Here it comes, I thought. I got ready to tell her the truth: The only girls Burke hung out with all summer were Manda, Sara, and me. Okay. So it wasn't the whole truth. When Bridget blew me off, she blew her shot at being set 100 percent straight. Let her find out the ugly truth by herself. Leave me out of it.

Looks like the fine line between lie and not telling the truth turned out to be irrelevant. Bridget wasn't interested in the truth at all: she never asked for it. Why should she when the fictionalized Burke offers her everything she ever wanted in her relationship and more?

Burke has been so sweet to me! Like, I can tell he really missed me all summer! I think he was worried I was going to run off with like, Brad Pitt or something! He was waiting at the airport with a dozen roses and a big box of Jujyfruits, my favorite! We would've totally started going at it like, right on the floor of the airport if my parents hadn't been there! This summer was tough, but soooooo good for us! It made us appreciate each other more than ever. Moremushygushymushygushy-mushygushgarbage!

I can't believe I was actually feeling bad about the idea of B. and B. breaking up.

They deserve each other. And as much as I am amused by the concept of watching the Clueless Crew lie to each other all year, the reality of all the bitchy backstabbing that is bound to occur makes me less excited about being a junior than ever.

September 1st

Hope,

Matthew Michael Darling died twenty years ago today. Although our situations are very different, I know you can relate.

I'm mourning him in a weird way: by trying on my back-to-school clothes.

I tried them on in my bedroom to see if I still looked like me when I wore them outside the dressing room. I tucked the tags up in the sleeve. Cutting them off meant commitment. And I was uncomfortable making that commitment because I felt like I was never going to wear them outside my bedroom. I felt as if they'd always be unfamiliar articles of clothing with no memories attached.

What would my mom do with them if I died? I can't ask her. Especially today.

Actually, is there an appropriate time to ask that question?

Every year girls like Sara wear their flyest fall clothes on the first day of school. They get all decked out like the September covers of *YM* and *Seventeen* in their turtleneck sweaters and wool miniskirts and boots, despite the fact that it's still eighty-five degrees outside. I used to think that they just wanted to show off how stylish they were. But maybe I'm not the only one afraid that I'll never get a chance to wear them.

I doubt it.

I know this is stupid, but every time I go back-to-school shopping, I always imagine that my purchases will bring me a new-and-improved life. Like that new T-shirt or lipstick will finally make Paul Parlipiano realize how amazing and offbeat I am. Only I don't even have Paul Parlipiano to hope for anymore.

Now what will I do to try to get my mind off the fact that you're gone?

Quixotically yours, J.

september

the third

I was lounging under the covers, bittersweetly enjoying my last Sunday morning free of school-on-Monday dread, when Bridget came bursting through my bedroom door.

"Everything was a lie!" she shrieked.

Wow, I thought. *I knew Sara would spill about Burke and Manda, but I expected her to hold out longer than this.*

"Like, everything about Hy was a lie!"

"What?"

"There's an article about her in today's *New York Times*!" Bridget yelled, waving a newspaper in my face.

"What?!"

"See for yourself!"

I wiped the sleep crust out of my eyes and took the paper from Bridget. There, on the front page of the "Styles" section, was a picture of a very bored-looking Hy, chin in one hand, cigarette in the other. The caption read: WILL CINTHIA WALLACE BE GEN-Y'S LITERARY "IT" GIRL?

"Cinthia Wallace?!"

"That's what the Park Avenue Posse calls her," Bridget said.

"Park Avenue Posse?!"

"It gets worse," Bridget said, nervously twisting her ponytail around her hand.

I read on, and finally found out the truth about Miss Hyacinth Anastasia Wallace.

Miss Hyacinth Anastasia Wallace, daughter of Pulitzer Prize–winning poet Wisteria Allegra-Wallace and banking billioniare Nicholas Wallace, who divorced when she was four years old. Miss Hyacinth Anastasia Wallace, "the cream of the crop of the hip-hop debutantes who zoom through their young lives at warp speed." Miss Hyacinth Anastasia Wallace, who, at thirteen, was caught by her nanny at her father's Park Avenue penthouse having sex with an underwear model twice her age. Miss Hyacinth Anastasia Wallace, "clubber, raver, precocious party girl," asked to leave no less than six chi-chi private schools for smoking, drinking, and drugging. Miss Hyacinth Anastasia Wallace, who, by sixteen, "was bored by champagne, cocaine, promiscuous sex, and Prada." Miss Hyacinth Anastasia Wallace, who "craved the normal life she never had" and decided to move in with a "normal" family acquaintance (a former maid) and attend a "normal" public high school in a "normal" town in New Jersey just to see what "normal" girls her age were like. Miss Hyacinth Anastasia Wallace, who claims that she was shocked to discover that these "normal" New Jersey girls were "just as superficial and sex-crazed as the girls in the Park Avenue Posse—only severely challenged fashion-wise." Miss Hyacinth Anastasia Wallace, who just snagged six figures to write her first novel, which she hopes will give her the credibility she needs to get accepted to Harvard on merit, instead of on money and family name. Miss Hyacinth Anastasia Wallace, whose fictionalized account of her "normal" New Jersey experience is tentatively titled (GASP!) *Bubble-Gum Bimbos and Assembly-Line Meatballers*.

"*Bubble-Gum Bimbos!*"

"I know! It's like, totally horrible!" Bridget yelled right back. "*She's* calling *us* bubble-gum bimbos!"

My stomach spun around faster than the Himalaya ride on Funtown Pier. Miss Hyacinth Anastasia Wallace wasn't the first one to refer to the Clueless Crew as bubble-gum bimbos. She stole the title from that conversation we had at her house over spring break. Then I thought: *What if she writes about the conversation we had at her house over spring break? What if she writes about me? What if I'm lumped in with the bubble-gum bimbos?*

Bridget read my mind. "Can she do this? Can she write about us? Is she like, gonna write about us?"

I couldn't answer her. I was speechless.

Within a half hour, Manda and Sara had arrived on the scene. It was the first time all four of us had been in the same room together since school let out. Only now we were joined by an elephant named *MandabangedBurkeallsummer* that stood quietly in the corner while we all ranted and raved about Miss Hyacinth Anastasia Wallace. It went something like this:

Sara: *Omigod! I should've known. I had a hunch she came from money,*
    too.
Manda: *I should've known. Virgin Mary? Puh-leeze.*
Bridget: *I should've known. Like, I sort of felt we were being used some-*
    how.
Me: *I should've known. Her street slang never sounded right.*

After hours of Hy-steria, the apex was a hilarious conversation about the ethics of friendship. It went something like this:

Sara: *Omigod! How could Hy lie to us like that? She was our friend.*
    Friends don't lie to each other.
Manda: *Grrrrrrr . . . I can't stand liars! Liars are the lowest of the low!*
Bridget: *I'd take the ugly truth over a lie any day. Like, at least you know*
    where you stand.
Manda and Sara: *So true!*

I couldn't make this stuff up if I tried. Junior year sure is starting off with a bang. More like a gunshot through the back of the head.

the fifth

I've imagined Marcus Flutie in many places.

I've imagined him sneaking up on me on my walk home from school.

I've imagined him hitchhiking on Route 9 in the rain.

I've imagined him in a bar years from now, ordering me a beer for old time's sake.

I never imagined him sitting in his assigned seat in homeroom this morning.

Or sitting right in back of me in History.

Or English.

Or Physics.

But that's where he was. Again and again and again. And that's where he'll be—because he's back.

Leave it to Marcus to outdo the Miss Hyacinth Anastasia Wallace scandal. All morning everyone was wondering, *Why the hell is the school's biggest drug addict in our honors classes? Why isn't Krispy Kreme with the Dregs where he belongs? And why is he wearing a jacket and tie?*

Of course, no one would dare open their mouths to ask him. And our teachers were no help. Once they acknowledged him during roll call (*Sara D'Abruzzi . . . Jessica Darling . . . Marcus Flutie . . .*) they ignored his presence altogether. For his part, Marcus just sat quietly and mysteriously in his seat. He knew that the longer he kept his mouth shut, the more mythological the PHS legend of his return would be. I couldn't even *look* at him, let alone talk to him. If I looked at him, I just knew I'd break out into a nervous, neo-Saint-Vitus' herky-jerky.

Our alphabetical destiny guarantees that he sits behind me in every class, and I could feel his eyes burning into the back of my head all day. I could feel it so intensely that I swear he was trying to tell me his story telepathically: *I'm back, Cuz. I told you I wouldn't narc on you.* But I didn't pick up on any signals. By our third silent class together, it was clear that Marcus wasn't going to say a word to me. I appreciated his stealth and understood that it was meant to protect me. Yet Marcus sitting six inches, yet a bizillion miles, away was bamboo-under-the-fingernails-variety torture. Especially when he wouldn't stop jiggling my chair with his feet. My seat vibrated all day.

Sara was pissed off at herself for having missed out on not one but *two* of the biggest Pineville High scandals of all time. Since the *New York Times* had already scooped her on Miss Hyacinth Anastasia Wallace, Sara took it upon herself to find out everything about Marcus's return. And by God, if she didn't redeem herself by getting the lowdown by lunchtime, she'd contemplate taking on another extracurricular activity other than gossiping. Of course, not even Sara could procure the bit of information I needed most: the message inside the origami mouth. Still, Sara's nosy tenacity makes her useful to have around sometimes.

"Omigod! You're not going to believe this!" she said. "Krispy Kreme is a *quote* genius *unquote*."

Apparently, the staff at Middlebury were flummoxed by Marcus's complex philosophical takes on his self-destruction. So much so, that they ordered a battery of intelligence tests to see if he was gifted or just plain insane. It turned out to be the former: His scores put him in the top 2 percent of the population. The staff concluded that Marcus wasn't being challenged in school, which is why he turned to drugs for amusement. With the support of his parole officer, Mr. and Mrs. Flutie threatened to sue the school system that had mislabeled him as a troubled kid way back in elementary school, and therefore did not encourage him to develop his many gifts. The administration caved, let him back in school, and placed him in our honors classes.

"He won't be bothering us for long, though," Sara said, smugly.

"Why?" I asked, a bit too concerned.

"If he's caught engaging in any illegal activity, he's out for good," she said.

"What makes you so sure he will?"

"Get real," Manda said. "Like he's gonna go straight-edge just so he can have the pleasure of sitting in our Physics class all year."

"Maybe he will, Manda," I said, wishing it were true. "Maybe he wants to turn his life around."

"Jess?"

"Yes?"

"Puh-leeze."

Puh-leeze. Please. Please, Marcus, please. If not for you, then for me.

the seventh

In the past week, I've received no fewer than two dozen *urgent* E-mails from nycinthia@hotmail.com. I've sent every single one into the trash, unopened. Any message from Miss Hyacinth Anastasia Wallace is more treacherous than the I Love You virus.

Still, every time I log on, I hope that in addition to my daily dose of Hope, there will be an E-mail in my inbox from a sender named krispykreme36@hotmail.com, containing a message that is cryptic, yet significant. Something like . . .

I have no idea. I can't even get inside Marcus's mind long enough to make something up. Maybe that's why I can't hear what he says to me in my dreams. For the past few nights I've been having almost the same dream. The setup is identical: Marcus and I are sitting side by side on the cot in the nurse's office. His mouth is moving. He's saying something but I can't hear him because there's too much noise drowning him out.

The noise is part of the dream that changes from night to night. The first time it was PHS football fans chanting in the bleachers: *PINE*-ville! *PINE*-ville! *PINE*-ville! The second time it was a stereo blasting a medley of treacly hits from the Backstreet Boys' first CD: "As Long As You Love Me," "All I Have To Give," and "Quit Playing Games (With My Heart)." Last night it was the boardwalk's buzzers and bells.

The point is, if there is any secret message, I'm not meant to find it out. And he's certainly not going to tell me. It's only been two days, but I know that this is how it's going to be for the rest of the year, or for as long as Marcus can stay on the level and in our honors classes.

the tenth

Be careful what you wish for.

Of all my twisted fantasies, why oh why did *this* one come true?

After falling asleep as soon as my head hit the pillow all summer, it took less than a week of school to restart my insomniac streak. Granted, as far as the first weeks of school go, mine were unbeatably bizarre. Every night I lay wide awake, trying to figure out what would be the next mind-blowing thing to happen—a slight variation on the bad-things-happen triptych.

Tonight I got my answer.

At about three-thirty this morning, I knew there was no chance I would fall asleep before sunrise. So I decided to go for a run in the dark, like I have dozens of times before, just not since the end of my sophomore year. Thankfully, it was as cathartic as ever. With each step, I felt more at ease with everything that was going on.

Maybe that's why something had to go wrong. I was only about a tenth of a mile away from my house when it happened: I tripped over an exposed tree root in the sidewalk and twisted into the pavement, ankle first. It was exactly how I had tried to orchestrate it last spring, only my dad wasn't there to hit me with his bike.

Or help me.

The pain in my right ankle was blindingly immediate. No way hydrogen peroxide would fix me up this time.

I literally baby-hopped home on my left foot. I cried every inch of the way. When I hopped through the back door of my

175

house, I called out for help. My parents stumbled down the stairs in their pajamas and freaked out when they found me on the floor of the kitchen, my ankle blown up like a purple balloon. They thought I had been kidnapped and beaten or something. When I explained through my tears that no, I had snuck out in the middle of the night to go running all on my own, they *really* freaked out.

They rushed me to the ER. I was given a major painkiller that made me feel like I was moving in syrup. I don't remember much about getting X rays or my cast.

Later at home, my mom read the doctor's word-for-word diagnosis, as she had transcribed it on a yellow legal pad in the ER: I fractured both my tibia and fibula bones where they join at the ankle. This requires complete immobilization in a cast for six weeks, and it will take months of physical therapy and maybe even surgery to heal properly. My stability will never be the same.

My mom told me all this because my dad isn't speaking to me.

I can hear him ranting and raving to my mother behind their closed bedroom door, though. *How could she be so careless? This is the year college coaches look at for awarding athletic scholarships! She's blown it! She could have been a superstar! What a waste of talent!*

So it looks like my dream has come true. I ended my running career. Of course now that it's happened, I can't believe I ever wanted it in the first place.

the eleventh

I knew my parents were taking this all too well. Mom had been too quiet and concerned for my health. Even Dad's rant was nowhere near as intense as I thought it would be. It turns out they were just waiting for the heavy narcotics to wear off so they could inflict some major parental pain on me when they got home from work today.

I was in my room, listening to the *Pretty in Pink* soundtrack, when I heard three short, sharp knocks on my door. They came in. Dad told me to shut off the stereo. They sat down on the bed, flanking me on either side. The wrinkle in Mom's forehead was more pronounced than usual. My dad's hands were tightly clasped, barely containing his anger, his bald head gleaming with sweat.

The interrogation was long, and relentless: *How long have you been sneaking out behind our backs? Who were you meeting? Where were you going? Why in God's name would you go running in the middle of the night? Is your coach not training you hard enough? Why don't we see any of your old friends? What's wrong with you?*

I answered each question honestly, because it seemed to be the path of least resistance. But they weren't the answers my parents wanted to hear. Sneaking out to meet a boy was something they could understand. Bethany had done that. Sneaking out to go to a rave, they could understand. They'd read about that in the *Asbury Park Press*. But sneaking out to go running because I couldn't sleep, *that* they couldn't understand. So they grounded me for a month. Total overkill since it's not like I can go anywhere anyway.

When they left, I put my CD back on and skipped to my favorite track. *Please, Please, Please.* I sang along with Morrissey, the depressed pop star of choice for melancholic music lovers in the UK and beyond:

For once in my life, let me get what I want
Lord knows it would be the first time.

At least *he* knew what he wanted.

the fifteenth

Grounded Gimphood

I. THE BEST THINGS ABOUT IT.

A. **I get to limp out of class five minutes early to ensure safe passage through the otherwise treacherously bottlenecked PHS halls.**

    1. Multiply that by eight academic classes and I miss 40 minutes of useless learning per day, 200 minutes per week.

    2. I miss 5 minutes of Clueless Crew lunch conversation per day, 25 minutes per week.

        a. This slightly ups the odds that I won't be around when Sara spills the news about the S.O.S.

        b. And spares the obliteration of countless brain cells.

B. **I have a bona fide excuse for my sucky moods that family and faux friends can understand.**

    1. The truth is that I'm no more or less depressed than I was before this happened.

    2. Blaming my sketchy ennui on my injury is easier than explaining it.

        a. If I could explain it to myself.

        b. Which I can't.

C. **I can't engage in any two-legged activities.**

    1. I'm a guilt-free no-show at the Clueless Crew's hoo-has of the season.

        a. Football games.

        b. Post-football-game keggers.

        c. Post-football-game kegger sleepovers.

    2. I'm out for the entire cross-country season.

        a. Dad can't strategize the hell out of me.

    b. No bad races for *Notso Darling's Agony of Defeat, Volume Two*.

    c. No practice every day.

       i. I can catch *The Real World*.

       ii. Or "new classics" on TNT.

       iii. Or sleep.

       iv. Or draw up elaborate outlines detailing the pros and cons of grounded gimphood.

II. THE WORST THINGS ABOUT IT.

A. The goddamn cast.

1. It hurts like hell.
2. It itches like hell.
3. It's starting to smell.
    a. Like warm, wet puppies.
    b. This is inexplicable and unpleasant.
4. It's covered in ugly Magic-Marker graffiti.
    a. It's an ever-present reminder of how unclever my classmates are.
       i. BREAK A LEG . . . OOPS! YOU ALREADY DID!
       ii. LIFE IS TUFF!
       iii. GET WELL SOON, SWEETIE!!!!!!!!!!!!!!!!!!!!!!!!!!!!
    b. If Hope were here, she would've painted something cool on it.

B. My mom hovers over me like I'm a drunk toddler.

1. I am forced to listen to her complain about how Bethany never visits.
2. I am forced to endure her lame attempts at girlie bonding.
3. I am forced to field her annoyingly inane questions about people she thinks are my friends.
    a. She doesn't understand why I had zero interest in Bridget's Hollywood exploits.
       i. Even after I explained how Bridget and I are equally skilled thespians (meaning, we aren't) but you don't see anyone encouraging *me* to fly out to L.A. to give acting a go.

       ii. She still thinks Bridget and I are bestest buds.

   b. She doesn't understand why Scotty doesn't call anymore.

       i. Even after I explained how he's gone through three bimbo-cious girlfriends in as many months.

       ii. She still thinks Scotty is "quite a catch."

   c. She doesn't understand why I refuse to take any phone calls from Miss Hyacinth Anastasia Wallace.

       i. Even after I explained how being the inspiration for a novel called *Bubble-Gum Bimbos* is incredibly insulting.

       ii. She still thinks I should give Hy a second chance.

C. My dad still isn't talking to me.

   1. His grunting is way more annoying than his strategizing the hell out of me.

   2. This just confirms the sad truth about our non-relationship.

     a. Running is all we have in common.

     b. If I don't run, I don't exist.

D. Marcus Flutie still isn't talking to me either.

   1. This has hardly anything to do with my temporary gimphood.

     a. His silence is more painful than my throbbing ankle.

     b. His silence drives me crazier than the unscratchable itch on the ball of my injured foot.

   2. I have more than enough time to think about it.

the eighteenth

My injury forces me to spend more time with my mom than I have since I was a zygote. Since my sister is too busy being Mrs. Grant Doczylkowski to set foot in Pineville, guess who gets to be Bethany by proxy.

Every day after school Mom plops down beside me on the

couch and tries to get me to engage in girl talk, which really is her and Bethany's specialty. I think she is trying to brainwash me so that by the end of my thirty-day prison sentence I will be the second daughter of her dreams.

When Mom isn't pretending I'm her beloved firstborn, she is giving me lectures on life. One of her favorites is called, "Get Some Perspective." My mom has always been very big on *perspective*, even more so lately. She's constantly telling me that I need to get some *perspective*. If I put things in *perspective*, I wouldn't make such a huge deal out of the teensy-weensiest things and I'd be a much happier person.

What always pissed me off about her whole *perspective* spiel was that she was writing off my feelings at that moment. If something crappy happens—say, when someone I thought was a friend betrays me for a book deal—my negative emotions are legit, right? It may not be as *vivid* as the crappiness one feels after contracting the Ebola virus, but it's just as *valid*. It's not *my* fault that these are the problems I've been put on this earth to deal with, right? They're petty, they piss me off, and they're *all mine*.

Besides, I've got perspective o'plenty. And to prove it, here are a few heretofore undocumented events that—in a less agitated stage of my life—inspired pages and pages worth of angst:

UNDOCUMENTED EVENT #1

"Bonjour, mademoiselle!"

It was the first day of school. The voice was unfamiliar. A baritone instead of a castrato. I turned to see who it was.

This *wasn't* Pepe Le Pew. No, this was a different guy altogether. One who had grown four inches and gained twenty-five pounds of muscle in less than three months.

This was Pepe Le Puberty.

"Pep—I mean, Pierre!" I gasped. "You grew up!"

He puffed up with pride.

"Thanks."

"En français, s'il vous plaît," singsonged Madame Rogan. She

181

didn't care if we talked before class started, as long as it was in French.

"*Comment était votre été?*" ("How was your summer?")

"*Eh. J'ai travaillé sur le boardwalk.*" ("Eh. I worked on the boardwalk.")

"*Moi aussi.*" ("Me too.")

"*Vraiment? Où?* ("Really? Where?")

"*J'étais . . . Le Geek.*" ("I was . . . The Geek.")

Jésus le Christ!

Pepe Le Puberty (né Le Pew) a.k.a. Pierre a.k.a. Percy Floyd a.k.a. The Black Elvis . . . was The Geek! The one who singlehandedly made the boardwalk's most degrading job into the coolest position ever! My appreciation of Pepe had reached a whole new level.

Our conversation was cut short by Madame Rogan's ramblings about her Francophilic summer vacation.

When the bell rang, I wanted to give Pepe props for being the best Geek of all time. Plus, I wanted to ask why he let himself get pulverized by paintballs that one depressing night. What had gotten him so down? I really wanted to know. He seemed invulnerable to that kind of sad resignation.

But I didn't get the chance. Pepe bolted from his seat, sped out the door—and into the arms of a tiny, freckle-faced freshman gymnast named Drea something-or-other. The only reason I know her first name is because I overheard Burke and P.J. pointing her out and calling her a "spinner," as in, *Sit on my dick and spin.* Ack.

Just then I realized that Pepe's voice and his bod weren't the only things that had changed. Pepe hadn't called me *"ma belle."* And that's because I wasn't anymore.

UNDOCUMENTED EVENT #2

Bridget doesn't know about Burke and Manda's S.O.S. and therefore, when she gets all mushy-gushy, she's totally unaware of how ridiculous she sounds.

"Going to L.A. didn't get me any closer to being an actress, but it was like, the best thing that ever happened to my relation-ship with Burke," she says. "Like, he's so much sweeter now."

Manda doesn't know that I know about the S.O.S. Thus, when she gets all booey-hooey (whenever Bridget is out of earshot), she's totally unaware of how transparent she sounds.

"Burke needs a strong woman," she says. "Bridget has been so clingy since she came back from L.A. Puh-leeze."

Sara doesn't want Bridget to know that she and I both know about the S.O.S. Hence, when she gets all friends-to-the-endly, she is totally unaware of how on-the-brink-of-spilling-her-guts she sounds.

"Omigod! Let's make sure junior year rocks," she says. "Let's make more time for each other. Friends are forever!"

I don't want anything to do with Bridget, Manda, Sara, and the S.O.S. So I say even less at lunch than usual, totally aware of how alone I am.

UNDOCUMENTED EVENT #3

Scotty dumped his summer chauffeur and is now dating a cheesy freshman cheerleader named Cory.

Kelsey. Becky. Cory. Apparently a cutesy-wutesy name is what Scotty looks for most in a sex partner. (For the record, I hate being called "Jessie," the diminutivization of my name favored by senior citizens and my parents.) The ironic thing is, Scotty doesn't go by the cutsified version of his own name anymore. At some point this summer, Scotty Glazer died and a sex-machine named "Scott" was born. (It's no coincidence that Robbie Driscoll was similarly replaced by "Rob" two Augusts ago.) If I had reason to say his name (and I don't), I know I'd flub up and call him Scotty. I have trouble remembering names of people I don't know.

I didn't bother to write about these events right after they happened because I was too preoccupied by the Bubble-Gum Bim-bos and Marcus the Genius episodes. Then I busted my ankle. Compared to that triple-whammy tsunami, the aforementioned tri-als were mere toilet swirlies.

Perspective.

Then I started thinking about the downside to perspective. Perspective basically guarantees that there's no such thing as a pure emotion. Every emotion is based on how sucky (or not) something is in relation to something else that has already happened. I realized that Hy and Marcus and my ankle wouldn't be so huge if I had experienced a Hiroshima-size disaster.

Hope's moving doesn't even count. I say this only because I remember her reaction to the news. She was upset by it, but she didn't have a tear-out-your-hair hissy fit like I did. True, she's more laid-back and go-with-the-flow by nature. But I think the real reason she didn't act like her life was ending is because she had already experienced what that really meant. Heath's death gave her *perspective*, and that made it possible for her to see that things weren't really as bad as I thought they were.

It kind of makes me wish that the worst thing that will ever happen to me will just hurry up and happen already. That way I could live the rest of my life in bliss, if only because I know how much worse things could be.

the twenty-fifth

We've been in six out of eight classes together every day for a month and Marcus will talk to everyone in class except me. Or anyone I associate with. For the latter, I can hardly blame him.

To his credit, Len Levy was the first person in our class to go out of his way to talk to Marcus. I don't think his motives were all that Samaritan, though. I think Len was threatened by Marcus's intelligence and was following the *Godfather* keep-your-enemies-closer philosophy. I don't know if Marcus is a genius, but he has definitely stunned everyone with his ability to always have the correct answer whenever any teacher calls on him, even if he's spent the entire class period doodling in his notebook. Regardless, Len and Marcus have become kind of tight in the past few weeks.

At first, I didn't mean to mooch in on their conversations. I literally couldn't help hearing them, though. I mean, Marcus is in back of me and Len sits next to me in every class. I was *right there.* Then I figured that listening to their conversations could have a therapeutic effect on me. I thought that as soon as I found out *anything* about Marcus, I'd stop being so psychotic about him. The real Marcus—not the reformed rebel/genius I'd created in my hyperactive imagination—would be sure to disappoint. Then I could stop being such a girl and just move on already.

Here, with as few editorial comments as possible, are

The Top 10 Things I've Learned about Marcus Flutie from Eavesdropping on His Conversations with Len Levy with One Ear While Sara Buzzes On and On about Nothing in the Other:

10. Marcus was diagnosed with ADD in elementary school. (This helps explain why he is always in motion. He never stops jiggling his foot, drumming his fingers on his desk, twirling and letting go of his tie, and so on.) He thinks this is a bogus condition designed by fascist headshrinkers who want to destroy any spark of individuality and foster conformity at a young age.

9. Marcus thinks the medications that doctors prescribe for his ADD (Ritalin, etc.) are worse for him than some recreational drugs, namely, pot, E, and 'shrooms.

8. Marcus had to do community service at an old-folks' home as part of his penance. After his 200 hours were up, he got a job there because he likes "kickin' it with the old fogues."

7. Marcus is teaching himself how to play guitar. He bought it not because he wants to be a rock star (let's face it, the only reason guys want to be rock stars is so they can get play from hot chicks, and Marcus already gets more play than he can handle) but because it gives him something constructive to do with his hands instead of smoking.

6. Marcus is trying to stop smoking. Tobacco, that is. He figures this will be harder to kick than all the illegal substances combined because he was never *addicted* to all that other stuff. He just did it because he was bored, which he now realizes was a sad lack of imagination on his part.

5. Marcus adopted his semiformal jacket-and-tie dress code in order to better look the part of a goody-goody honors student. (Besides, what could be more subversive in a world of casual Fridays in which Internet gazillionaires dress like skater punks?) Now he does it because the chicks are digging it.

4. Marcus is currently "chillin'" with a senior named Mia. She's six foot two, which makes her the first girl he's ever been able to look in the eye. This, he has found, makes it much harder to lie to her. He hopes this will stop him from hurting her feelings, which he always seems to do with girls he's chillin' with, but never intentionally. Mia is not that bright, but she has a cartoonish Saint Bernard named Bubba that Marcus likes to play with.

3. Marcus spends a lot of time alone now. When he got out of Middlebury, he knew that he had to ditch anybody who knew him only as Krispy Kreme, which was everyone.

2. Marcus often has the urge to talk to people in the middle of the night. He tried chat rooms, but he found the idea of talking nonsense to a worldwide web full of strangers extremely depressing. He thinks we're losing the ability to touch each other in a personal, human kind of way. (Me too!)

1. Marcus writes—in longhand—in a journal when he can't sleep. Usually this helps him fall asleep. (ME TOO!!!!!!!!!!!!)

Do I even need to tell you that my plan royally backfired? I thought that learning about Marcus would demystify him. That I'd find out there was nothing more to him than tired, nonconformist clichés. But he's more like me than I ever imagined. I listen to Marcus talking to Len, and I wish he were talking to me. This punishment for peeing in the yogurt cup is far worse than anything the administration could have come up with.

October 2nd

Hope,

Exactly one year ago today, I sprinted the last 100 yards to win a cross-country meet against Eastland and nailed a new PR (19:32) in the process. I was feeling proud and happy. I rented *Heathers* at Blockbuster and was looking forward to what new insights/analysis we would come up with in our tenth VCR viewing. I got ready to make two bowls of Chubby Hubby—mine topped with Cap'n Crunch, yours without—when you arrived for our Friday Night Food and Flick Fest. You wore the slouchy gray Old Navy cargo pants I'd persuaded you to buy and a white Fruit of the Loom T-shirt you had embroidered with pink and aqua daisies. You didn't burst through the kitchen door cracking a joke about the Clueless Crew or doing a dead-on imitation of one of Christina Aguilera's white-girl soul riffs or bearing a construction-paper-and-glitter gold medal that you'd insist I wear on my chest all evening. Your face was sad and serious in a way that I hadn't seen since Heath died. I knew something was wrong. Then you said it.

"We're moving to Tennessee."

As horrible and impossible and all-other-ibles as the news was, I knew it was true. You put the ice cream back in the freezer so it wouldn't melt, and I cried for hours.

Today I dug past layer upon layer of microwave dinners and foil-covered leftovers in the freezer. I found that pint of Chubby Hubby covered in flowery frost, unopened, uneaten. And I cried all over again.

I still miss you.

Nostalgically yours, J.

october

the ninth

No one at PHS gives a crap about anything even remotely resembling an intellectual after-school activity. Plus, any student interested in writing channels that creativity into home pages full of bad poetry or fanfic. Not to mention that the only issue of the school paper that anyone reads is the one with the Senior Class Last Will and Testament, and that doesn't come out until May. So no one was shocked when Miss Haviland, our English teacher, announced that not one student showed up for the planning meetings for the September or October issues of the *The Seagull's Voice*.

Miss Haviland (who, on account of her unmarried antiquity and love of lacy blouses and long flowing skirts, will be referred to as Havisham here on out) is a former make-love-not-war hippie who has been both the junior honors English teacher and *The Seagull's Voice*'s advisor for thirty years. To her, the lack of interest in this fine publication was simply "a travesty." Don't we realize that "the school paper is a forum for discussing the issues that are important to us? The school paper provides a platform for voicing criticism of school policies and procedures! The school paper is an outlet for creativity! The school paper gives us the opportunity to resuscitate the written word!"

Blah-diddy-blah-blah-blah.

Needless to say, no one was moved by her speech. We figured *The Seagull's Voice* had squawked for the last time. Oh, how wrong we were. Havisham announced that starting today, participation on the school paper would be mandatory for all juniors and seniors in honors English. Juniors are responsible for writing and reporting all the stories. Seniors are responsible for editing and laying it out. We were all pretty pissed off.

Our class is known for being particularly apathetic, debunking the media myth that Gen-Y is made up of a bunch of optimistic, wanna-do-gooders. But goddamn, do we galvanize against any oppressive force that wants to better us through academics. The Clueless Crew spoke up first, saying they couldn't possibly work on the paper because they needed to devote their after-school hours to perfecting their cheerleading routines *and* planning the homecoming festivities. Scotty and P.J. complained that it would interfere with football practice. Soccer guys, field-hockey girls, and band nerds voiced similar objections.

The class was too busy whining to hear Havisham explain that we'd use *class time* to work on our stories. When it finally hit them that the paper could be a time-waster extraordinaire, most of the bitch-and-moaners quieted down. Then Havisham revealed that she had most of the stories for the first issue already planned out because of the time crunch. We just needed to decide which ones we wanted to write. So the rest of the period was spent determining which intrepid reporters would write such groundbreaking stories as, "Cheerleaders Work Hard on Homecoming" and "Football Team Gears Up for Winning Season."

I refused to volunteer for any of these sorry-ass stories. Miss Hyacinth Anastasia Wallace gets a six-figure book deal, while *I* get to write for *The Seagull's Voice*? Thanks, but no thanks. As the period wore on and we got down to the less plum assignments ("Cafeteria Gets New Pepsi Machine"), I was happy as hell when I could make my early break for it. I was almost out the door when Havisham said, "Jessica, I'd like to talk to you after class. I'll give you a pass."

That's when I knew my luck had run out.

Once we were alone, Havisham sat down at the desk next to me. I could literally hear her bones creaking.

"How important is free speech to you?"

"Uh . . . free speech?"

"Yes."

"Uh . . . I don't really think about free speech."

Havisham's nose twitched involuntarily, like a rabbit. She often does this when she's disgusted with today's youth.

"Well, you should think about it more," she said.

"I'll take that under advisement," I said, reaching for my crutches.

"I've been very impressed with your writing," she said, placing her bumpy, veiny hand on my arm to keep me in my seat. "You put a unique spin on the holistic essay topics. Your essay about how technology has affected society, for example."

She was referring to the latest of the snooze-fest writing assignments designed to prepare us for these proficiency exams that all eleventh-graders are forced to take in the third marking period. Screw the SATs; the majority of PHS students struggle to pass these basic equivalency exams. A humiliating one-third of the Class of '01 failed the English section last year, so now the administrators are trying to make up for it with relentless essay writing, vocab memorization, and reading comprehension. They're only about ten years too late.

"You noted how no advance in technology can be a substitute for real interpersonal interaction. I was particularly touched by your admission that being able to get in touch with your long-distance friend twenty-four hours a day is sometimes more of a burden than a blessing because it just makes you wish she were here."

"Thanks." I squirmed in my seat, suddenly uncomfortable. Whenever I turned in an essay, I generally forgot about it until I got the paper back with an A on it, then I promptly forgot about it again. Hearing Havisham talk about Hope reminded me that someone actually _read_ what I wrote. I had shared something personal, and the very idea of it made me kind of queasy.

"Not many students can imagine a world without E-mail and the Internet," she said. "Let alone see the advantages to the way things used to be."

I started wondering what Marcus had said in his essay. I know how he feels about technology, yet Havisham hadn't called him after class to talk about it.

Havisham waved a wrinkled finger at my cast, snapping me out of my reverie. "_The Seagull's Voice_ needs your voice, Jessica."

"My voice? What voice?"

"I think you would make an outstanding op-ed columnist . . ."

193

Oh, Christ. I really, really didn't want to do this. Why waste my time writing for a paper that no one reads? And besides, I'm not a writer. I don't go to coffeehouses and smoke, wear black, and analyze Sylvia Plath to the point of depression. Okay. I do get depressed. But not for amusement's sake.

"And I assume that you won't be up and running any time soon."

"Well, uh, yeah," I said, grasping for any excuse to get me out of this, "But I'm still really overloaded. . . ."

"It will look very impressive on your college transcript."

She was a shrewd woman, this Havisham. She knew this would suck me in. I had the athletic stuff, the service stuff, and the leadership stuff, but I didn't have any creative stuff on my transcript to make me the type of well-rounded person that Ivy League schools love.

So that's how I ended up the op-ed columnist for *The Seagull's Voice*. I have to come up with a topic for my piece by the end of the week. Havisham already ruled out my first idea, "Why Forced Participation in School Activities Sucks." Free speech, my ass.

Finally, an interesting little P.S. To help me brainstorm, Havisham gave me a list of all the stories in the issue and who was writing them. As I scanned it, I discovered that I wasn't the only one who hadn't volunteered for a story. Yet I was the only one Havisham noticed, or cared about. Marcus Flutie's name was missing. I thought, *Good for him, too bad for us. The Seagull's Voice* needs his voice, too. Or at the very least, I do.

the sixteenth

Indulge me, as I document the transcript of this evening's telephone glory:

Miss Hyacinth Anastasia Wallace: *Hi, Jess.*
Me: *This isn't Hope! My dad said Hope was on the phone!*
MHAW: *I lied to get you to take the call.*
Me: *Lying is what you do best, isn't it? Bye-b—*
MHAW: *Don't hang up! Let me explain. . . .*
Me: *Why should I?*
MHAW: *Because you're the only one I feel guilty about . . .*
Me: *You have ten seconds . . .*
MHAW: *I genuinely like you. Why do you think I stopped rollin' with you?*
Me: *Five seconds . . .*
MHAW: *Manda and Sara gave me much better material. . . .*
Me: *Time's up.*
MHAW: *I wanna talk to you. . . .*
Me: *Why? So I can provide the plot of your TV-movie-in-the-making?*
MHAW: *Girl, I . . .*
Me: *I'm not your girl. Don't ever call or E-mail me again.*
Click.

After everything she's done, Hy had the audacity to imperson-ate my best friend in the universe. What makes this even dirtier is that Hope is someone who has never intentionally backstabbed anyone in her life. (And do I even have to point out how sad it is that my dad fell for it? He's so out of touch with me that he doesn't even know the sound of my best friend's voice on the phone. Pathetic!)

I don't know why I was so surprised. Miss Hyacinth Anastasia Wallace is just living the footloose, fucked-up, and fancy-free lifestyle of a NYC trustafarian. Her suburban experiment was just an extreme example of her feeling entitled to whatever she damn well wants. Only, in this case, she couldn't use her parents' names or bank accounts to get it. No, she needed *us* to get the one thing that eludes pampered, privileged girls with famous parents: Credibility.

Boo-hoo! What a burden being born into a high-class caste. Every-thing comes too easy for me! Sex. Drugs. Manolos. Boo-hoo! I'm such a cliché! No one takes me seriously. If only I were . . . middle class. Then

195

my life would be simple and rosy! So you know what I'll do? I'll slum in (ick!) New Jersey and pretend to befriend some poor mallrats who have no idea what it's like to live on the right side of the VIP velvet ropes. I'll win their confidence, learn their secrets, then exploit the hell out of them. While the rest of the Park Avenue Posse fucks and snorts and shops, I'll write a novel about how my suburban nightmare was far worse than anything I saw after-hours in the meat-packing district. The world will be so impressed by my transformation from addict to author that no one will accuse me of getting into Harvard because of my parents. . . .

The upside of the conversation is that I now know the subject for my essay. "Miss Hyacinth Anastasia Wallace: Park Avenue Poseur."

the seventeenth

A*re we ready for a World War?*

In homeroom this morning, I told Sara all about how I'd dissed Miss Hyacinth Anastasia Wallace on the phone. She's the perfect person to share these types of triumphs with, if only because she asks for so many details that the retelling lasts a bizillion times longer than the actual event.

Omigod! She said what? Omigod! You said what? Omigod! What did you do then? Omigod! Didn't you want to strangle her? Omigod! You're really gonna write an editorial about her? Omigod!

And so on.

With five minutes left, I put on my backpack and picked up my crutches to get a head start on the PHS student body. That's when I saw his hand go up in the air.

"Mr. Flutie?" said Rico Suave with the condescending, mock-polite tone teachers use to mask their dislike of certain trouble students.

"I have to tell Jessica Darling something before she leaves," Marcus said.

"Okay. But be quick about it," said Rico Suave.

Marcus got up from his seat and walked right up to me. Then he deliberately turned to look at Sara, whose eyes were springing out of her head like a pair of novelty googly-glasses. He looked at me again and said, "Ask yourself this: Who's the real poseur?"

Then he walked back to his seat.

He had no idea how long I had waited to hear those seven words. Well, not those specifically, but just words in general.

Needless to say, I tried hobbling out of there before Sara had a chance to pick her chin up off the floor. But I couldn't limp fast enough.

"Omigod! What was *that* all about?" asked Sara, who had snuck up behind me.

"Jesus Christ!" I yelled, twitching with shock. "What are you doing here? You scared the crap out of me."

"I told Suave you forgot your Chem book," she said. "What is up with you and Krispy Kreme?"

"I have no idea, Sara."

"*Really?*" she said, her tongue dripping with venom. "If I didn't know better, I'd think that you actually understood what he was talking about."

"Well, I don't."

"If you don't ask Krispy what the hell his problem is, I will," she said with a steely determination I knew she would make good on.

It didn't take too long. Six minutes later, before the start of History class, Sara was already on her way to getting to the bottom of it.

"Why are you always messing with my friend Jess?" she demanded, flapping her arms in his face before he had a chance to take two steps inside the classroom. But Marcus didn't even break his stride. He walked over to his assigned seat and sat down.

"Don't ignore me!" she said, following right behind him. "I want to know why you're messing with my friend."

Marcus laughed. Actually, it was more of an *idea* of a laugh. His shoulders shook and his eyes crinkled and bursts of air came out of his mouth. But there was no noise that resembled anything close to a laughing sound. Sara got the point anyway.

"What's so funny?" Sara asked, her fists clenched tightly at her sides.

Marcus kept right on laughing his silent laugh.

"WHAT'S SO FUCKING FUNNY?!"

The whole honors class held their breath. Everyone had been waiting for something like this to happen since school started. But to their disappointment, Marcus had defied his controversial, provocative rep and had basically kept to himself. Until now.

"You're not Jessica's friend," Marcus said. "She can barely tolerate any of you."

For the first time since I've known her, Sara was at a loss for words. She huffed and puffed in the aisle for a few seconds. Then came the mother of all hissy fits.

"OMIGOD! WHERE DO YOU GET OFF SLAMMING ME AND MY FRIENDS?! I DON'T CARE THAT YOUR IQ TESTS SAY YOU'RE A *QUOTE* GENIUS *UNQUOTE*. YOU'RE A FUCKING DREG WHO IS GONNA WIND UP PUMPING GAS IN PINEVILLE FOR THE REST OF YOUR FUCKING LIFE!"

Just then, Bee Gee entered the room, oblivious to the sweeps-week-level drama that was going on in Room 201.

"Okay, people. Are we ready for a World War?"

Sara was ready, that's for damn sure.

"I CAN'T WAIT UNTIL YOU FUCK UP AND GET KICKED OUT OF HERE FOR GOOD. BETTER YET, WHY DON'T YOU DO US ALL A FAVOR AND JUST OD AND GET IT OVER WITH, YOU FUCKING LOSER?"

And Bee Gee, in a rare moment of PHS jurisprudence, sent Sara to the principal's office, which was just for show since Masters is tight with Sara's dad.

As Sara stormed out of the classroom, Marcus leaned across his desk, pushed back my hair, and whispered in my ear.

"I'm trying to repay the favor, Cuz."

WHAT?! This is the thanks I get for The Dannon Incident? Since when does repaying the favor mean not talking to me for two months, then trying to make sure that no one else at Pineville High School talks to me either?

Of course, I didn't say any of this.

Sara was sprung from the office by lunch, which was spent drilling me about Marcus.

"What the hell is going on with you and Krispy Kreme?"

"I have no idea," I said, keeping it simple.

"You're the only one he makes these smart-ass remarks about."

"You must be working his nerves in some way," Manda chimed in. "Maybe he's threatened because you're an intelligent female, since he's supposed to be the genius."

"I have no idea," I repeated, making my point and sticking to it.

"No, that's not it," said Sara, matter-of-factly. "This started last year, before that Dreg was declared a *quote* genius *unquote*. There was that time he went off outside the principal's office, then that other time in homeroom before spring break, remember?"

Sara never forgets *anything*.

"What do you want me to say? I have no idea why Marcus started doing any of this. I have no clue why he singled me out for his mind games."

This was all true. So far.

"Why would he say *quote* she can't stand any of you *unquote?*"

"I have no idea."

Okay. That was a lie. The first of many I told throughout the remainder of lunch.

I don't hate you guys. I haven't done anything to provoke Marcus. I'm totally innocent in this.

Then just like that—BAM!—I had an epiphany. Marcus was right. My lies made me a bigger poseur than Miss Hyacinth Anastasia Wallace.

At that moment, I knew exactly what I needed to do.

I was snapped out of my revelation by Sara's nasal noise.

"Jess! What's up? You have this totally bizarre look on your face right now."

I touched my teeth with my fingers. I was smiling. A goofy, toothy, *genuine* smile. One Sara couldn't recognize. No wonder I looked so bizarre.

the twentieth

I had no trouble convincing Havisham to let me tweak my essay, as long as I turned it in by 9 A.M. this morning so it could be sent to the printer.

"What a perfect idea!" she said. "It's still topical, but will affect readers on a personal level. It might even inspire some changes around here."

"I doubt it," I said. "No one even reads the paper."

She twitched her nose. "Then why do it at all?" she asked, with great gravity.

I wasn't sure of the answer. Maybe I assumed Havisham would shoot me down and I wouldn't have to go through with my idea. As soon as I got her approval for the eleventh-hour change, I had no clue how to say what I wanted to say without sounding trite. I'd had no problem dissing Hy in my first draft. But now that I wanted to lay a school-wide guilt-trip, 400 words might as well have been four bizillion.

The annoying thing is, I have no trouble going on and on in here whenever I can't fall asleep. Of course, the difference is, none of *this* stuff really matters. This is just stupid stuff that I can't burden Hope with because she's got heavy issues of her own to deal with or because she wouldn't approve or understand. This is the stuff I shouldn't give a damn about, but keeps me awake anyway. The editorial is different. It's important, even if no one reads it but me.

Anyway, after two sleepless nights at my computer, too much

cutting and pasting and deleting to keep track of, and the final spell check, which almost killed me, I turned it in. Now excuse me while I go into a weekend-long catch-up-on-sleep coma.

Miss Hyacinth Anastasia Wallace: Just Another Poseur

By Jessica Darling

By now, everyone knows the true identity of the PHS student we knew as Hy Wallace. But those who thought they were tight with Hy or Cinthia or The Artist Formerly Known As Miss Hyacinth Anastasia Wallace (or whatever she's calling herself these days) were shocked by the September 2 *New York Times* article revealing that the street-smart, straight-up homegirl was actually a former junkie and private-school flunkie with a fat trust fund.

Even those who weren't friendly with Miss Wallace were peeved about getting played, especially when they found out that the book she's writing about her PHS experience is called *Bubble-Gum Bimbos and Assembly-Line Meatballers*.

"I would never lie like that," students cried. "That's the lowest of the low!"

Hy faked her way through friendships because she thought that was the only way she could get what she wanted. She morphed her identity in order to win favor with the people she wanted to pimp out. She sold out her "friends" to get ahead. It's easy for us to get all high and mighty and point a disappointed finger at her. But ask yourself this: Is her deception any different than the lies we tell each other—and ourselves?

Think of cliques whose members smile in each other's faces, then whip out the knives when backs are turned. Jocks who act like jerks and can still buy dozens of donuts. Social Climbers who drop less popular buds as they move their way up to the Upper Crust.

Sure I'm tired of all the backstabbing and social climbing and B.S. that goes on here. But how can I expect it to stop unless I stop doing it myself? I've looked in the mirror and faced the sad truth: I'm as big a poseur as Miss Hyacinth Anastasia Wallace.

Since my best friend moved away, I've censored my true feelings more and more, replacing them with lies that I know everyone wants to hear. I've felt like I've lost my right to have an opinion, just because I know no one will back me up. But we should all have the courage to speak out about what's bothering us about this school and beyond. Maybe people won't like what you have to say. Perhaps you'll find that you're not alone.

Be willing to take the risk. Because if we continue to keep our mouths shut about all the nasty stuff we do to each other on a daily basis, then Miss Wallace is right. We are bubble-gum bimbos and assembly-line meatballers. Every last one of us.

the twenty-third

The paper came out today. I had stupidly thought that merely opening the paper would all at once unleash the floodgates of girlie fury. But it was much slower than that. More like the steady drip . . . drip . . . drip . . . that precedes a pipe-bursting explosion.

Havisham passed out copies at the end of the class period. Everyone turned to the story that he or she had written. Even though the Clueless Crew's cheerleading–homecoming coverage comprised no more than 500 words, it spawned enough giggly conversation to suck up the rest of the class period without so much as a glance at any other stories in the paper. So it wasn't until lunch that the Clueless Crew got around to reading my editorial.

"*Quote* Just Another Poseur *unquote*," Sara cooed. "*Ooooohh . . .* this should be good."

As they read, I watched their eyes grow wide with surprise.

"Omigod!" Sara said after looking it over for about five seconds. "I can't believe you did this."

"Did what?" I asked. "You didn't even finish it yet."

"I don't have to," she said, putting the paper down on the table. "You finally owned up to how fake you've been since Hope left. . . ."

What?

"We've been waiting for you to see how the whole *I'm deep and brooding* thing isn't winning you any popularity contests," interrupted Manda.

"It's about time you got over yourself," Sara said.

"Yeah," said Manda. "Puh-leeze."

I couldn't take it anymore. They couldn't even take the time to finish the essay and figure it out for themselves. I was going to have to spell it out for them. So I did. Very loudly, I might add.

"I WAS TALKING ABOUT YOU!" I screamed. "MARCUS FLUTIE WAS RIGHT. I CAN'T STAND TO BE AROUND ANY OF YOU. I'M SICK OF KEEPING SECRETS BECAUSE I DON'T WANT TO STIR UP TROUBLE."

"Hey!" Bridget said, "Like, chill out. You're screaming."

I took a few deep breaths and lowered my voice. "You don't want me to chill out," I said to Bridget. "Because if I chill out, you'll never find out the truth."

Sara and Manda exchanged panicked, guilty-as-sin looks. Bridget seemed as blank and bewildered as ever.

"What is she talking about?" Bridget asked, quietly.

"If you don't tell her, I will," I said.

"Don't!" begged Sara.

"How does *she* know?" said Manda, through clenched teeth, looking at Sara because she already knew the answer.

"*What* does she know?" asked Bridget.

I looked at Manda and Sara, giving them one last chance to come clean. They passed it up. So I said the words responsible for the bubble-gum bimbo blow-out:

"Manda banged Burke all summer."

Have you ever witnessed a high-school catfight? There are four universal elements: 1. Hair-tearing. 2. Fingernail face-scratching. 3. Pierced-earring pulls. 4. Gut-wrenching screams. This catfight was no different, only it amassed a huge audience in half the time of the average Hoochie on Hoochie brawl because of the uniqueness of the participants. How often do you see three honors *cheerleaders* rolling on the floor? Right; it's a rare occurrence. Therefore, it attracted the attention of the teachers on lunch duty and was broken up in about ten seconds.

But this was long enough for some Tyson–Holyfield moves to

go down: Bridget smacked Manda and sent her glasses sailing through the air; Manda grabbed a fistful of Bridget's silky hair; Sara was tripped and stepped on by Manda's size-seven Steve Madden boot; and Sara pulled on Manda's skirt and sent her rolling on the sticky tile floor.

It was, in a word, *awesome*.

When it was over, they were all crying. I escaped unscathed, simply because Manda couldn't get to me fast enough. A miracle, considering I was on crutches. Eyewitnesses backed up my claims that I hadn't thrown a single punch, so I was set free. Bridget, Manda, and Sara were sent down to the principal's office. They all got a week's suspension for fighting. I shouldn't find that positively hysterical. But I do.

Catfights are a favorite PHS topic, so I wasn't looking forward to providing my in-the-trenches commentary. Fortunately, I escaped everyone's inquiring minds because my mom had to pick me up from school early for a doctor's appointment. I got my cast removed today. (By the way, have you ever seen someone's leg right after it's been released from a cast? It's so disgusting that just thinking about it now and knowing it was my leg makes me want to puke.)

By the time I got home, I'd received a half-dozen E-mails.

Bridget's said that she would never forgive me for keeping the truth about Burke to myself. (She never asked for the truth!)

Manda said she would never forgive me for ruining both her friendship with Bridget *and* her reputation just because I couldn't handle such an aggressive exhibition of female sexuality. (*She* ruined them—not me!)

Sara said she would never forgive me for blabbing when everything was just fine the way it was. (Everything was *not* fine the way it was!)

Burke said I was a bitch who was just jealous because I didn't get a chance to ride his hog. That is, if I were even interested in dicks. (This confirmed my suspicions: Burke is an asshole.)

Scotty said he didn't hate me, but out of respect for Burke he can't talk to me anymore. (Such a shocking revelation considering we didn't talk to each other anymore anyway.) He also asked why I have to be such a pain in the ass all the time. (Valid point.)

Hope said some funny stuff about a guy she has a crush on that has nothing to do with any of this. (Which actually made me appreciate her absence.)

Instead of responding to the hate mail, I examined my pale, hairy, shriveled, sorry excuse for an extremity.

Some things are just too coincidental not to be a message from whatever higher power controls synchronicity. The comparisons between getting my cast off and getting the secret off my chest are inevitable: One is physical emancipation, the other an emotional one. Both are painful, yet they leave me feeling free, clean, and ready to build myself up and be stronger. Maybe even happier.

the twenty-seventh

I was in front of my locker this morning, bent over, adjusting the Velcro straps on my air cast, when I felt a tap on my shoulder.

"Hi. Jessica. Um. I."

My first reaction was, _Len Levy. Ugh._ This repulsion is the result of years of Valentine's Day resentment combined with intense head-to-head academic competition. But my conditioned response was quickly replaced by "Oh, hi, Len!" when I remembered that he might be my way in with Marcus.

"Um. Your article. Um. In the paper."

For as long as I've known Len Levy, I have never heard him utter a complete sentence. This has been confirmed in all my Len–Marcus eavesdropping sessions.

"Uh-huh?"

"It was. Um. Rad," he said. "And. Um. You said what. Um. A

lot of people think. Um. But don't say. And. Um. I'm looking forward to. Um. Future articles. And."

I managed to mumble some sort of thank-you before he walked away.

About two minutes later, I felt another tentative tap. This time I turned around to see a trio of band nerds, ID'd by the black music cases they clutched in their hands.

"You're Jessica Darling, right?" asked one with an overbite and a red, pulsing pimple on her chin that looked like it could keep time with the music. A built-in metronome.

"Yes."

"Your article in the paper. My friends and I . . . think it's cool," she said meekly.

"Thanks."

They scurried away.

I didn't think my essay would have any effect on the student body. But when word got out that my editorial caused yesterday's brawl, there was more interest in this issue of *The Seagull's Voice* than ever before.

"There's no excuse for violence," Havisham said to me before English class. "But if a little sensationalism gets students reading *The Seagull's Voice*, so be it. I just hope your next editorial is as rabble-rousing as the first one. Power to the people!"

Right on, sista. But my *next* editorial? I hadn't thought beyond the first.

As other freaks and geeks quietly thanked me for speaking out throughout the day, I realized that I was going to have to think about it carefully. "Miss Hyacinth Anastasia Wallace: Just Another Poseur" actually had a *positive* impact on those who felt most oppressed at PHS.

Who knew my editorial would even renew my faith in Pepe Le Puberty?

"*Bonjour, mademoiselle!*"

It had been *so* long since he had said anything to me, that I was a bit taken aback by his greeting, even during a week when

I'd been approached by people I'd never spoken to before in my life.

"Your editorial was off the hook," he said. "It made me think about the wack stuff I've been doing, you know, to fit in."

It was strange to hear Pepe talking to me again. Especially in English.

"*En français, s'il vous plaît!*" sang Madame Rogan.

Pepe paused, grasping for the right words. "*Je n'ai pas eu . . . les boules . . . à casser vers le haut avec ma petite amie . . .*"

What?

"*Comment?*" I asked. Either my French was off, or what he said made no sense.

He dropped his voice to a whisper, "I didn't have the balls to break up with my girlfriend until I read it."

That's what I thought he was trying to say.

"*En français!*"

Pepe looked up toward the ceiling, as if the right English-to-French translation were written there. After a few seconds, he shrugged and said, simply, "*Merci, Jessica.*"

I can only imagine what my essay had to do with his breaking up with his girlfriend. Maybe he dated her only because he was under the same couple-up pressure that had made me consider getting back together with Scotty last spring. Maybe he thought he needed a girlfriend to prove just how testosterrific his new bod really was. Maybe, of all his identities—Percy Floyd, Pierre, Pepe Le Pew, The Black Elvis, The Geek—Pepe Le Puberty was one he *didn't* identify with. Maybe he didn't identify with *any* of them, which is why he jumped from persona to persona in the first place, hoping to find one that fit. Maybe that very realization is what defeated The Geek that night. Maybe the supreme self-confidence I envied in Pepe was nothing more than cleverly masked insecurity.

It's irrelevant really. Because Pepe is clearly happy about his decision. And to think that I'm the one who helped him come to it. Cool. Maybe my op-ed pieces *can* make a difference.

Still, my newfound notoriety doesn't change the fact that I've alienated my suck-ass excuses for friends and don't have anyone to sit with in the cafeteria. I now spend my lunch periods rehabbing my leg with the athletic trainer. My father and Coach Kiley are thoroughly impressed by my *Will to Win*. Ha! Truth is, the flesh-ripping pain of the fifteenth and final rep on the Cybex leg press is preferable to sitting through lunch with another assemblage of pseudo pals.

I know I should be thrilled about all this success—*¡Viva la revolución!*—as Hy said, back when she was still Hy to me. Yet, I can't stop thinking about the one person who apparently hasn't read it. The one person I haven't affected at all. The one person who inspired me to write it in the first place.

the thirtieth

A Titanic, '70s-era brown Cadillac slowed down, then pulled over onto the shoulder right in front of me on my limp home from school today. The owner had tied a fake flower to the antenna for quick sightings in shopping center parking lots. Bumper stickers: HONK IF YOU LOVE YOUR GRANDCHILDREN and SEXY GRANDPA. Five never-been-worn baseball caps were lined up against the back windshield, proudly on display. Sun glare on the windows made it impossible to see who was inside, but I was expecting a blue head to pop out and ask for directions to the local V.F.W. Naturally, that's not who I got.

"Hey, Cuz. Need a ride?"

!!!

"I said, do you need a ride?"

!!!

I thought Marcus would pull away. But he stayed there, with his head out the window, waiting for me to respond.

"Uhhhh . . . I live less than a half mile from here. Twelve Forest Drive."

Pause.

"So I don't need a ride . . ."

Another pause.

"But do you *want* one?" he asked.

God, did I want one.

He knew it, too. He leaned over the front seat and popped open the passenger-side door. "Come on, I want to talk to you," he said. "I'll drive around in circles if I have to." Happyhappyjoyjoy-happyhappyjoyjoyhappyhappyjoyjoyhappyhappyjoyjoyhappyhappy!

Because I'll never see Marcus's bedroom, here's what the inside of his car reveals about his personality.

> **Marcus's car:** Luxe leather backseat littered with empty packs of Marlboro reds, wadded-up balls of notebook paper, and no fewer than four crushed sixty-four-ounce 7-Eleven Super Big Gulp cups. Caramel droplets trapped in straws chewed and bent beyond any successful suction. On the front seat, amid more crumpled paper, but still in plain sight, a teensy, quarter-inch bit of wrapper printed with the letters ROJA, instantly recognizable as the heart of the word TROJAN, as in condom.
> **Conclusion:** !!

He cleared the clutter. If he noticed the condom wrapper, he didn't let on.

I didn't have trouble maneuvering myself into the car. There was ample leg room. I placed my backpack on the seat between us and slammed the door, making a yellow palm-tree deodorizer swing from the rearview. The car smelled like coconuts. The beach. Suntan oil and brown skin.

Marcus wasn't saying anything as he drove. I felt like one of us needed to break the silence. So I said the first thing that came to mind.

"Uh, nice car," I said.

"I love this car."

"Really?"

"Yeah, it belonged to one of the coolest fogues I know," he said. "I work at an old fogies' home."

I almost said, *I know*, until I remembered that I wasn't supposed to know that.

"Really?"

"Yeah, he's dead now, though," he said.

"Oh. That's too bad."

"It is," he said. "But he left me his car."

"Oh."

"And all the eight-tracks that go with it."

"Oh?"

"That's why I love this car," he said. "It's festooned with all the trappings of the elderly."

I laughed out loud. That was one of the funniest things I had ever heard in my life. *It's festooned with all the trappings of the elderly.* Then it suddenly occurred to me that Marcus and I were actually having a conversation. A *real*, two-sided conversation. I felt the heat creep up from the middle of my chest and spread red across my clavicle.

ROJA. "Red" in Spanish.

Since school began, I've sat in front of Marcus Flutie in six out of eight classes. When he isn't jiggling the back of my chair, he often stretches his long legs out into the aisle, so I can see his feet without having to turn my head around. Until this afternoon, I could say far less about his face than I could about his feet: no socks; faded blue Vans; the big toe wearing a hole in the canvas of the foot closest to me; the left one, rubber sole coming undone, opening and closing like a puppet mouth every time he taps his heel to the floor, which is quite often.

I knew that sitting beside him in the Caddie could be a one-time-only opportunity, so I looked him full in the face for the first time ever. This is what I saw, in the order that I saw it: adobe-red buzz cut, no more dreads; feline eyes; sunburnt skin peeling off his nose; two thread-thin lines bookending his mouth.

He lightly poked my shoulder with his index finger and I involuntarily twitched like a spasmodic. We were already at my house.

"Twelve, right?"

"Uh, yeah."

He stopped the car and turned off the ignition.

"I figured that I've been a good boy long enough to talk to you without arousing suspicion," he said, flicking a cigarette lighter open and shut. Open and shut.

"Uh-huh." I chewed my lip.

"We could be talking about homework." Open and shut.

"Uh-huh." Chew.

"Comparing notes." Open.

"Uh-huh." Chew. Chew.

"Making a study date." Shut.

"Uh-huh." Chew. Chew. Chew.

Marcus threw the lighter in the backseat and spun in his seat to face me. He paused long enough for my skin to get all electric and tingly in anticipation, like every hair on my body was standing on end, but wasn't.

"I never read *The Seagull's Voice* because I think it's a big, steaming turd," he said. "An opinion that has only deepened since my literary contribution was rejected."

I knew all about this. Havisham had discovered Marcus's lack of participation on the paper and assigned him a story about the improved nutrition guidelines for the cafeteria. He turned in a poem titled, "Requiem for Sloppy Joes." It didn't make it into print. I only know this because Havisham complained to me about his insubordination. I, of course, was dying to read it, but Havisham had already turned it over to his guidance counselor to be put in his file.

"Len told me to check out your editorial today."

Len Levy. My man, I owe you big-time.

"I'm sorry I didn't read it sooner," he said, twisting his blue-and-white polka-dot tie. "It was the first good thing that heap of dung has ever printed. An instant classic."

211

He liked it. Marcus Flutie liked my editorial.

"If I had known that calling you a poseur would have inspired you like that, I would've pissed you off sooner."

He let go of the tie and it unfurled in a blue-and-white blur.

Too many words at once. I was overwhelmed.

Suddenly, my mom's Volvo pulled into the driveway. Christ! I had to get out of there and fast.

"Uh, that's my mom," I said, pointing at the high-strung blond woman straining to see who had the audacity to park this huge Cadillac in front of her perfectly landscaped front yard. As any Realtor knows, appearance is everything. "I gotta go."

"It's too late," he said. "You're already caught."

True, I was going to have to face the Guy Inquisition, no matter what. I wanted to get out of there before she rapped her rings on the window and screamed, *Get away from my property!* But I needed to ask him a question first, and somehow, I finally got up the nerve to do it.

"Marcus?"

"Yes?"

"Uh, that note you wrote me? You know, after the uh, *incident* last year?"

"Yessssssssssssssssss."

"Uh, what did it say?"

He jerked his head quickly, as if to shake the words he'd just heard out of his ears.

"You didn't read it?"

"Uh, well, I uh, kinda lost it before I got a chance to."

He rested his head on the steering wheel, saying nothing.

"Was it important?"

After a few seconds of silence, Marcus snapped to attention.

"You know what?" he said. "It's better you didn't read it."

Now I was totally confused.

"What? Why?"

"It's just better," he said, "Trust me."

212

Trust him. Trust Marcus Flutie. Oh, dear God. Why did I feel like I could?

My mom was pacing on our front porch, seconds away from pouncing. I really had to get out of there before she totally embarrassed me.

"Thanks for what you said about my editorial."

"Thanks for writing it."

Marcus then leaned across me to open the passenger-side door. He was invading my personal space, as I had learned in Psych class, and I instinctively sank back into the seat. That just made him move in closer. I was practically one with the leather at this point, and unless I hopped into the backseat, there was nowhere else for me to go. Marcus was within whispering distance.

"I'll talk to you later."

In any other context, that would have been a throwaway, something to say to put a nice tidy end to a conversation. But in this case, it meant more. I just know it.

Why must tomorrow be Saturday?!

Milliseconds after the Caddie pulled out and I was safe at my doorstep, my mom asked me who the driver was.

"Nobody you know," I said.

"Is he your *boyfriend?*"

"No way, Mom."

"A friend?"

"Uh, no."

"Well then who is he?"

"Just a boy, Mom," I said. "He's nobody."

"He can't be nobody, Jessie."

I can't remember the last time my mom was so right about something. Marcus Flutie had zero chance at being my boyfriend and had even less of a shot at being a real friend to me. But that conversation in the Caddie guaranteed that Marcus Flutie would never be nobody. At least, not to me.

November 1st

Hope,

I thought the Clueless Crew's return yesterday would make for the most terrifying Halloween ever. I imagined that while they were suspended, they had all settled their differences with each other and joined forces to retaliate against me in a revenge plot that involved pigs' blood. (I caught *Carrie* on cable this weekend.) Fortunately, they all still hate each other, so their scare tactics won't go beyond giving me really dirty looks.

It's tough to keep track of the tension from 1,000 miles away. That's why I devised this handy chart during study hall today. It puts things in "perspective." (Wink-wink.)

Who Hates Whom and Why

		HATER			
		Bridget	**Manda**	**Sara**	**Me**
HATEE	**Bridget**	Hollywood failure and Burke's cheating shows her that she may not get by on looks alone.	Burke never dumped B. because he really does love her—even if he thought with his penis throughout the S.O.S.	She's thin and pretty and has guys lining up to replace Burke.	She's not you.
	Manda	She banged Burke all summer then acted like her bestest bud when she got back.	She knows what she did was skanky and now has to live with herself.	If she hadn't banged Burke, this whole fight wouldn't have happened and she wouldn't have had to cancel the 16th-birthday bash she planned for last weekend.	She's not you. And she's a skank.
	Sara	She witnessed the S.O.S. then spearheaded the conspiracy to keep it quiet.	S. spied on M. and Burke, then couldn't shut up about what she saw going on in the backseat.	She'll never be a thin, pretty boy magnet, especially because she repels them with her big, fat mouth.	She's not you. And she's annoying.
	Me	I humiliated her by blowing up about the S.O.S. in the very public cafeteria, instead of in private.	I blew up when I should have shut up.	I blew up when she thought I promised to shut up. But I never did. Promise, that is.	I shut up when I should have blown up.

Analytically yours, J.

november

the fourth

Lalalalalalalalalalalalalalalalalalalalalalalalalalalalalalaladeeda.

There is only one reason why I am able to stay so calm about the Clueless Crew. One reason why I don't care that they're conspicuously ignoring me or—in Sara's case—starting an E-mail campaign to the entire junior class to make everyone hate me as much as she does. One reason why my physical therapy sessions don't seem to hurt as much anymore. One reason why I'm not bothered by the sudden and renewed interest my dad has in my life now that it looks like I might be rehabilitated in time to run some races during indoor track season. One reason why my mom's endless chatter about Bethany's Thanksgiving visit hasn't made me puncture my eardrums with a sharp stick.

And that reason is Marcus Flutie.

Talk to you later, he said. Really, he meant it.

It all seemed so hopeless on Monday morning. He didn't talk to me before homeroom because he was too busy macking with Mia, his moronic girlfriend. He didn't talk to me during homeroom. He didn't talk to me after homeroom because he was too busy macking with Mia. Again.

When he sat down in back of me in first period, I assumed we were back to our silent-partners-in-crime routine. But then he tapped me on the shoulder, and said something so random that I was afraid he was back on the junk.

"Did you know that the average American spends six months of his or her life waiting for red lights to turn green?"

"What?"

"Six months wasted, waiting for permission to move on," he said.

"Uh-huh."

"Think of all the other stuff you could do with that time."

I was totally confused. "In the car?"

"In your life," he said.

"Oh."

Then Bee Gee started talking about FDR's New Deal and that was the end of that.

And so it went for the rest of the week. Before History class, Marcus would tap me on the shoulder and ask me a question that, on the surface, had nothing to do with anything. But then it would evolve into a conversation about something much more than I expected, considering the randomness of the opening statement. It's hard to explain. It was like a verbal Rorschach test.

By Friday, I wasn't surprised that asking me to pick my favorite actor wasn't *really* about choosing between John Cusack and the guy who played Jake Ryan in *Sixteen Candles*, but a way to launch into a discussion about how every magazine article or TV appearance that brings a star "closer" to his fans actually adds another brick to the towering altar at which we worship the cult of celebrity.

Or something like that.

These conversations are like a shot of schnapps with a Tabasco-sauce chaser. Short, sweet, and strange, as well as capable of making me hot, wobbly, and confused.

What a difference a week makes. Just 168 hours ago, we didn't talk. Now we do. Of course, the downside to this maxim is that by next Friday, it could all be over between us.

I can't let that happen. There are too many issues we haven't discussed that need to be covered before we can continue this . . . *whatever* relationship: The Dannon Incident. The Origami Mouth. Middlebury. Mia. Three boxes of donuts. Heath's death. Hope.

Knowing what I do about his need for nocturnal amusement, I've decided to take control of Monday's conversation by asking Marcus a more straightforward question: *I can't sleep at night. Can you?*

Let's see how this evolves.

the ninth

He called!

Caller ID is the best invention ever, ever, ever. Because seeing Marcus's name and number in the tiny window gave me just enough time to take a long, deep, anti-hyperventilation breath before speaking.

"Hello?" I said, high-pitched, as though I'd just taken a drag off a helium tank.

"Tonight I'm not going to ask you a question to make you talk," Marcus said, without so much as a *hey*, *hi*, or *how's it going*.

"No?"

"Nah," he said. "The question was a conversational construct."

"A what?"

"Just something I threw out there to get us started."

"Oh."

"But we don't need it anymore."

"We don't?"

"We don't," he said. "We can talk just fine without it."

For one hour and forty-seven minutes, we proved him right.

Here, an incomplete list of topics from tonight's convo: pregnant chads, the Olsen twins, the AIDS epidemic in Africa, fake tattoos, *Igpay Atinlay*, the universe's unseen dimensions, cloning, clichéd guitar gods in leather pants, year-round schooling, plastic-surgery junkies, Napster.

I can't remember the last time I had a conversation like this. I discovered I had opinions about things that I didn't even know I had opinions on. Unlike computer-genius Cal, whose conversational shtick now seems so . . . *Cal*culated in retrospect, talking to Marcus is an exercise in spontaneity. He jumps from topic to topic, often without finishing up one train of thought before branching off into another, which splinters off into another, and another, and so on. So one conversation with him contains a bizillion schizophrenic discussions. ADD all the way. Or maybe it's all the drugs. Who knows? All I do know is that he told me to call him at midnight whenever I'm in the mood to talk because that's when *he's* in the mood to talk.

Talking to Marcus reinforced for me what I already know: I have such a narrow, PHS-obsessed worldview. I've almost lost the ability to carry on a conversation about anything other than myself. Even with Hope. Most of our convos are spent catching up on daily comings and goings—the parts I can tell her. It didn't used to be this way, of course, when she was here. But even then, we didn't have talks like the one I had with Marcus tonight. Not worse, just different. Perhaps it's because Marcus is so different.

I'm trying to convince myself that this isn't a bad thing. I mean, anything that helps me sleep must be good for me, right? Because after I got off the phone with Marcus, I crashed like a narcoleptic. A slumber so blissfully uninterrupted by worry that I woke up this morning feeling wide-eyed, alive, and ready to face whatever PHS crap came my way today.

I had thought that as soon as I got Marcus alone, on the phone, I would bombard him with a bizillion questions about his side of our history. But after last night's talk, I hope Marcus and I continue to sidestep the tricky issues that exist between us, because I feel like the moment we acknowledge out loud who he is and who I am and why we shouldn't be talking to each other, we'll stop talking to each other. And that can't happen.

the thirteenth

Knowing what I know about Marcus through my spying, it would be easy for me to bring up subjects that interest him, if I had to. He doesn't know my bio like I know his. This is why, after five consecutive nights of conversations, I am continually amazed by his ability to bring up subjects that I want to talk about.

"I was watching *The Real World* tonight . . ."

"You watch *The Real World?*" I asked, excitedly. "I loooooove *The Real World*. Even with all the new reality shows, it's still the best. It's one of the few forms of entertainment targeted at our generation that I just eat up."

"Oh you *do*, do you?"

"I'd rather watch real kids make total asses out of themselves than watch Kevin Williamson's creations be so goddamn perfect and profound all the time."

"I think that's sad," he said.

"Why? They're setting themselves up. They're asking for it."

"They're setting *you* up," he said.

"How?"

"Did you ever stop to think that the term 'reality TV' is an oxymoron? Once these people agree to be filmed, it guarantees that these shows have nothing to do with reality."

Marcus is the only person who even comes close to one-upping me knowledge-wise. And it kind of bothers me, to tell you the truth. "I know all about the Heisenberg Uncertainty Principle, genius boy," I said, getting testy. "What's wrong with entertainment as escapism?"

"Nothing," he said. "Unless you have no problem spending an evening watching a bunch of people you don't know live life instead of going out there and living it yourself."

He had a point. My obsession with *The Real World* had only gotten out of hand after Hope moved away.

"And how can you live life in Pineville, especially in the middle of the night?"

I heard the flick of his lighter in the background. A pause. Then a burst of breath.

"Well, I used to fire up Puff Daddy."

"Puff Daddy," I repeated, totally stymied.

"Yes. Puff Daddy. My bong."

"You named your bong?"

"Sure. I spent more time with Puffy than anyone else, so it made sense."

Another pause. Another lungful of nicotine, tar, and tobacco. I remembered the pre-pube boy on the Boardwalk. Wacky for Tobacky.

"I'd also find girls to have sex with."

He said it so casually. *Find girls to have sex with*. No big deal. But it was because this is the closest we'd come so far to talking about anything personal. Then he took a long drag on his cigarette, no doubt to give me a moment to imagine him having sex with every scintillating, fleshy detail intact. I had to let him think this talk didn't freak me out.

"So sex and drugs are a way of living life?"

"Yeah," he said. "Isn't that what being young is all about? These are our prime years for experimentation, for exploration. I thought I'd experiment and explore to the extreme."

"That's so . . . *jackassinine*," I said.

"Yeah, it's jackassinine," he said. "But that's what made it fun."

This was making me really angry. How could he be so blasé and blatantly self-destructive? Especially when one of his best friends died because of all of it. Not to mention that as a result of that death, my best friend was taken away from me. But I opted not to directly confront him about Heath. His guilty confession should come naturally or not at all.

"If it's so much fun, why don't you do it anymore? Why not give Middlebury the finger and just go back to your old ways?"

"Because it's been done," he said. "About the only thing I *hadn't* done was go straight-edge, all the way."

Of course. After his teenybopper T-shirt experiments last year, Marcus must've known that making himself into the model student would be the ultimate method for messing with everyone's minds.

"Besides, I've found other things to do with my time," he said.

"Like what?"

"Like playing Nirvana songs on my guitar, writing in my journal, talking to the fogues. I use my wisdom to help Len get laid. And I'm having my first completely nonsexual relationship with a female."

"Wait," I said, totally confused. "So you're *not* having sex with Mia?"

Marcus laughed harder than I've ever heard anyone laugh in my life. A stereophonic, surround-sound laugh. It was the kind of laugh that squeezes all the air out of your belly and leaves you gasping for oxygen. It was the kind of laugh that could leave you with permanent brain damage, which is what I must have in order to have said what I did in the first place.

"You're too funny," he said. "Good night, Cuz."

Marcus finds me completely nonsexual. No tension to complicate our whatever relationship. I should be relieved. Right?

the fifteenth

Today my second editorial came out: "Homecoming King and Queen: Democracy at Its Dumbest." It got the expected reaction: The people who already hate me still do. The people who don't hate me still don't—and thanked me for my visionary remarks.

"Students care more about the homecoming elections than they do about the presidential controversy," I said. "They should just eliminate the whole homecoming court because it gives popular people power and prestige that goes right to their heads."

"So I take it you're boycotting the homecoming dance," he said.

"Of course I'm boycotting." My moral crusade was a very convenient way of dealing with the fact that no one had asked me.

"Too bad."

"Why too bad?"

"Mjdfuwx bv nlkhr'po ydrhext," he said, muffling his mouth with his hand.

"I must have wax buildup," I said. "Could you repeat that?"

"Because we could have doubled," he said.

"You're going to homecoming?"

"Yes," he said.

"*You're* going to homecoming?"

"*Yes.*"

"You, Marcus Flutie, are going to homecoming."

"I think we've adequately covered the fact that I am going to the homecoming dance."

"You *want* to go to homecoming?"

"I could live without it," he said. "But Mia really wants to go."

It's very easy to forget Marcus even has a girlfriend, so infrequently does he mention her. It's only at times like this, or when I catch them tonguing down in the halls, that I remember this fact: I am his first nonsexual female friend.

"That's so hypocritical!" I cried. "You're totally selling out. You're turning into exactly the type of homecoming-going, goody-goody honors student the administration wants you to be."

Marcus chuckled.

"Selling out? I'm not the one who wrote the anti-homecoming editorial."

"But you agree with it."

"I've never been to homecoming, so I don't know whether I agree with it or not."

This Hy-inspired excuse just infuriated me.

"You don't need to go to a homecoming dance to know it's an evening devoted to worshipping the Upper Crust and U.C. wannabes!"

"I, unlike you, like to form educated opinions."

I was getting madder by the millisecond.

"What's that supposed to mean?"

"It means that you're quick to pass judgment on things you know nothing about."

I hung up on him.

Thirty seconds later, I called him back.

"I'm sorry I hung up on you," I said. "That was lame."

"It was a genuine reaction," he said. "I pissed you off."

"I'm still pissed off."

"Good."

"Good."

Pause.

"Talk to you tomorrow?" he asked.

"Yes. Good-bye."

It wasn't until after I hung up the phone the second time that I saw this as a major breakthrough. I was pissed off by something Marcus said. His words weren't automatically intoxicating anymore, just because they were *his* words.

Marcus is demystified.

And I still can't wait to talk to him tomorrow.

the twentieth

My mom was standing in front of the bathroom mirror in tears when I got home from school today.

"Am I so terrible to be around?" she asked.

"What?"

"There must be a reason why both of my daughters hate me," she said, tearing apart a soggy tissue.

Either my mom was having a menopausal episode, or something very bad had happened.

"Did something happen?"

"Bethie isn't coming home for Thanksgiving," she whimpered, wiping away tears. "She and Grant are going to a business dinner party thrown by a bunch of *dot-com* brats instead."

Mom likes throwing around words like "dot-com" and "IPO." It makes her feel *très* twenty-first century, which is sad considering technocracy is clearly on the decline. Bethany and G-Money are in denial about this.

"I guess making money is more important than family. I bet the whole thing will be catered. Let's see if *they* make Bethie's favorite mashed sweet potatoes."

I really couldn't believe that even Bethany could be such an überbitch. I hadn't been looking forward to seeing her, but this was the third time she'd bailed on my mom since she moved out to California.

"As though turning forty-seven weren't bad enough," she said, pulling back the skin around her eyes. "I'm old *and* my daughters hate me."

For Christ's sake. My mom's birthday is the twenty-fourth. The Friday after Thanksgiving. I totally forgot.

"Mom, we, *I* don't hate you," I said.

"You never talk to me," she said. "So I feel like you do, so it's the same th—" She stopped mid-sentence, turned on the faucet, and splashed water on her face.

I looked at my mom, water dripping from her nose, mascara running, congealed concealer clumping in peach patches on her cheeks, blond bangs wilting on her forehead. And for the first time ever, I saw my mom not just as my mom, but as a real person. A flesh-and-blood person who was hurt by rejection just like anyone else.

Just like me.

I suddenly felt guilty about every bitchy thing I had ever said or done to her. I wasn't like Bethany. I was better than that.

"Hey, Mom," I said. "Why don't we do something together on your birthday?"

She looked puzzled. "Isn't Friday the night of the homecoming dance?"

Leave it to Mom to have the PHS homecoming marked on her internal Palm Pilot.

"Yeah."

"So you're really not going to the homecoming dance?"

Why did she have to make it so hard to be nice to her?

"I think we've adequately covered that I'm *really not going to the homecoming dance*." I did a pitch-perfect imitation of my mother using Marcus's words. A very bizarro hybrid.

"Why not?" she said. "You should go to homecoming instead of hanging out with your old mother."

"Mom! You were just complaining about how I don't hang out with you enough!"

"But I don't want to deprive you of special high school memories."

It's statements like this that make me seriously question whether I came out of her womb.

"Mom! I wasn't going anyway."

"Why?"

"Well, I don't have a date, for one," I said.

"You can't get a date?"

I growled and grabbed a hand towel to chew on.

"Moooooooooommmmmm," I whined through clenched teeth.

"I just find it hard to believe that you can't get a date, that's all," she said, fluffing her bangs with her fingertips.

"Can we *please* drop this?"

"Okay," she said. "I'm sorry."

I unclamped my teeth and made my mom an offer I knew she wouldn't refuse.

"Why don't we fight the masses at the mall and do dinner afterward?"

"Just the two of us," she said, her face brightening.

"Just the two of us," I said.

"I'd love that," she said. "Shopping with you."

"Yes," I said. "We'll look for an anti-homecoming dress."

And my mom laughed.

the twenty-second

I was finishing up a brisk walk around the neighborhood when I heard a voice calling me from across the street.

"Hey, Jess!"

Bridget was standing in her driveway, waving me over. But I was totally baffled by why she would be trying to get my attention. We hadn't spoken all month. And as far as I knew, she still held me personally responsible for her breakup with Burke, even though *I* wasn't the one who snaked her man.

"Jess! Come here. I'd like to talk to you."

She appeared to be unarmed. So I slowly walked across the street.

"Hey," she said.

"Hey."

She grabbed her ponytail and started stroking it. She was nervous.

"Are you like, doing anything right now?"

"Uh, not really."

"Can you come in so we can talk?"

"Sure," I said. "Okay."

I hadn't been inside her house in a very long time. There was more Precious Moments knickknackery than ever. But it smelled exactly as I had remembered it, a combination of Pine Sol and decades of cigarette smoke.

"Can I get you something to drink?"

"Sure," I said. "Is your fridge still filled with nothing but Diet Coke and condiments?"

She laughed and opened up the fridge. Inside were two cases of Diet Coke, half-empty containers of mustard, ketchup, and mayonnaise, and a few indistinguishable foil-wrapped objects.

"Some things never change," she said.

"Is your mom around?" I asked.

"Is my mom *ever* around?"

I took that to mean that Mrs. Milhokovich was as absent as ever. Bridget's parents were divorced. Even though her father was good about alimony, Mrs. M. still had to work long hours as a hostess at the Oceanfront Tavern to make ends meet. It was a typical Jersey Shore establishment, with $12.99 surf-and-turf specials, and bathrooms designated by driftwood signs painted BUOYS and GULLS in nautical blue. When we were growing up, Bridget almost always came over to my house to play.

"Some things never change," I said.

We walked upstairs in silence. At each step, there was a different school picture of Bridget, framed and mounted on the wall. The higher we got, the younger she got. When we got to the top, we were greeted by a grinning pigtailed preschooler in pink-and-white checkered Osh Kosh B'Gosh overalls. That's the Bridget I remember best.

I barely recognized her room. Gone is all B. and B. paraphernalia, replaced by posters of matinee idols: Marilyn Monroe, Audrey Hepburn, and James Dean.

She sat on the very edge of her bed. Very businesslike. I flopped down on a beanbag chair, trying to appear as cool and casual as possible.

"I know you're like, wondering why I asked you here," she said.

"Well, yeah," I said.

"Remember that first editorial you wrote? 'Miss Hyacinth Anastasia Wallace: Just Another Poseur'?"

"How could I forget the article that caused the infamous cheerleader catfight?"

She giggled nervously. "Oh yeah."

Bridget got up and turned on the radio. Orlando's latest (and lamest) prefab boy band warbled about a girl who was *2 Good 2 B 4 Me*. I sipped my Diet Coke. It tasted like ass and needed three sugar packets. At least.

"I totally got what you were trying to say the first time I read it," she said. "I just never told you because, like, everything blew up before I had the chance to."

"Right."

"Anyway, I found that paper when I was cleaning my room today. I was about to throw it out, but I read it again instead."

"Uh-huh."

"And when I reread it today, I was like, *duh!* It's stupid for me to be mad at you," she said.

"Really?"

"I never asked you to tell me the truth about Burke," she said. "I, like, did the total opposite. I went out of my way not to ask you. I didn't want to know the truth because, like you said in the essay, it's easier to tell lies that others want to hear. Except, like, I was telling lies to myself. Get it?"

I really couldn't say that I did.

"I'm not like, expressing myself very well," she said. She stuck her ponytail between her mouth and her nose, like a mustache. Then she let go.

"Do you know the real reason I went to L.A. this summer?"

"Uh . . . to be an actress?"

"Sorta," she said. "You said it yourself before I left. I'm not an actress," she said, sweeping her arm in the air at the icons on her walls. "Not yet anyway." She stuck her tongue out at her reflection in the mirror.

"Oh." I had no idea where this was going.

"That was like, the excuse for the trip. The only way my mom would agree to it."

"Uh-huh." I still wasn't getting this.

"The real reason I went was because I thought that if Burke missed me while I was away, he'd appreciate me more when I got back," she said. "Like, what a *duh* move."

"Things weren't cool between you and Burke before you left?"

Bridget shook her head.

"What was so bad?"

"I don't really want to get into that," she said. "It wasn't bad. It was just like, boring. We'd been together for three years and things had gotten boring."

I don't know why this surprised me. Burke *was* boring. I just assumed that Bridget was boring too, and therefore didn't care. Much like Bethany and G-Money don't mind.

"I should have just broken up with him."

"Why didn't you?"

She took a deep breath and held it for a few seconds before answering.

"Because I was afraid of being alone."

The words resonated inside me, like a favorite song. *I was afraid of being alone.*

"But you had Manda and Sara. . . ."

She sighed. "I know you were too busy being miserable about Hope to notice, but like, I hung out with them outside of school like about as much as you did."

"What?" How could that be?

"It's true," she said. "I was left out on as many things as you were."

Then she pointed out a bunch of examples that I had missed: Bridget wasn't invited to the spring-break ho-down. Bridget didn't make the N.Y.C. shopping trip. Bridget wasn't at the post-prom party. During the Hy heyday, Bridget had become an innocent bystander. But because she wasn't Hope, I'd seen her as being as guilty as Manda and Sara.

"The tighter they all got, the more like, desperate I got to stay with Burke."

I thought about how close I'd come to getting back together with Scotty just so I'd have something to do in my downtime. And I really couldn't blame Bridget for what she'd done. Not one bit.

"I just don't see why we have to go on not talking to each other," she said. "It's like, *duh.* Especially like, when you're one person who I know relates to what I'm going through. We both hung out with one person all the time. And now that person is gone."

Whoa. I'd never once considered the similarity of our situations. At least Hope was still around in the emotional sense. For Bridget, Burke was obliterated. Permanently.

I thought Bridget had a better shot at inventing cold fusion than surprising me in a good way. I can admit when I'm wrong. And I was wrong about Bridget. She's no genius, but she's not as brainless as I thought she was.

There. I said it.

Still, this conversation doesn't change things in a monumental way. Bridget and I are not going to be best friends again. But there's one less person in the world who hates me. And that can't be a bad thing.

the twenty-third

Everything happens earlier on Thanksgiving.

You get up at eight A.M. (a full four hours ahead of what's normal) to watch the Rockettes get rained on in the corny Macy's parade. By nine A.M. you've already pissed off your father by telling him you'd rather rebreak your leg than don red-and-white face paint and accompany him to Pineville's homecoming football game. At eleven A.M. you point out to your mom that she's prepping way too much food for four people, which drives her to the first of many glasses of chardonnay. At noon, your grandmother Gladdie has already asked you a bizillion times if you have a boyfriend, then forgotten she's asked, and asked another bizillion times, and forgotten, and so on until she leaves. By one P.M., you turn off the TV for the day when you realize there's nothing on but football and more football. Turkey on the table at three-thirty P.M.

Dessert served at four P.M. The tryptophan kicks in and you're asleep before the five o'clock news.

That's how it happened this year in my house, anyway.

I woke up from my food coma at eight P.M. There was nothing to do. It was too early to call Marcus. I always called him at midnight. That was our schedule. That's how we did it. However, I thought maybe everything was happening earlier for him, too. So I picked up the phone and dialed his digits.

One ring. Two ring. Three rings.

Then an unfamiliar click, kicking me into voice mail. "Marcus here, but I'm not really here . . ."

I panicked and hung up before he finished. I couldn't bring myself to leave a message. Leaving him a message was so . . . *desperate* or something.

At midnight, as was our custom, I called again.

No answer again.

This was the first time Marcus had not been there for me and I was really rattled by it. I almost had to tape my hands together to stop myself from calling every five minutes until he picked up. The only reason I didn't do it is because I don't know if he has caller ID. I didn't want him to see my number backlogged a bizillion times. That's psycho stuff.

I was kind of glad this happened because it helped me to come to my senses: I will not call him anymore. I'm giving this whatever relationship way too much power. Yes, he helps me sleep through the night. Yes, he makes me feel like a better person when I wake up. But if I continue using Marcus as my Tylenol PM, I might get addicted to him. And no twelve-step program has a cure for that.

Besides, it's not like I'm his girlfriend or anything. Then it would be different. Then I'd have a right to be upset by his absence. But I'm not. So I've got to get a grip. Or rather, I've got to loosen it. As part of that, I will make a point not to even think of him and Mia at the homecoming dance tomorrow night.

I just can't believe it, though. It's harder than I thought.

the twenty-fourth

Black Friday.

How appropriate, I thought, when I woke up after a restless, Marcus-less night. Why did I ever take it upon myself to brighten my mother's birthday? Where did I get off improving anyone else's mood?

She was already dressed and ready to go when I went down for breakfast.

"Happy birthday, Mom."

"I thought you were never going to get up!" she said. "I was going to wake you but I know how cranky you get!"

It's her birthday, I said to myself. *Don't be a bitch.*

"It's already ten-thirty!" she said, pointing to her watch. "We've got to get out there if we're going to find anything! I'm sure the stores have already been ransacked by now!"

It's her birthday. It's her birthday. It's her birthday. Don't be a bitch. Don't be a bitch. Don't be a bitch.

I shoved a fistful of dry Cap'n Crunch in my mouth and headed back upstairs to get dressed. I spent five minutes standing in front of my closet in my underwear, contemplating the outfit that would be least likely to offend. I settled on a pair of tan cords and a beige hoodie. Neutrals. Neutrality. Peace.

I brushed my teeth, washed my face, stuck a barrette in my hair, and spread Carmex on my lips. Seven minutes after I'd gone up, I was back down in the kitchen.

"Let's go."

My mother popped out of her seat with surprise. "Already?"

"This is as good as it gets, Mom."

"You know," she said, grabbing her camel coat, "that's the advantage of going out with you instead of Bethany. I don't have to wait forever for *you* to get ready."

Well, I was certainly glad there was any advantage. That's one more than I'd thought there was.

The mall put up its Christmas decorations *before* Halloween. So the red and green jingle-bellsy atmosphere might have gotten me in a holiday spirit, but who the hell knows which one.

"Isn't this *fun?*" my mom said, cutting off the circulation in my arm with her overly enthusiastic grip.

I smiled with all my teeth.

Mom wanted to separate for an hour so we could shop for Christmas presents without ruining the surprise. This was fine by me. I had already taken care of everyone's presents. I stuck to a magazine theme. I ordered subscriptions for everyone in my family. (*Martha* and *House Beautiful* for Mom. *PC World* and *Cycling* for Dad. *Cosmo* and *People* for Bethany. Some boring trade mags for G-Money.) And for Hope, I made a fake teen-mag cover. I wanted to make something for *her* wall for a change. It didn't require any artistic skill, just a computer. I scanned her picture and wrote cover lines like:

HOPE WEAVER TELLS ALL: "IT'S NOT EASY BEING A TEEN QUEEN"

THE ALL-GIRLS-SCHOOL GUIDE TO GETTING A GUY (WHEN THERE AREN'T ANY AND THE JANITOR IS LOOKING TASTY)

MAD ABOUT PLAID: 101 WAYS TO WORK THAT DRESS CODE

ARE JERSEY GIRLS THE BEST IN THE WORLD? TAKE OUR QUIZ!!!!

It cracks *me* up.

I didn't let Mom know I was done with my holiday shopping. It would have broken her already fragile heart. So I spent sixty minutes in the food court, fueling up on Cinnabon and Coke, because when we reunited, it would be time to begin our search for the anti-homecoming dress and I would need to tap into my sugar reserve for energy.

I know that as a red-blooded American teenage girl, I should be thrilled that she considers buying something for *me* a better present than the tiny bottle of Chanel No. 5 my dad and I'd already given her. Yet it was an excruciating process anyway.

"*Ooooooooh,*" my mom cooed, putting down her shopping bags

so she could rub a swath of burgundy velvet between her fingers. "You would look lovely in this."

"Mom, you're missing the point," I said. "This is supposed to be an *anti*-homecoming dress. *Anti* meaning something I *wouldn't* wear to homecoming."

"Oh, right," she said, her voice as flat as my chest. "Like what?"

"Like nothing in the 'Midnite Expressions' juniors section of Macy's."

I dragged her to Delia's, which is sometimes too trendoid for me, but where I can usually find something sorta cute for my pathetic, size-nothing bod. After I ruled out about a dozen of my mom's girlier ideas, she finally pulled out a hanger that I could say yes to: a slate-blue corduroy, zip-front shirtdress. Cute, but not too cute. I tried it on in the dressing room and was actually pretty pleased by my reflection. So much so, that I actually stepped out and let my mom see me in it. Big mistake.

"You really live up to your name in that dress," she said, brimming over with maternal pride. "You look so darling in it."

Darling. I looked darling, which means I didn't look like me. And that's when it dawned on me: I was making my mom happy on her birthday by being like Bethany. Suddenly, this whole venture seemed stupid. I didn't really need to get this thing. I had no reason to look darling for anyone or anything. I unzipped the dress, stuffed it on the hook, opened the door, and told my mom it was time to go.

"You're not going to get it?" She looked crushed.

"No."

"Why not?"

"I don't need it, Mom," I said.

"Nonsense," she said, grabbing it off the hook. "I'm getting it for you."

"Moooooom," I said, tugging it away from her. "I have nowhere to go in it."

"You'll have somewhere to go in it, I promise."

If she wanted to max out her credit card for no reason, who was I to stop her?

Finally, four major department stores and 170 specialty shops later, we were done.

"The mall wasn't crowded at all today," Mom observed, over a salad at TGI Friday's.

I shoved a fistful of fries in my mouth, so as not to spew venom Linda Blair–style.

"I bet everyone is home getting ready for the homecoming dance," my mom said, spearing a cherry tomato.

Daggers. From my eyes. Through her heart.

"What?" she asked.

"Can you go for two seconds without reminding me about the goddamn homecoming dance?"

"Watch your language, honey," she said, her voice tight. "I just can't believe that you're the only girl in your class who couldn't find a date."

"Well, Bridget isn't going either."

"Bridget?" she sat up in her seat. "*Bridget* didn't get a date? What about Burke?"

"She and Burke broke up."

"They broke up? When? Why? How?"

My mom lives for this stuff. It was her birthday, so I decided to throw her a juicy bone. Besides, I thought she should know how disgusting my former fake friends really were. Then she might get off my case for not hanging out with them anymore.

"It all started when Manda had sex with Burke while Bridget was in L.A. . . ."

And I told her the whole sordid story. When I finished, she was dumbstruck.

"I don't believe it."

"It's true."

"That poor girl," my mom said. "Such a pretty girl home alone on homecoming night."

Homecoming again. Jesus Christ! I was barely keeping it together.

"She's not home alone," I said, my throat tightening. "She

flew to her dad's for the Thanksgiving weekend because her mom had to work."

"We should've invited her out with us," she said. "It would have been fun! Just like the old days . . ."

That was it. The end.

"You're right," I shouted, throwing my napkin on the table in disgust. "How could I have been so stupid. I should've rented Bridget out for your birthday! Rent-a-Daughter. So you wouldn't have to go through the torture of walking around with me."

"Keep your voice down!"

"I'm outta here!" I screamed.

The thing about making a dramatic exit is this: It helps when you have a way of getting beyond the parking lot. I hadn't thought to swipe my mom's keys, or grab my backpack so I could call a cab. I was stuck. I had to resort to sitting on a bench outside the entrance until my mom came out.

I heard her heels clicking on the floor before I saw her. She walked right past me and straight to the car. I followed her. She unlocked the door to let me in, so she wasn't going to drive away without me.

"Do you want to tell me what that was all about?"

Part of me did. And part of me didn't.

"I'm not leaving here until you give me an explanation."

I couldn't tell if she meant it or not, but I felt like every second in that car took a year off my life.

"I . . ."

When I opened my mouth to talk, I had fully intended on only telling her enough to make her put the key in the ignition and drive home. But once I started, I couldn't stop.

"I . . . feel like you only want to be with me if I can be someone else, someone beautiful like Bethany or Bridget. And I feel like Dad only wants to be with me if I can be like the star athlete he wanted his son to be. It's like when I try to be me, you're not happy with who that person is. You're constantly trying to talk me out of my feelings or make me feel bad for thinking differently than you do. I'm sorry I'm not popular and born to shop and I don't have a ton of boyfriends like Bethany. I'm sorry that Matthew died and Dad never got to coach him! But that's not my fault! And I'm sick and tired of you both taking it out on me! "

Tears were streaming down both our faces when I finished. I didn't know if my mom was going to hug me or hit me.

"Jessie," she said. "I had . . . no idea . . . you . . ." She then wrapped her arms around me and started stroking my hair. Her body was soft and warm and as comforting as it was when I was kid.

She released me and held my face in her hands. "I don't want you to be Bethany. And your father doesn't want you to be . . ." She couldn't bring herself to say his name. ". . . anyone but you. Neither one of us does."

"It doesn't feel that way," I said.

"I understand Bethany better than I understand you. She was no picnic, but she was definitely less . . ." She cocked her head to the side, trying to find the right word. "Less *complicated* than you. And as a parent, I sometimes can't help but think that things would be easier if I had two children like her. But then you wouldn't be you."

"And what a joy it is for us all that I am."

"You have to stop saying things like that," she said. "I know things are hard for you right now. And I know I'll never quite understand why. But I think these difficulties are going to make you a much better person in the long run."

"But why do some people, like Bethany, seem to coast right on through high school and college and life?"

"I love Bethany, you know that. But she is so used to getting her way that it has made her a very spoiled, selfish person. And I'm partly to blame for that," she said. "Sooner or later, that's going to catch up with her, though."

This all sounded very familiar, like dialogue straight out of the touching Parent-Bonds-with-Misunderstood-Teen scenes in my favorite flicks. Normally, a revelation like that would make me crack up. Or cringe. Or cry. Why? Because it proves that I'm just a cliché, and not the complex iconoclast I (deep down) like to think

I am. But at that moment, I didn't give a damn that my mom was being totally corny, and that I was being corny by association. She made me feel better.

When we got home, I decided to show Mom my editorials. If she really wanted to know what went on inside her second daughter's head, so be it.

"You write for the school paper?"

"Yeah," I said. "It's no big deal."

"Why didn't you tell me?"

"Like I said, because it's no big deal."

She put on her reading glasses and opened up *The Seagull's Voice*. I had to leave the room because I couldn't handle watching her reaction.

About ten minutes later, I heard a knock on my bedroom door.

"Boy," she said. "You are your father's daughter."

That was not the reaction I'd expected at all.

"Me and Dad? No way."

She sighed and sat next to me on the bed. "You're both perfectionists. You're both hardheaded. You both have trouble dealing with people. You both get depressed when things don't go your way. You both think too much. You both keep your feelings inside, then explode at inopportune moments," she said, tracing the triangles in the quilt with her shiny fingernail.

"If we're so alike, how come the only thing we can talk about is running? Otherwise we don't talk at all."

"It's the one thing he feels he has in common with you," she said. "It's his way of trying to connect with you."

"But he puts so much pressure on me! I start to hate him and the sport, and I don't want to do it anymore."

"I know," she said. "Just try to remember that every time he talks to you about running, it's because he loves you, not because he lives to torture you."

Deep down, I already knew that. But that's so much easier said than done.

"Thank you for showing me your editorials," she said, getting up to go. "That's the best birthday present I've ever gotten."

the twenty-sixth

Hope called tonight, gasping, choking, sobbing.

Heath would have turned twenty today.

The most upsetting thing about it was that she'd been so caught up in the minutiae of private-school life that she forgot her brother's birthday until her parents called to ask her how she was coping on this sad occasion.

"How could I let my life go on so easily?" she asked me. "How could I?"

I was silently asking myself the same thing. *How could I?*

Yes. How could I talk to Marcus, someone indirectly responsible for the death of my best friend's brother, someone so indifferent about it that he's never once brought it up? Never once apologized or expressed any grief or regret or *anything*.

And to think I almost caved in and called him last night.

How could I?

the thirtieth

So I haven't heard from you in a week. What's up?"

Marcus had tapped me on the shoulder before History class. He had fresh, faint Mia lipstick smears on his neck, right above his shirt collar. Brownish enough to blend in with his still-tanned skin, but clearly visible.

"Nothing's up. I just haven't called. That's all."

Truth was, I had wanted to lift my moratorium on Marcus before it even began. But the guilt of our midnight phone calls ultimately won out over the need for sleep. Plus, I just couldn't handle getting the details on the homecoming dance. I was starting to feel like *half* of his perfect woman. Mia was the body. I was the brains. And when I saw him and Mia together, they reminded me of the Twin Towers. I was any anonymous curb.

"Oh," he said. "So does this mean that you want me to call you?"

Did I want him to call me? Did I want *him* to call *me*?

Yes. No. Yes?

"Don't answer that," he said. "I know I want to call you. So I will. And if you want to talk to me, we'll talk. If you don't want to talk to me, you can hang up."

He held out his hand. "Deal?"

I hesitated. He reached for my hand. We shook on it, skin on skin. *Yes.*

Then a lightning bolt shot straight through my skivvies. Sha-ZAM!

December 2nd

Hope,

   No charts necessary this month.

   Bridget and I are talking again. And Manda and Sara are talking again,
I assume in response to the fact that Bridget and I are talking again. Very,
very lame.

   Without Burke, Bridget isn't so brainless. In fact, their breakup has
brought on a sort of metamorphosis. Bridget actually quit the cheerleading squad and is trying out for the school play. She wants to take acting
seriously. Rah-rah for her. Seriously.

   Now if only I could get a boyfriend to break up with me so I could go
through a similar life makeover . . .

   I'm kidding.

   All of this is just a way for me to avoid writing about what's really on
my mind right now anyway.

   Could you really be here on New Year's Day?

   I can't think of a better way to make up for last year's suckfest.

   Here's the thing: Don't say it unless you mean it. I don't think I could
handle another psych-up and letdown. I know it wasn't your fault that
we had to cancel my summer trip. I don't blame you, but it was really
hard to get over anyway.

   So please don't say you're coming unless you know you're coming.
And don't visit unless you really want to visit. Coming back when you
really don't want to would be even suckier than spending New Year's
alone. For me, anyway.

Brutally but honestly yours, J.

december

the fourth

Today is the one-year anniversary of the first day of my last period.

I'm not exactly celebrating.

When I lied to my mom about getting my period, it was just the easiest escape route at the time. I didn't think much of it because I was sure that sooner or later, it would turn out to be true. So every twenty-eight days I take tampons out of the box under the sink and flush them down the toilet to make her think that I'm cycling as I should.

But I can't tell her now that my ovaries still aren't back from vacation. She'll not only freak out and ground me for lying, but she'll force me to go to the gyno. And the very thought of getting into the stirrups and letting a total stranger go elbow-deep and up to my uterus . . . Jesus Christ! I can't handle it. I just can't. I'd puke all over the exam table. I swear.

What is wrong with me? Will it ever come back? Why would my female equipment break before I even got a chance to use it? Why was my womanhood revoked? Why am I back to prepubescence?

Oh, the irony. I'm decades ahead of my classmates psychologically. Physically, however, I'm a goddamn kindergartner.

the sixth

PAUL PARLIPIANO IS GAY.

Jesus Christ O'Mighty.

Our whole school is buzzing about it. He came out to his family over Thanksgiving. His family tried to be supportive, but they didn't want the news spread all over town. They wanted to keep it secret. But yesterday Mrs. Parlipiano ran into a neighbor at Super-

Foodtown and broke down right in front of the deli counter. "My son is gay!"

Apparently, Paul Parlipiano had suspected his gayness for a very long time. But it wasn't until he moved to NYC that he got in touch with his inner George Michael and was ready to be seen as the rainbow-flag-waving fag he is.

I know. Shame on me. How Slim Shady. I know I should be happy for Paul Parlipiano. He's not lying to himself anymore. Yet I can't help but be pissed. Not because I don't have a chance with him now, because God knows I *never* had a chance with him, even when he was "straight." No. I'm pissed because I can't fantasize about him anymore. I've created this stellar little imaginary world around him and now he's ruined it. It's one thing to get all torqued up over a guy who doesn't know you exist. It's quite another to get all torqued up over a guy who doesn't know you exist *and* likes to take it where the sun don't shine. One is fantasy. The other is just plain masochistic.

You only think you love me, he said. *If you knew me, you would know better.*

I'm starting to think I don't know a damn thing about anyone. Or anything. My entire notion of sex and love is totally, completely, and irreversibly screwed.

the seventh

What does it mean when your true love turns out to be a homosexual?" I asked Marcus on the phone tonight.

"Well, Darlene, I'd assume that means he's not really your true love."

Darlene is my alter ego. She was born last week. Marcus was lying on his bed, smoking a cigarette, waiting for me to call. He said he started saying my last name over and over and over like a mantra until *darlindarlindarlindarlin* became Darlene. Marcus says Darlene has sort of a trailer-trash allure that makes her more fun than I am. Jessica Darling had always sounded too cute, a cheerleader or head of the Clueless Crew or someone else I'd hate. So I welcomed the mutilation.

I tried to explain how much I thought I loved Paul Parlipiano.

"I was totally convinced I loved him, even though I barely knew him."

I could hear Marcus suck on his cigarette. I pictured the orange tip growing and glowing, and Marcus closing his eyes and holding his breath.

"There's an explanation," I said. "I learned in Psych that sometimes the sensory receptors send impulses straight to the amygdala, which controls emotional responses, bypassing the hypothalamus, which processes and relays the information to the brain."

There was a thoughtful pause.

"I'm not going to pretend I know what you're talking about," he said. "But you're basically blaming your love on biology."

"Biology," I repeated, imagining a thin ribbon of smoke reaching for the ceiling, the sky.

"That's interesting . . ."

"What?"

"It just makes me wonder what subject you blame for talking to me every night."

I'm still settling on an answer for that one. Probably Chemistry. Jesus Christ. I can't believe I just wrote that.

the ninth

Marcus called me tonight and said, "Let's do something."

We've been talking for two months. Not only have we never "done something" together before, but he's never even called me on a Saturday night. It was understood: Weekdays at midnight were for me. Weekends were for Mia.

"Where's Mia?" I asked.

"Mia?"

"Yeah, the girl you mack with in the hall every day."

"Oh, *her*." I knew he was joking around even though he sounded serious. "Mia is in Philly for her grandmother's birthday."

"Oh."

"So I was thinking, I'm free, why not see if you wanted to do something with me? Maybe go to Helga's?"

My tongue inflated to a bizillion times its normal size. It must have, because I could barely breathe, let alone speak.

"Darlene, are you there?"

I had to be cool about this. I had to be his nonsexual female friend who could care less if he was asking me to do something on a Saturday night, which was the closest thing I've had to a date, uh, *ever*. I had to make a joke out of this. Or else.

"So I'm sloppy seconds, is what you're saying."

"Oh no, Jessica," he laughed. "You're sloppy *firsts*."

Have truer words *ever* been spoken?

I sighed and told him I'd be ready in fifteen minutes.

Sixteen minutes later, we were cruising in the Caddie on Route 9. I was surprisingly not nervous. The Caddie was in the same exact condition it was in the last time I rode in it. Only no ROJA. The fact that he hadn't cleaned it up especially for me reinforced that this was no big deal. Just two friends, going to the diner on a Saturday night. The radio was busted, so Marcus popped Barry Manilow into the eight-track player. Rain pounded on the roof, and the volume was turned way up:

When will our eyes meet?
When can I touch you?

"I know this song!" I shouted over the crescendo. "My mom plays it when she does housework."

"Did you know that *Rolling Stone* called him 'the showman of our time'?"

Wow. I actually did know that. It's what my mom says every time I complain about Manilow on the stereo. But the fact that Marcus knew it freaked me out. I mean, how many seventeen-year-old guys know that Barry Manilow is the showman of our time?

Fortunately, we got to Helga's Diner before I had a chance to obsess about this for another minute.

Marcus hopped out of the car and didn't even attempt to open my car door for me. Good. Again, he reminded me that this was not a date.

We walked into Helga's lobby. Bam! Mirrors everywhere. A million Marcus-and-me's to remind us that we were actually doing this. We were going out in public on a Saturday night—together.

"Smoking or non," growled Viola, our waitress. She intimidated me pretty well for someone who came up to my chin.

"Non," I said before Marcus had a chance.

Non-smoking. Non-date, I thought.

We slid into our booth. He took off his wool pea coat and I was made instantly happy over his decision to ditch his shirt and tie in favor of an oldie but goodie.

"Backstreet's back?!" I asked, pointing to the boys smiling on his chest.

"What?"

"No jacket and tie?"

"Nah," he said. "That's just for show at school."

Helga's was decked for the holidays in the sad but well-intentioned way that diners and gas stations and other public places often are.

"Fake Christmas trees depress me," I said, pointing to a shabby evergreen with plastic, toilet-brush-like branches.

"Me too," he said. "How about fake Christmas trees spray-painted with fake snow?"

"Yes!" I said. "How about fake *Xmas* trees spray-painted with fake snow?"

251

"Yessssssss! I hate that word," he said. *"Xmas."*

Then we rattled off a list of things that depressed us about the holidays: pop divas who mess up holiday classics with their show-offy vocal gymnastics; fruitcake; when people don't write anything but their names inside mass-produced greeting cards; Salvation Army bell-ringers; animatronic Nativity scenes . . .

"This would've been great to write about," I said. "Too bad I already turned in my next editorial."

"What's the topic?" he asked.

" 'Rudolph Revisited: A Red-Nosed Nerd's Revenge.' "

"Classic," he said, nodding his head in approval.

We stopped bah-humbugging when Viola chucked our plates on the table. I poured on the ketchup and dug in.

"You eat," Marcus said, after a few minutes of face-stuffing silence.

"Yes," I mumbled in between mouthfuls of cheeseburger.

"Most girls don't eat."

He was doing it again. Marcus was reminding me of all the other girls he's had before me. Well, *I* was going to remind *him* that this didn't bother me a bit. Not one bit.

"You would know, wouldn't you?" I said, popping a fry into my mouth. "Because you've dated *most girls*, haven't you?"

"Most," he said, with a sly smile. "But not all. Not yet."

I barely had time to savor these lip-smacking words when I was bitch-slapped back to reality with one shrieky *Omigod!*

Sara, Manda, Scotty, and Burke had just burst through the door on a gust of ice-cold air. This was my fault. I should have known they would come here on a Saturday night. There was no way Marcus and I would get out of this without being seen.

"What's wrong?" Marcus asked.

I jerked my head in the direction of their noise.

"Why do you care?" he asked, leaning back in the booth.

Why did I care? Did I care? How could I still care what the Clueless Crew and Co. thought?

I looked at Marcus. He was sitting still, with his hands folded calmly on the table. A serene smile on his lips. He wasn't tapping his foot or drumming his fingers on the table or flicking his lighter open and shut. Marcus wasn't all hopped up and hyperkinetic. He was loose and relaxed in a way that I haven't seen him since he stopped using. And then I realized that I hadn't felt nervous around him all night either. I'd felt more comfortable in my own skin than I had, well, since Hope moved away.

So did I care about what these assholes thought? No. Let them see us. I—*we*—belonged here.

Too bad I didn't get the chance to tell this to Marcus.

"OMIGOD!" screamed Sara so loud, I thought she'd shatter the lobby mirrors. "Look who it is! The Class Brainiac and Krispy Kreme."

All heads turned in our direction. Eight eyes on us.

"I'm still thinking she's a dyke," said Burke.

"Puh-leeze," said Manda. "She just got tired of being the last virgin in school."

"Mutherfucker," was all Scotty had to say.

Finally, after what seemed like back-to-back life sentences, plus twenty-five years for good measure, Sara said, "Omigod! Maybe we'll have to arrange a two-for-one drug test."

Her words stunned me like a taser.

The next thing I knew, I was watching a million Marcuses leading a million mes through the lobby and out the door, into the cold.

Once inside the car, Marcus tried to ease my mind. "She doesn't know anything. She was just being a bitch."

Holyshitholyshitholyshit! Did Sara say what I thought she said? Was it directed toward both of us? Or just Marcus? Did Sara know about The Dannon Incident? How could Sara know? No way she knew. If she knew, she would've busted me already. Right? Or maybe seeing us together was all the evidence she needed to nail us?

I was too busy thinking about all this to talk, let alone notice that Marcus had turned down a dark dirt road off Forest Drive. He pulled over to the side of the road and turned off the engine.

"Why are we stopping?"

The only light shone from high beams. Marcus got out of the car, walked around the front, came over to the driver's side, opened the door, and held out his hand.

"What?"

He just stood there with his arm outstretched.

I unbuckled my seat belt and grabbed his hand. He pulled me out of the car. A chill shot through me from the inside out.

"Keep your eyes closed," he said.

He took my other hand in his.

I was so freaked out, I didn't know what to do with myself.

He pulled me close. I inhaled the earthy, autumnal scent of his skin—the scent that had inspired fantasies about stealing his BSB T-shirt and using it as a pillowcase so I could breathe him in as I sleep.

I felt his smoky breath on my face.

Hot.

And at that moment, I just knew he was going to kiss me. I was petrified. So much so, that I hadn't even noticed that I'd been chewing the left side of my lip—until I felt a sharp nibble on the *opposite* side.

Marcus bit me! He nipped my lip!

I nearly jumped out of my boots—not because it hurt, but because no one had ever chewed on my mouth besides me. I couldn't believe that the first person to do that to me was *him*. Marcus Flutie. I opened my eyes and there he was, looking at me. Grinning.

"Shall we?" he said.

He opened the door and slid inside, and I followed suit.

I don't know how I managed to make it through the drive home. Or how I got the word *good-bye* out when he dropped me off. I don't know much of anything right now. But what I really don't know is if that lip nip counts as our first kiss.

the tenth

All night I repeated his name over and over and over again out loud. *Marcusmarcusmarcus.* And after a while, I started to hear what it really meant.

Markissmarkissmarkiss.

Marred kiss.

Jesus Christ.

So let's just preface this by saying that I was very desperate for advice this morning. And now, after seeking that advice, I'm more desperate for advice than ever.

Bridget was still in her pajamas when I knocked on her door. Even at her groggiest, she looked as fresh and dewy as Sleeping Beauty. I needed to tell someone about what happened last night. I've created such a complex inner world for myself that I was starting to believe that I'd made it all up. And no matter how much I wanted to, I couldn't talk to Hope about it. She would *die* if she knew Marcus and I had done uh, whatever we had done last night. Bridget hated the Clueless Crew and Co. as much as I did, so I figured she was my best bet. She was my only bet. Make no mistake, I hated myself for telling her instead of Hope. I mean, what does it say about our friendship when I'm hiding more than I'm sharing? But I had to get it all out.

So I told Bridget everything that had happened, from Marcus's invitation to Burke's lesbo comment to the bit lip. The only thing I didn't get into was why Sara's comment stung as much as it did. The Dannon Incident had to remain a secret.

"He bit your lip?"

"Yeah."

"That's like, so weird."

"I know."

"Does that mean you're the girl Marcus is using to cheat on his current girlfriend?"

I leapt out of the beanbag. "No!" I protested. "I mean, I don't think so. . . . Uh . . . It wasn't a kiss. I mean, I don't know. . . . Uh . . ."

Bridget clapped her hands and jumped in the air.

"You *like* him!"

"I like him as a friend."

"No," she said. "You *like* him like him."

"No I don't!"

"Then why are you acting like a total spaz?"

Why was I acting like a total spaz? Why? I knew better than this.

"There's just something weird between Marcus and me," I said. "Since last year, there's been this . . . *energy* between us."

"Sexual energy."

"Bridget! Stop it!"

"I'm just trying to help," she said, twirling her ponytail around her finger. "Like, what kind of energy?"

"I don't know," I said. "Once we acknowledged each other's existence last year, he started popping up all over the place. He was always around, causing controversy."

She put her ponytail in her mouth for a few seconds, deep in thought.

"I think the biting thing is maybe just another way to keep me guessing. It's all part of his game."

Bridget kept on sucking on the end of her ponytail. I wanted to tell her more about Marcus and me. More than was necessary. Just enough to make it real and get it all out of my system.

"He slipped a note in my back pocket once," I said. "He had it all folded up origami-style, like a mouth. But I lost it before I got to read it. And when I asked him about it, he wouldn't tell me what it said . . ."

Bridget dropped her ponytail.

"It was shaped like *what*?"

"It was folded up, so it opened and closed, you know, like a mouth or something."

"You're kidding, right?"

"Uh, no." I didn't understand why Bridget was so hung up on

the shape of the note when there were so many other details that needed to be analyzed to death.

She leapt off the bed, bounded over to her dresser, and opened the top drawer. She pulled out a box with cherubs and hearts on it. She rifled through some papers before pulling out . . . *the origami mouth I was just talking about.*

I almost peed all over Bridget's comforter—which wasn't living up to its name.

"Is this it?"

I fell backward on the bed and slammed my skull against her headboard. She took that as a yes.

Bridget sat down next to me and bounced up and down on the bed. "I can't believe it!" she squealed. "I can't believe this is for you! I can't believe that it's from Marcus! I thought I'd like, never find out who it was to or from!"

I started coming to. "How did you get it to begin with?"

"I found it on the locker-room floor last spring."

The locker-room floor! It fell out of my pocket as I changed for gym! I should have known!

"I kept it because it's only, like, the sexiest thing I've ever read!" she squeaked.

"Sexy?"

"Sexy."

"Really?"

"*Really.* It was better than anything Burke wrote me in four years. I wished it were for me," she said, heaving a sigh and hugging a lacy pillow to her chest. "That's why I held on to it. As proof that someone out there thought sexy meant more than sleeping on the wet spot so I wouldn't have to."

Huh?

"Sleeping on the wet spot? What? But you and Burke never . . ."

Bridget dropped the pillow.

"Oh, Jess," she said with a touch of condescension.

"*Oh, Jess,* what?"

"I thought you of all people would've seen through that."

"Seen through what?" I asked, not liking the sound of where this was going.

"I never said I was a virgin," she said, breathily.

And that's when I discovered that Bridget might have an acting career ahead of her after all.

"I did it with Burke in like, ninth grade. I just made it sound like I was still a virgin to get Manda, Sara, and Hy off my fat ass about the statutory rape stuff."

"But you said . . ."

"I think I said, 'Who says Burke and I are having sex?' which like, implied that we weren't," she said. "And when I said it, we'd stopped having sex, so it wasn't a lie."

What did I tell you? Bridget does not lie. She really doesn't.

"Why did you stop?"

"I just wasn't into it anymore," she said.

"Why?"

She took a second to come up with the perfect answer.

"It got like, old. By the time I left for L.A., I was like, a born-again virgin. So in a way, I don't blame Burke for screwing Manda. He was really horny."

"That doesn't make it right."

"I know. Which is why I'm like, never going to speak to them again."

She started waving her hands wildly in the air, as if to wipe out the previous conversation. "Enough about *that* and back to this," she said, holding up the note. "All I can say is, you are a very lucky girl."

"I am?"

"Now I know how Marcus gets so many girls to sleep with him," she said. "He knows how to like, woo."

Woo? I was freaking out at this point.

"Can I read it?!"

Bridget rolled up into a ball and giggled hysterically. "Oh, you can read it," she said. "But its gonna like, blow away your whole just-friends idea."

And it did. Because here's what Marcus's origami mouth had to say:

FALL

We
are Adam and Eve
born out of chaos called
creation
Ribbing me gave you life
yet you forget
there will always be
a part of me in you
yes
I taunted and tempted
you
with my forbidden fruit
does that make
me
the serpent too?
Believe what you will
but if I am exiled
alone
I know we will be
together again someday
naked
without shame
in paradise
My thanks to you
for being in on my
sin

the eleventh

I couldn't stop thinking about "Fall" all weekend. Or the quasi-kiss. And what one had to do with the other.

I must have read the poem a bizillion times. And every time I finished, sweat was pouring from my armpits, down the inside of my T-shirt. Every time, it was too much. Sensory overload.

I know we will be/together again someday/naked/without shame/in paradise.

What else can that mean but what I know it means?

At first I tried being blasé about it. He wrote that poem when he still deserved to be called Krispy Kreme, before he even knew me. We were different people now. Friends. He even said himself when we had our first talk in the Caddie that it was probably better that I never got to read it.

But the more I read it, the more it disturbed me. Because it reminded me of the fling with Cal on *the big day*. Cal had convinced me—albeit briefly—that we had a connection, one that he concocted to get his rocks off. What if my phone friendship with Marcus was the same sort of thing? What if it was nothing more than the second phase of his plot to make me another donut?

If we were going to continue talking, there had to be zero doubt that our phone friendship was *not* going to lead to sex. That meant no more lip-nipping. Nothing. Of course, Marcus didn't make this confrontation easy for me. I had to hover at my locker for a few minutes before homeroom, waiting for him to finish feeling up Mia.

Mia. Did she know about the lip nip? Did that count as cheating?

When the spittle settled, I walked up to him. He leaned against the locker Mia had been pressed up against only seconds before. I bet it was still warm from their body heat.

"I read your poem," I croaked. " 'Fall.' "

Then something I never thought would happen, happened: Marcus Flutie was shocked by something I said.

"You did?" he said. "I thought you lost it!"

"Well, someone found it for me. Where do you get off saying," I lowered my voice, "we'll be *naked without shame in paradise?*"

He didn't open his mouth.

"I know what that means, you know. Who do you think I am?"

He didn't open his mouth.

"We are *never* going to be naked without shame in paradise."

He didn't open his mouth.

"We're NEVER going to have sex," I whispered, clearly overstating my case.

He didn't open his mouth. The mouth that he used to bite mine.

"And I'm just going to forget about that biting thing from the other night," I said.

He looked me right in the eyes. If he'd focused hard enough on my pupils, he could've seen his own reflection, his own face smirking at me.

"You couldn't forget it if you tried," he said, before walking away.

He's right. And I don't know if I hate him or love him for that.

the twelfth

I can't stop thinking about sex.

Specifically, that everyone at PHS has had sex except me. I mean, even Pepe Le Puberty used to grope his pixie chick like *un homme qui a beaucoup de sexe*.

Am I a dysfunctional freak for *not* doing it?

I'm not a prude. I've just never imagined myself being devirginized by just *any* guy. It's not that I've been suckered into that *why-marry-the-cow-when-you-can-get-the-milk-for-free?* crap. And I don't cherish my virginity as a precious jewel, or a delicate flower, or any other of the corny metaphors used to describe it by Holy Rollers. I just have high standards, that's all.

I've always wanted to have sex with the first guy I had a Hope-like conversation/connection with. The vast majority of boys are too farty and horny and corny all the time. (Scotty, Burke, Rob, P.J., etc.) Why would I want anyone sticking *anything* on his body into *anything* on my body if I can hardly stand to talk to him for more than thirty seconds? Most of the time when they're sweet and smooth, they're only being sweet and smooth so they can get into my pants. (Cal.) Then there are the worst kind of guys. Guys who've got a good game and therefore think that the few dozen girls who've been inside their boxers are representative of all femalekind. (No example necessary.)

Oh, I see right through them all. Why doesn't everyone else?

the fourteenth

Hallelujah. I'm not a shriveled-up spinster-in-the-making.

This morning, I rediscovered the real reason why I'm not a ho-bag. One that I've never told anyone. Not even Hope. Here it is:

I'm what *Cosmo* would call a "highly orgasmic woman."

I know. Certifiable, right? Especially since I'm in a hormonal shutdown that has no signs of starting up again. (I'm not thinking about that right now.) But you haven't heard the *really* insane part: I don't even masturbate. It's true. And not because I think I'll go insane or grow hair on my fingers. I don't think masturbation is nasty or dirty or a one-way ticket to hellfire and damnation. I know that it's "a safe and healthy way of getting in touch with [my] burgeoning sexuality" (page 92, *Learning About Your Body*, copyright

1998). But the fact is, all my forays into self-stimulation have been failures. I can't get over the ridiculousness of rubbing one out.

No matter; I can have orgasms without so much effort. I used to get off just by having XXX-rated Paul Parlipiano daydreams. (That era has ended.) Sometimes I don't even have to try to think sexy thoughts—my subconscious takes care of it for me. I've woken up numerous times to that telltale throb in the middle of the night, the girlie equivalent to nocturnal emission, I guess. And don't ask me why, but I always feel one coming on whenever I do push-ups, which can be problematic at track practice.

I have orgasms so easily that for the longest time I didn't even realize they were orgasms. It's not something they teach you in Sex Ed. And women's mags make such a big O fuss that I figured that my below-the-belt thumping just meant that I was really turned on. The hard-to-get orgasm *had* to be on a whole other level than what I've experienced since I was eleven and discovered scrambled soft porn on cable, right? The thought kind of scared me, to tell you the truth. Last year when I overheard Carrie P. describing them as "waves of sensation so [fucking] intense, so [fucking] insane, they almost hurt [like fucking hell]," I realized I'd been having them all along.

So I'm not sexually dysfunctional. I'm sexually self-sufficient. My body takes care of biz all by itself. I've got a built-in sexual-tension escape valve that will stop me from doing it with a total loser. I can get off *without* any boy's help, so *what's the point* of getting one involved when he's only going to disappoint me later?

There's just one teensy-weensy detail that I've conveniently left out: It was a full-on freaky-deaky dream about Marcus that helped me come to this conclusion. (Ha. In more ways than one.)

the twenty-second

I got in trouble today. But this time I really didn't do anything. Sort of.

The intercom call came during homeroom: "Mr. Ricardo. Could you please send Jess Darling down to the counselor's office?"

PHS is nothing, if not discreet.

Even though Marcus and I hadn't talked to each other since our awkward hallway showdown, I instinctively shot him a look as I got up to leave. He shrugged. I glanced at Sara. She smirked. Something was up.

In the eleven months since our last rap session, Brandi had grown out her foot-high bangs in favor of a shaggier metal-head mane. Think: Bon Jovi, *Slippery When Wet* tour, 1987. She was as supernaturally perky as ever.

"Your teachers and peers are a bit concerned about you, Jess," she began.

I sneered. "My *peers?*"

I knew it. This had Sara all over it. This was a way of getting back at me. She had looked too pleased in homeroom not to have something to do with this.

"Right!" bubbled Brandi. "It seems that they've seen you talking to some (ahem) unsavory characters."

This wasn't fair. There was only one (ahem) unsavory character, not unsavory characters plural. And we haven't even been talking much lately. But it just goes to show you how out of touch the powers-that-be at PHS really are.

"You mean Marcus Flutie."

"Right! Marcus Flutie!"

I didn't say anything.

"You see, Jess, you're a role model for the younger students," Brandi said.

Me. The most ridiculous role model ever. Hadn't my editorials taught them anything about me?

"And it worries the administration when someone as bright as you gets caught up in a bad crowd."

Marcus Flutie. A bad crowd of one. How bogus was this, since he hadn't even done anything bad since he got back to school. No matter. They still saw him as Krispy Kreme, even though he'd been totally reformed. Well, drug-wise, at least.

"Are your new friends pressuring you to say the things you say in your editorials?"

I almost fell out of my chair. The administration *did* read my editorials. But they didn't think they were mine. They believed that I was a mouthpiece for Marcus Flutie. That the subjects of my editorials were coming from his heart, not mine.

This was too much.

I knew I could've bullshitted my way out of this like the last time I was dragged down here. But I realized I could probably cause a bigger scene by speaking up. If Brandi wanted to judge me by my rah-rah-sis-boom-bah, so be it.

"Are my grades going down?"

"Well, they don't seem to be. No."

"Am I ranked number one in my class?"

"Well, you seem to be. Yes."

"Does Miss Haviland have a problem with what I've written in the paper?"

"Well, no . . ."

"There's no problem here," I said, flouting authority in a way I never had before. "And I don't appreciate being pulled out of class to be told who I can and can't talk to."

I gathered my books and left.

I was too angry to enjoy my moment of rebellion. PHS is so goddamn hypocritical. I get called down to the office for merely *talking* to Marcus Flutie. Christ, if the administration found out that the number-one-ranked student was banging the captain of the football, basketball, and baseball teams, they'd probably throw us a fucking parade.

Ha. Make that, a Fucking Parade. With a capital "F."

Still, the meeting wasn't a waste of time. It made me realize that I need Marcus back in my life. Anything met with disapproval by the PHS authorities must be good for me. When I called Marcus tonight, I told him just that.

"I'm glad you feel that way, Jessica," he said.

Unfortunately, he's visiting his brother in Maine for the holidays. So I can't have him back in my life until next year. Next year is really next week. Just ten days away. But saying "until next year" sounds more traumatic. As traumatic as it felt when I realized that Hope and Marcus are due back in Pineville on the same day and I'm not sure who I need to see more. If Marcus is the male equivalent to Hope that I've always dreamed of, does that make her obsolete? No. It can't. I won't let it.

It's so unfair that I have tons of room in my life for people I hate, yet have to choose between the only two real friends I've ever had. Why can't I have both?

the twenty-fourth

In the mail today arrived the best card ever, folded into the shape of a star, postmarked Bangor, Maine.

WISHING YOU A MERRY XMAS

'Tis the season
for fireproof evergreens
covered in pine-scented
aerosol snow

Hip-hop carols
performed by prepackaged teen divas
backed by one-man synthesizer orchestras
Drunken Santa Clauses for
every gas station
And the latest in nativity scene technology:
"Hear the baby Jesus cry!"
Do genuine kisses exist
in a world of plastic mistletoe?
Merry xmas '00

the twenty-fifth

Bethany and G-Money have already departed, barely twelve hours after their arrival—eight of which were spent sleeping. They're headed for the airport, where they will hop on a plane to Turks and Caicos, where they will be staying with G-Money's family through New Year's Day.

Bethany neglected to tell my parents this until after we had opened each other's presents and were about to sit down for breakfast. Nat King Cole crooned. The house smelled of pine needles and cinnamon buns. The tree twinkled. Everyone was warm with holiday cheer, so it was the perfect moment for Bethany to Grinch it up.

Upon hearing the news, my father grabbed his coat, bolted to the garage, and hopped on his bike, muttering *Goddammits* under his breath. G-Money just sat at the kitchen table, useless as usual. This left me alone to deal with my mother.

"I can't believe you, Bethany!" my mother shouted. "You promised you'd spend the holidays with us! Why didn't you tell us sooner?"

"We *did not* tell you because we knew that you would overreact."

Sometime since our last conversation, Bethany had dropped her faux Euro accent in favor of the clipped, crisp, over-enunciated dialect favored by the Mid-Atlantic upper class, which was just as ridiculous since she lived in California now.

"*Overreact?*" screamed my mother, in tears. "I haven't seen you since your wedding and you can't even bring yourself to spend an entire day with us! It's Christmas, for Christ's sake!" She stormed out of the kitchen and locked herself in the bathroom.

Bethany pouted. "It was a lot of trouble get-ting out here at all. And this is the thanks I get for trying to be the good daughter."

The good daughter. Ha! I don't know if either of us qualified as the good daughter, but the way she was outbitching herself, I was definitely coming out ahead.

"You know what, Bethany? Do us all a favor and don't try so hard next time."

"And what is that supposed to mean?"

"It means, don't burden yourself by gracing us with your presence if you're going to be such a bitch about it."

The insult whizzed right past her. She had already focused on something more important. "Enough talk!" she snapped, waving her diamond-dripping fingers in my face. "We must get Mother out of the bathroom."

"That's the first decent thing you've said since you've been home."

Maybe Bethany isn't such a monster after all, I thought. *Maybe she's capable of thinking about someone other than herself.*

"My makeup is still in there. I desperately need it for my vacation."

At that moment, I decided that no matter how much my parents pissed me off—which was sure to be a sizable amount—I would never be like this. Never.

Makeup be damned, my mom stayed in the bathroom until after Bethany and G-Money's hasty departure. Eventually, I was able to persuade her to come out with the promise of hot cider and a plate of cookies. She slowly opened the door.

"You called your sister a bitch. . . ."

Great, I thought. *Grounded again. Is there no justice in this world?*

She jerked her fingers through her hair, as though she were about to rip it out.

"I'm glad you said it before I did."

My mom and I sat in front of the Christmas tree, sipping cider and biting the heads off gingerbread men. We surveyed all the super-pricey presents Bethany and G-Money had given us.

"You know she hired a personal shopper to pick out these gifts," my mom said, rubbing a pink silk robe against her cheek. "She didn't have time to do it herself."

"That explains why these presents are so perfect," I said, picking up a slick leather journal and fountain pen. "The personal shopper knows us better than she does."

Mom smiled, shook her head, and said, "Why do you have to be so smart?"

"As long as I'm not a smart-*ass*, right?"

Mom gently brushed a lock of hair behind my ear. "Then you wouldn't be you."

I held up the journal. It was so shiny that I could see the reflection of my mom and me laughing together on the couch. And even though I know that's not what we *really* look like, it was close enough.

the twenty-eighth

The operator said, "Collect call from Marcus. Do you accept?"

As if I had a choice in the matter.

"I accept."

"Thank you," said the operator and Marcus simultaneously.

"Marcus, where are you?"

"Still in Maine with my brother."

"Why are you calling?"

Was he calling just to chat? Was he calling for no reason at all? Just because . . . ?

"Mia broke up with me," Marcus said. "This is a first for me."

My head pounded, knowing that this meant things were about to become a lot more complicated. Or easier. Depending on the way you looked at it.

"She did? When?"

"She mailed me a Merry Christmas-I'm-Breaking-Up-with-You card. I'll read it to you," he said. He cleared his throat. "*Dear Marcus. Merry Christmas. I'm breaking up with you. Mia.*"

"It does not say that."

"You're right," he said. "But it would be so classic if it did."

"So why did she break up with you?"

"Well, she said it's because I'm no fun. I don't drink or drug anymore, so I'm no fun. I go to AA meetings instead of hanging out, so I'm no fun. And I do homework instead of having sex, so I'm no fun. I guess she wanted to break up with me before New Year's Eve so she could finally have fun."

I was too busy thinking about him doing homework instead of having sex to reply.

"The reason I'm calling is because I need to spend New Year's Eve with you."

Need. Not want. *Need.*

"Why?"

"Can't you hear the devastation in my voice?"

"No," I said. "You sound holly-jolly to me." He really did.

"It's all an act," he said. "I need to be consoled."

"By who?"

"By who?" he said, insulted. "By *you,* of course."

Of *course.* Consoled. Consolation prize. Runner-up. Second best. Oh, wait. Not sloppy seconds. Sloppy *firsts.*

"So I'll see you on New Year's Eve," he said, hanging up before I could refuse.

the twenty-ninth

Reasons Why I Should Not Have Sex
with Marcus Flutie

1. I don't want to ruin my friendship with Hope by telling—or not telling—her.
2. I don't want to give him the satisfaction of fulfilling the "Fall" prophecy.
3. I don't want to be just another donut—I'd rather be remembered as the one girl he *couldn't* have.
4. I don't want to destroy this weird whatever relationship we have.
5. I don't want to end up proving the naysayers right.
6. I don't want to embarrass myself with my lack of ability.
7. I don't want him to see my sorry boobage.
8. I don't want to get pregnant. (This is highly unlikely since I haven't ovulated in over a year, but knowing my luck I'd get knocked up anyway.)
9. I don't want to catch some nasty-ass STD that he has possibly contracted from one of his Hoochiest lays.
10. I don't want to get caught because no way my last name will save me.

Reasons Why I Should Have Sex with Marcus Flutie

1. I want to. Oh, God, do I want to.

the thirty-first

So it was settled. New Year's Eve was Devirginization Day. D-Day.

I even had the perfect outfit. The anti-homecoming dress. Just one long unzip down the middle and I was ready for action. In theory, that is.

"I told you you'd have a reason to wear that," said my mom, popping her head into the bathroom as I wiped off the mascara I had just jabbed onto my cheek. "Who is this boy you're going out with?"

"He's just a friend from my classes, Mom." I hoped she didn't notice how badly my hands were shaking.

"Does this friend have a name?"

I hesitated. I'd already lied about our destination—a party at Scotty's house—and I didn't want to push my luck. If I didn't tell her, she'd torture me until I did.

"His name is Marcus," I said, reapplying the lip gloss I had already chewed off. "Marcus Flutie."

"Marcus . . ." She tapped her finger to her forehead. "Marcus Flutie. How do I know that name?"

She probably recognized it from the police blotter.

"He's really smart, possibly a genius," I said. "Maybe you know him from that."

"Is he smarter than you?" she asked.

Is he smarter than me? I wondered. "Maybe," I decided.

"He'd better be if he's going to have a shot," she said.

Then the doorbell rang. The finger pushing that doorbell belonged to Marcus Flutie. Marcus Flutie was ringing my doorbell just as if he were any other boy. I thought for sure he'd honk and wait in the driveway. But he was actually going to meet and greet my parents. Jesus Christ. This really couldn't be happening. I fumbled my hairbrush into the toilet.

"I've never seen you this nervous before," my mom said, reaching under the sink to pull out a pair of rubber gloves so she could fish it out.

I'd never decided to have sex before.

I went to the top of the landing and saw Marcus shaking hands with my dad. I felt like I was wearing a cast again—on both legs this time. I couldn't move. My mother nudged me from behind and I almost tumbled head-over-ass down the staircase. As I gripped the railing, and gingerly took each step, I prayed Marcus wouldn't ask one of his bizarre questions before I got to the bottom: *Mr. Darling, did you know that the Japanese have a word to describe the hysterical belief that one's penis is shrinking?*

"Jessica!" my dad exclaimed, as though the last time he'd seen me had been on the back of a milk carton.

Marcus looked me up and down.

"*Ain't you jus' darlin'?*" he drawled, exactly like the first time in the principal's office last year. So long ago.

"She is, isn't she?" my mom said, not getting the joke. "I told her she was!"

I think I got out the *th* of thanks through my stifled giggles, but the other letters got stuck in my throat.

Good-byes are a blur. The next thing I knew, Marcus and I were in the Caddie.

"Your parents love me," he said. "They obviously don't know who I am."

"Obviously," I said.

Marcus popped in an eight-track. It took a few seconds of snare drum and bass to figure out what it was.

"This is *Kind of Blue*," I said.

"Yes."

"Hy said it was *the* essential jazz recording," I said.

"Hy was right," Marcus said.

"I hate that she was right," I said. "It would be so much easier to hate her if she were wrong about everything."

I listened to the music, wondering how and where my devirginization would take place. Would we go back to his house? To mine? My parents were going to a party, but their return time was unpredictable. How about right here in his car? The Caddie had a big enough backseat. . . .

"Aren't you even curious about where we're going tonight?" He didn't wait for my answer. "Well, tonight, I'm going to take you on a tour. A tour of what I like to call The Five Wonders of Pineville, the strangest landmarks our town has to offer."

I snorted. "There are five? I find that hard to believe."

He turned the car into an abandoned parking lot. "Behold," he said, waving his arm with a flourish. "The Champagne of Propane."

The Champagne of Propane is a twenty-five-foot high cement structure in the shape of a wine bottle. When we were kids, it advertised a liquor store. But when the liquor store became a gas station, the clever owners repainted the label, tweaking it to suit their needs.

"You probably pass by the Champagne of Propane every day of your life," he said. "From the road, it's kind of tacky. But have you ever looked at it up close before?"

I admitted that I hadn't.

"It's been painted over so many times that each color that chips or wears away reveals a whole new layer of color. Modern art."

He pointed to a section where green popped through pink, speckled with aqua, flecked with red. He was right. Inch by inch, it was kind of pretty.

"I know how much you hate Pineville," he said. "I thought tonight I'd show you what you miss when you don't look hard enough."

For the next hour, we visited the other "Wonders" of the town in which we were both born and raised: the fiberglass purple dinosaur inexplicably erected outside Magic Carpets and Remnants that predates Barney by about twenty years and has been beheaded by out-of-control automobiles no less than six times; Der Wunder Wiener, the tiny hot-dog-shaped shop-on-wheels that has been parked across the street from the abandoned Woolworth's for as long as we remember, yet never seems to have any customers. After the fourth Wonder—the white Volkswagen Beetle perched on top of the roof of Augie's Auto Parts—I got a bit anxious about, well, getting the action going. Especially when Marcus made a right at the light at the entrance to my development.

"Are you taking me home?"

"Not quite."

He drove past my house (no lights on) and slowed down when we got to the kiddie park. The one I used to run to in the middle of the night.

"And this," he said, "is the park that time forgot. It's the only one in town that hasn't been Disneyfied or Pokémonized. It's exactly the same as it was when we were in elementary school. The tire swings, the monkey bars, the merry-go-round. It's all exactly the same."

The park is one of my favorite places. I loved that he brought me here. It made me want to tell him things.

"I used to run here in the middle of the night when I couldn't sleep."

"Really?"

I pointed up at the leafless tree. "I'd hop on a swing and try to hit the branches with my feet," I said, feeling bold enough to look Marcus right in the eye. "It was just a game I used to play."

"A game."

"Yes." I tried, and failed, to suppress a smile. "Now I talk to you instead."

Marcus stuffed his hands into his front pockets. He suddenly looked incredibly uncomfortable, as though he wished *he* could climb inside his pants and hide.

Then, without saying anything, he ran toward the merry-go-round. I followed and sat down inside the big red circle in the middle. Bull's-eye. Marcus hopped on and sat Indian style, facing me. The wind inched the merry-go-round in circles, but I felt like I was spinning out of control.

Megan McCafferty

"I made my first New Year's resolution," he said.

"Really? I would think that you'd already given up all your vices."

"Almost," he said.

"So?" I said, sitting up on my heels. I was eager to hear what vice he was giving up. God help me if he chose now to go celibate.

"Well, it has to do with you."

I tried to say, *With me?* but no sound came out.

"I promised myself that I'd stop jerking you around."

"What . . . ?!"

He put his finger to my lips to shut me up. Did I ever want to put it in my mouth and suck on it until it got pruny. Then I'd move on to the next one . . .

"You never should have read that poem," Marcus said. " 'Fall.' "

Our knees were touching.

"Why?" I asked. "I like your poems."

"But it gives you the wrong idea about what I want from you."

He was going to apologize for wanting to have sex with me. I just knew it. I learned from watching addicts on *The Real World* that saying *I'm sorry* is number nine on AA's twelve-step program. But Marcus didn't have to take this step with me.

"You don't have to apologize," I said, leaning in closer. Close enough for him to kiss my forehead, my cheek, my mouth . . .

"Yes, I do," he said, arching back and away from me. He tapped his fingers against the merry-go-round metal, *ping-ping-ping.* "I wrote that before I really knew you. I only thought I knew you. Or maybe I did know you then, and you've changed."

Now I was confused. "Changed? How?"

He looked away, his foot tapping a bizillion beats per minute.

"Well," he said. "When I used to listen to you and Hope talk . . ."

I jolted to attention, as though a puppeteer had jerked my marionette strings. "You listened to me and Hope?!"

His words came rushing out, almost too fast to hear.

We'd be in Heath's room too stoned to move and I could hear you through the wall complaining about how much you hated your friends and this town and your goody-goody label and I thought hey here's some-

one who has something to offer the world if only she had someone to help her bust out and why couldn't I be that person I admit it was sort of an experiment to amuse myself to see how far I could push you but when I asked you to fake my test I never thought you'd actually do it so when you took that bait I wrote the poem to see if I could tempt you with sex too just to see if I could but that was before I really knew you . . .

Holy shit!

I couldn't believe what I was hearing. None of it was real. From our mutual mistrust of technology, to Barry Manilow, to Xmas, the things that made us click weren't signs of kismet or synchronicity or even mere coincidence. It was all about calculation, orchestration, manipulation. He knew what to say to me because he'd heard me say it before, to Hope.

Nothing that had happened between Marcus and me was real.

I sprinted away—but not far or fast enough. Christ, I wish I hadn't taken the fall that wrecked my leg.

"Jessica, listen to me for a second!" he yelled, grabbing my arm.

"Why should I?" I screamed, trying to pull away. "This whole thing was fixed from start to finish! You're no better than Hy!"

"Come on, Darlene!"

"Don't call me that! I'm tired of being a joke. I'm tired of being played."

"I know!" he said, gripping my arm tighter. "That's what I was trying to tell you. I don't want my relationship with you to be a game."

I was all ice and silence.

"Jessica, don't you see?" He cupped my chin in his hand.

"See what?" I said, thawing with the warmth of his touch.

"You are the one who changed my life."

NONONONONONONONONONNOONOONOONNONO!

Why did Marcus have to say that? Why? WHY? None of the girls he's messed with wanted to be just another donut. They—we—*all* wanted to be the one who changed his life. The one who made him forget all the other girls who came before. He was telling me exactly what I wanted to hear, not because he meant it, but because he knew I wanted to hear it. What had made all our conversations so wonderful was their weirdness. Saying this, the "perfect" thing, ruined everything. *Everything.*

"Did you hear what I said?" he said again, now softly brushing my hair behind my ears with the very tips of his fingers.

"Fuck you."

"What?" he asked, eyes blinking madly.

I had never said *Fuck you* straight to someone's face before. All forms of the word *fuck* are way overused—kids said *Fuck you* like it was *What's up?* I always thought that if I ever were to say it, I would have to hate that person with a genocidal fury.

And that's how much I hated Marcus at that moment.

"You heard me, Krispy. Fuck you."

He pulled his hands away from my hair, like he'd been electrocuted. I took off, and he didn't try to catch me.

I ran all the way home, until my barely mended bones screamed in pain. I bolted up to my bedroom, unplugged the phone, and sobbed until I was sore, until I felt as though I'd twisted my body tight like a wet towel and wrung myself dry of tears.

Marcus and I didn't have a connection.

One big mind game. Like Hy.

Like Cal, but way worse because I was about to peel off my panties.

How could I be such a moron?

How could I have jeopardized my friendship with Hope for THIS?

I played my conversations with Marcus over and over in my head. After hours of mental rewinding and fast-forwarding, one question kept repeating itself—first as a whisper, then louder—until I clamped my hands over my ears, vainly trying to shut it up:

Doesn't his confession prove that he cares more about me than the others?

Others chimed in, no matter how hard I tried to drown them out:

Wasn't it true that we didn't really know each other then?

Didn't we talk about things I'd never discussed with Hope?

Hadn't I eavesdropped on him and Len Levy?

Maybe it's not too late for us . . .

I was still floundering in a maelstrom of love, lust, and loathing when I felt an ache in my abdomen. I went to the bathroom, pulled down my tights, and saw the blood in my underpants.

Blood.

BLOOD!

Blood where there hadn't been blood in over a year. My period made its comeback on the very night I'd planned to have sex. With Marcus.

Jesus Christ.

I've been laughing ever since this discovery—hard, loud, and crazy—because this is way too bizarre to be just a coincidence.

Is it a message from the higher power that controls synchronicity? Is it another one of my body's built-in emergency antisex mechanisms? Is it a sign of the Y2K+1 apocalypse? Like the one doomsdayers predicted for *last* New Year's Eve? Maybe my world is coming to an end a year later than I expected.

Or maybe, just maybe it means something else entirely. No matter what his initial motivations were, Marcus's words rocked me to sleep. His strange lullabies soothed my anxieties, which made it possible for my period to return.

Without Marcus, would my body ever have caught up with my brain?

I have no clue what to think about Marcus anymore. But I am certain of one thing: I have to do what I should've done ages ago.

January 1st

Hope,

Your plane touched down in Newark about an hour and a half ago. Any minute now, your parents' rental car will drop you off in my driveway. I can't wait until you're here and I can hand-deliver this letter. Until then, I'm writing. Waiting.

By the time you read this, I will have already told you everything. *Everything*.

God, I hope you're reading this. I mean, I hope you don't hate me so much that you rip it up without looking at it first.

I can't see you doing that.

I wanted to tell you all that stuff about Marcus sooner. But I just wasn't ready. I was afraid that my "whatever" relationship with him would ruin the real relationship I had with you. And though I didn't feel right hiding it from you, it wasn't something I wanted to tell you on paper, over the phone, or via the information superhighway. It was face-to-face stuff. Heart-to-heart stuff.

Stuff I'm dying to tell you right now.

I'm just wasting time until you arrive.

Instead of making New Year's resolutions, I'm starting to think about *The Real World*. And how weird it must be for cast members to see themselves in reruns. I mean, they've moved on with their lives. But whenever there's a *Real World* marathon they have to relive moments that they probably would've forgotten about had they not been immortalized on video and broadcast to millions of TV viewers.

I wonder how I'd feel if I saw this year of my life on TV. Even with good editing, it would be tough to take. So many crazy-good and crazy-bad things have happened since you left. I thought I knew people so well. Marcus. Hy. Scotty. Bridget. Paul Parlipiano. Pepe. Even my mom. But they all blindsided me. And the thing is, I know people will continue to shock me next year, and the year after that. Forever.

I just realized that if I had been on *The Real World* this year, you never would've made an appearance on the show with me. That seems so strange, considering the huge influence you have on my life, every single day. Obviously our friendship will never be the way it was before you moved. And if we try to force it to be that way, we'll fail. But for the first time I can remember, I'm optimistic about both our friendship and the future in general.

Maybe it's because I hear your car in the driveway. You're here. Finally here.

Love, J.

Acknowledgments

Many thanks go out to:

My agent, Joanna Pulcini, whose very first words to me ("You're Megan? I love your book!") I will always appreciate, and never forget.

John Searles, whose incredibly generous introduction made it possible for me to hear those words at all.

My editor, Kristin Kiser, whose appreciation of the title told me everything I neeed to know about her understanding of Jessica Darling's world. Her assistant, Claudia Gabel, who also gave me precisely the feedback I needed to write the book that I'd always wanted to read. And everyone at Crown—especially Steve Ross and Andy Martin—whose enthusiasm confirmed that this book would appeal to readers of both sexes who were way beyond high school.

Liza Nelligan and Kate Burns, whose early suggestions helped me figure out why I was telling this story, and the best way to do it.

The ill-fated writers group—particularly Nancy Miller—who had no clue that a positive review of a ten-page short story would encourage me to quit my job and write a novel.

Alan, Ellen, and Sean McCafferty, whose W.T. tales were an invaluable source of humorous inspiration.

Ryan Fitzmorris, for being a master storyteller in his own right. And Renée Darling, who was gracious enough to let me steal her last name.

Sean, Donna, and Caitlyn Fitzmorris, for making Tuesday my favorite day of the week.

My parents, Tom and Laurie Fitzmorris, whose unique combination of nature and nurture got me here.

And finally, Christopher, my husband and best friend, for making me laugh every single day.

About the Author

MEGAN McCAFFERTY is a former editor for *Cosmopolitan*, *YM*, and *Fitness* magazines. Her work has appeared in *Glamour*, *CosmoGIRL!*, *Maxim*, *Details*, and other national publications. McCafferty created "You Think *Your* Life is Crazy," a fiction serial for teens featured on Twistmag.com. She lives with her husband in New Jersey, where she is curently writing her second novel about Jessica Darling.